C. C. (Charles Carroll) Goodwin

The Comstock Club

C. C. (Charles Carroll) Goodwin

The Comstock Club

ISBN/EAN: 9783743306028

Manufactured in Europe, USA, Canada, Australia, Japa

Cover: Foto ©Andreas Hilbeck / pixelio.de

Manufactured and distributed by brebook publishing software
(www.brebook.com)

C. C. (Charles Carroll) Goodwin

The Comstock Club

THE COMSTOCK CLUB.

BY

C. C. GOODWIN,

EDITOR SALT LAKE DAILY TRIBUNE.

Neither radiant angels nor magnified monsters, but just plain, true men.

1891.
TRIBUNE JOB PRINTING COMPANY,
SALT LAKE CITY, UTAH.

CONTENTS.

TO THE

MINERS OF THE PACIFIC COAST,

THIS BOOK,

WHICH WAS WRITTEN WHILE WORKING FOR AND AMONG THEM,

IS RESPECTFULLY DEDICATED

BY

THE AUTHOR.

Salt Lake City, Utah, December 15, 1891.

THE COMSTOCK CLUB.

CHAPTER I.

"The pioneer! Who shall fitly tell the story of his life and work?

"The soldier leads an assault; it lasts but a few minutes: he knows that whether he lives or dies, immortality will be his reward. What wonder that there are brave soldiers!

"But when this soldier of peace assaults the wilderness. no bugles sound the charge; the forest, the desert. the wild beast, the savage, the malaria. the fatigue. are the foes that lurk to ambush him, and if, against the unequal odds, he falls, no volleys are fired above him; the pitiless world merely sponges his name from its slate.

"Thus he blazes the trails, thus he fells the trees. thus he plants his rude stakes, thus he faces the hardships, and whatever fate awaits him. his self-contained soul keeps its finger on his lips, and no lamentations are heard.

"He smooths the rugged fields, he turns the streams, and the only cheer that is his is when he sees the grain ripen. and the flowers bloom where before was only the frown of the wilderness. When over the trail that he has blazed. enlightenment comes joyously, with unsoiled sandals, and homes and temples spring up on the soil that was first broken by him, his youth is gone, hope has been chastened into silence within him ; he realizes that he is but a back number.

"Not one in a thousand realizes the texture of the manhood that has been exhausting itself within him ; few comprehend his nature or have any conception of his work.

"But he is content. The shadows of the wilderness have been chased away : the savage beast and savage man have retired before him ; nature has brought her flowers to strew the steps of his old age ; in his soul he feels that somewhere the record of his work and of his high thoughts has been kept ; and so he smiles upon the younger generation and is content.

" May that contentment be his to the end."

It was an anniversary night in Pioneer Hall, in Virginia City. Nevada. one July night in 1878. and the foregoing were the closing words of a little impromptu speech that Alex Strong had delivered.

A strange. many-sided man was Alex Strong. He was an Argonaut. When the first tide set in toward the Golden Coast. he, but a lad, with little save a pony and a gun, joined a train that had crossed the Missouri and was headed westward.

The people in the company looked upon him as a mere boy. but, later, when real hardships were encountered and sickness came, the boy became the life of the company. When women and children drooped under the burdens and the fear of the wilderness, it was his voice that cheered them on ; his gun secured the tender bit of antelope or grouse to tempt their failing appetites ; his songs drove away the silence of the desert. He was for the company a lark at morn, a nightingale at night.

Arriving in California, he sought the hills. When his claim would not pay he indicted scornful songs to show his "defiance of luck." Some of these were published in the mountain papers, and then a few people knew that somewhere in miner's garb a genius was hiding. Amid the hills, in his cabin, he was an incessant reader, and with his books, his friction against men and in the study of nature's mighty alphabet, as left upon her mountains, with the going by of the years he rounded into a cultured, alert, sometimes pathetic and sometimes boisterous man, but always a shrewd, all-around man of affairs.

When we greet him he had been for several years a brilliant journalist.

He had jumped up to make a little speech in Pioneer Hall, and the last words of his speech are given above.

When he had finished another pioneer, Colonel Savage, was called upon. He was always prepared to make a speech. He delighted, moreover, in taking the opposite side to Strong. So springing to his feet, he cried out:

"Too serious are the words of my friend. What of hardships, when youth, the beautiful, walks by one's side! What of danger when one feels a young heart throbbing in his breast!

"Who talks of loneliness while as yet no fetter has been welded upon hope, while yet the unexplored and unpeopled portions of God's world beckon the brave to come to woo and to possess them!

"The pioneers were not unhappy. The air is still filled with the echoes of the songs that they sung; their bright sayings have gone into the traditions; the impression which they made upon the world is a monument which will tell of their achievements, record their sturdy virtues and exalt their glorified names."

As the Colonel ceased and some one else was called upon to talk. Strong motioned to Savage and both noiselessly sought some vacant seats in the rear of the hall.

Colonel Savage was another genius. He was a young lawyer in New York when the first news of gold discoveries in California was carried to that city. He, with a hundred others, chartered a bark that was lying idle in the harbor, had her fitted up and loaded, and in her made a seven months' voyage around the Cape to San Francisco. He was the most versatile of the Argonauts. Every mood of poor human nature found a response in him. At a funeral he shamed the mourners by the sadness of his face ; at a festival he added a sparkle to the wines ; he could convulse a saloon with a story ; he could read a burial service with a pathos that stirred every heart, and so his life ran on until when we find him he had been several years a leading member of a brighter bar than ever before was seen in a town of the size of Virginia City.

He was a tall, handsome man, his face was classical, and all his bearing, even when all unbent, was that of a high-born, self-contained and self-respecting man.

Strong, on the other hand, was of shorter statue ; his face was the perfect picture of mirthfulness ; there was a wonderful magnetism in his smile and hand-clasp ; but when in repose a close look at his face revealed, below the mirthfulness, that calm which is the close attendant upon conscious power

As they reached their seats Alex spoke :

" You were awfully good to-night, Colonel."

"Of course; I always am. But what has awakened your appreciation to-night ?"

" I thought my speech was horrible."

" For once it would require a brave man to doubt your judgment," said the Colonel, sententiously.

" I was sure of it until I heard you speak ; then I recovered my self-respect, believing that, by comparison. my speech would ring in the memories of the listeners, like a psalm."

" You mean Sam, the town-crier and boot-black. His brain is a little weak. but his lungs are superb."

" I believe you are jealous of his voice, Colonel. But sit down : I want to tell you about the most unregenerate soul on earth."

" Proceed, Alex. only do not forget that under the merciful statutes of the State of Nevada no man is obliged to make statements which will criminate himself."

" What a comfort that knowledge must be to you."

" It often is. My heart is full of sympathy for the unfortunate, and more than once have I seen eyes grow bright when I have given that information to a client."

" The study of that branch of law must have had a peculiar fascination to you."

" Indeed, it did, Alex. At every point where the law draws the shield of its mercy around the accused. in thought it seemed made for one or another of my friends. and, mentally. I found myself defending one after the other of them."

" Did you, at the same time, keep in thought the

fact that in an emergency the law permits a man to plead his own cause ?"

"Never, on my honor. In those days my life was circumspect, even as it now is, and my associates—not as now—were so genteel that there was no danger of any suspicion attaching to me, because of the people I was daily seen with."

"That was good for you, but what sort of reputations did your associates have ?" asked Alex.

"They went on from glory to glory. One became a conductor on a railroad, and in four years, at a salary of one hundred dollars per month, retired rich. One became a bank cashier, and three years later, through the advice of his physicians, settled in the soft climate of Venice, with which country we have no extradition treaty. Another one is a broker here in this city, and I am told, is doing so well that he hopes next year to be superintendent of a mine."

"Why have you not succeeded better, Colonel, financially ?"

"I am too honest. Every day I stop law suits which I ought to permit to go on. Every day I do work for nothing which I ought to charge for. I tell you, Alex, I would sooner be right than be President."

"I cannot, just now, recall any one who knows you, Colonel, who does not feel the same way about you."

"That is because the most of my friends are dull, men, like yourself. But how prospers that newspaper ?"

"It is the same old, steady grind," replied Alex, thoughtfully. "I saw a blind horse working in a whim yesterday. As he went round and round, there seemed on his face a look of anxiety to find out how much longer that road of his was, and I said to him, compassionately: 'Old Spavin, you know something of what it is to work on a daily paper.' I went to the shaft and watched the buckets as they came up, and there was only one bucket of ore to ten buckets of waste. Then I went back to the horse and said to him: 'You do not know the fact, you blissfully ignorant old brute, but your work is mightily like ours, one bucket of ore to ten of waste.'"

"How would you like to have me write an editorial for your paper?"

"I should be most grateful," was the reply.

"On what theme?"

"Oh, you might make your own selection."

"How would you like an editorial on—— scoundrels?"

"It would, with your experience, be truthfully written, doubtless. but Colonel, it is only now and then in good taste for a man to supply the daily journals with his own autobiography."

"How modest you are. You did not forget that, despite the impersonality of journalism, you would have the credit of the article."

"No, I was afraid of that credit, and I am poor enough now, Colonel; but really, that credit does not count. If, for five days in the week. I make newspapers. which my judgment tells me are passably good, it appears to me the only use that is made of them is for servant girls to kindle fires with, and do up their bangs in: but if, on the sixth day, my heart is heavy and my brain thick, and the paper next morning is poor, it seems to me that everybody in the camp looks curiously at me, as if to ascertain for a certainty, whether or no, I am in the early stages of brain softening."

"A reasonable suspicion, I fancy, Alex; but what do you think of your brother editors of this coast as men and writers?"

"Most of them are good fellows, and bright writers. If you knew under what conditions some of them work, you would take off your hat every time you met them."

"To save my hat?' queried the Colonel. "But whom do you consider the foremost editor of the coast?"

"There is no such person. Men with single thoughts and purposes, are, as a rule, the men who make marks in this world. For instance, just now, the single purpose of James G. Fair, is to make money through mining. Hence, he is a great miner, and he, now and then, I am told, manages to save a few dollars in the business. The dream of C. P. Huntington is to make money through railroads, so he builds roads, that he may collect more fares and freights, and he collects more fares and freights so that he may build more roads, and I believe, all in all, that he is the ablest, if not the coldest and most pitiless, railroad man in the world. The ruling thought of Andy Barlow is to be a fighter, and he can draw and shoot in the space of a lightning's flash. The dream of George Washington, he having no children, was to create and adopt a nation which should at once be strong and free, and the result is, his grave is a shrine. But, as the eight notes of the scale, in their combinations, fill the world with music—or with discords, so the work of an editor covers all the subjects on which men have ever thought, or ever will think, and the best that any one editor can do is to handle a few subjects well. Among our coast editors there is one with more marked characteristics, more flashes of genius, in certain directions, more contradictions and more pluck than any other one possesses.

"That one is Harry Mighels, of Carson. I mention him because I have been thinking of him all day, and because I fear that his work is finished. The last we heard of him, was, that he was disputing with the surgeons in San Francisco, they telling him that he was fatally ill, and he, offering to wager two to one that they were badly mistaken."

"Poor Harry," mused the Colonel; "he *is* a plucky man. I heard one of our rich men once try to get him to write something, or not to write something, I have forgotten which, and when Mighels declined to consent, the millionaire told him he was too poor to be so exceedingly independent. Here Mighels, in a low voice, which sounded to me like the purr of a tiger, said: 'You are quite mistaken, you do not know how rich I am. I have that little printing office at Carson; paper enough to last me for a week or ten days. I have a wife and three babies,' and then suddenly raising his voice, to the dangerous note, and bringing his fist down on the table before him with a crash, he shouted, *'and they are all mine!'*

"The rich man looked at him, and, smiling, said: 'Don't talk like a fool, Mighels.' The old humor was all back in Mighels' face in an instant, as he replied, 'Was I talking like a fool, old man? What a sublime faculty I have of exactly gauging my conversation to the mental grasp of my listener!' But, Alex, do you not think there is a great deal of humbug about the much vaunted power of the press?"

"There's gratitude for you. You ask *me* such a question as that."

"And why not?" inquired the Colonel.

"You won a great suit last week, did you not—the case of Jones vs. Smith?"

"Yes. It was wonderful; let me tell you about it."

"No : spare me," cried Alex. "But how much did you receive for winning that case?"

"I received a cool ten thousand dollars."

"And you still ask about the influence of the press?"

"Yes. Why should I not?"

"Sure enough, why should you not? If you will stop and think you will know that three months ago you could not have secured a jury in the State that would have given you that verdict. There was a principle on trial that public opinion was pronounced against in a most marked manner. The press took up the discussion and fought it out. At length it carried public opinion with it. That thing has been done over and over right here. At the right time, your case, which hung upon that very point, was called. You think you managed it well. It was simply a walk-over for you. The men with the Fabers had done the work for you. The jury unconsciously had made up their minds before they heard the complaint in the case read. The best thoughts in your argument you had unconsciously stolen from the newspapers, and the judge, looking as wise as an Arctic owl, unconsciously wrung half an editorial into his charge. You received ten thousand dollars, and to the end of his days your client will tell (heaven forgive his stupidity) what a lawyer you are, but ask him his opinion of newspaper men and he will shrug his shoulders, scowl, and with a donkey's air of wisdom, answer: 'Oh, they are necessary evils. We want the local news and the dispatches, and we have to endure them.'

"I am glad you robbed him, Colonel. I wish you could rob them all. If a child is born to one of them we have to tell of it, and mention delicately how noble the father is and how lovely the mother is. If one of them dies we have to jeopardize our immortal souls trying to make out a character for him. They want us every day: we hold up their business and their reputations, beginning at the cradle, ending only at the grave."

"What kind of character would you give me, were I to die?"

"Try it, Colonel! Try it! And if 'over the divide' it should be possible for you to look back and read the daily papers, when your shade gets hold of my notice, I promise you it shall be glad that you are dead."

"But what about that unregenerate soul that you were going to tell me of—has some broker sold out some widow's stocks?"

"No: worse than that."

"Has some one burglarized some hospital or orphan asylum?" suggested the Colonel.

"Oh, no. Old Angus Jacobs, you know, is rich. Among strangers he parades his thin veneering of reading, and poses as though all his vaults were stuffed with reserves of knowledge. Well, while East last spring, he ran upon a distinguished publisher there, with whom he agreed that he would, on his return, write and send for publication an article on the West.

"He came and begged me to write it, confessing that he had deceived the publisher, and asserting that he must keep up the deception, or the integrity of the West would be injured in the estimation of that publisher.

"I went to work, wrote an article, became enthused as I wrote, wrote it over, spent as much as three solid days upon it, and when it was finished I looked upon my work, and lo, it was good.

"Then, at my own expense, I had it carefully copied and gave the copy to old Angus. He sent it East. To-day he received a dozen copies and a letter of profuse praise and thanks from the publisher.

"I saw the old thief give one of the copies to a literary man from San Francisco, telling him, cheerfully, as he did, that he dashed the article off hastily, that most of the language was crude and awkward, but it might entertain him a little on the train going to San Francisco."

"I never heard of anything meaner or more depraved than that," indignantly remarked the Colonel, "except when I read the funeral service over an old Dutchman's child once, in Downieville. Speaking of it afterward, the old Hessian said:

"'Dot Colonel's reading vos fine, but he dond vos haf dot prober look uf regret vot he ought to haf had'—but here comes the Professor."

Professor Stoneman joined the pair, and when the greetings were over the Professor said:

"I am just in from Eastern Nevada: went to Eureka to examine a mine owned by a jolly miner named Moore. It is a good one, too—a contact vein between lime and quartzite. The fellow worked, running a tunnel, all winter, and now he has struck, and cross-cut, his vein. It is fully seven feet thick, and rich. I asked him how he felt when at last he cut the vein.

"'How did I feel, Professor,' he said, 'how did I feel? Why, General Jackson's overcoat would not have made a paper collar for me.'

"There are a great many queer characters out that way. Moore is not a very well educated man. In Eureka I was telling about the mine—that Moore ought to make a fortune out of it—when a man standing by, a stranger to me, stretched up both his arms and cried: 'A fortune! Look at it, now! Moore is so unspeakably ignorant that he could not spell out the name of the Savior if it were written on White Pine Mountain in letters bigger than the Coast Range. But he strikes it rich! His kind always do.' Then he added, bitterly: 'If I could find a chimpanzee, I would draw up articles of copartnership with him in fifteen minutes.'

"And then a quiet fellow, who was present, said: 'Jim, maybe the chimpanzee, after taking a good look at you, would not stand it.'

"I was sitting in a barroom there one day, and a man was talking about the Salmon River mines, and insisting that they were more full of promise than anything in Nevada, when another man in the crowd earnestly said:

"'If my brother were to write me that it was a good country, and advise me to come up there, I would not believe him.'

"Quick as lightning, still another man responded: 'If we all knew your brother as well as you do, maybe none of us would believe him.'

"That is the way they spend their time out there. But I secured some lovely specimens: specimens of ore, rare shells, some of the finest specimens of mirabilite of lead that I ever saw. It is a most interesting region. But I don't agree entirely with Clarence King on the geology of the district: You see King's theory is—"

"Oh, hold on, Professor," said the Colonel, "it does not lack an hour of midnight. You have not time, positively. Heigh ho. Here is Wright. How is the mine, Wright?"

"About two hundred tons lighter than it was this morning, I reckon," replied Wright.

"But tell us about the mine, Wright," said Alex, impatiently. "How is the temperature?"

"How is your health?" responded Wright, jocularly. "If you do not expect to live long, you might come down and take some preparatory lessons; that is, if you anticipate joining the majority of newspaper men."

"No, no; you are mistaken," said Alex. "You mean the Colonel. He is a lawyer, you know."

"It is the Professor that needs the practice," chimed in the Colonel. "Just imagine him 'down below,' explaining to the gentleman in green how similar the formation is to a hot drift that he once found in the Comstock."

"I will tell you a hotter place than any drift in the Comstock," said the Professor. "Put all the money that you have into stocks, having a dead pointer from a friend who is posted, buy on a margin, and then have the stocks begin to go down; that will start the perspiration on you."

"We have all been in that drift," said Alex.

"Indeed, we have," responded Wright.

"I have lived in that climate for twelve years. One or two winters it kept me so warm that I did not need an overcoat or watch, so I loaned them to—— 'mine uncle,'" remarked the Colonel.

"But, do you know any points on stocks, Wright?"

"No, not certainly, Alex. I heard some rumors last night and ordered 100 Norcross this morning. Some of the boys think it will jump up three or four dollars in the next ten days."

"I took in a block of Utah yesterday. They are getting down pretty deep, and there is lots of unexplored ground in that mine," said the Colonel, quietly.

The Professor, looking serious, said: "I have all my money the other way, in Justice and Silver Hill. They are not deep enough in the north end yet."

Alex got up from his chair. "You are all mistaken," said he, "Overman is the best buy, but it is growing late and I must go to work. What shift are you on, Wright?"

"I go on at seven in the morning. By the way, you should come up of an evening to our Club. We would be glad to see all three of you."

"And pray, what do you mean by your Club?" asked the Colonel.

"Why," said Wright, "I thought you knew. Three or four of us miners met up here one night last month. Joe Miller was in the party, and as we were drinking beer and talking about stocks, Miller proposed that we should hire a vacant house on the divide—the old Beckley House—and give up the boarding and lodging houses. We talked it all over, how shameful we had been going on, how we were spending all our money, how. if we had the house, we could save fifty or sixty dollars a month, and eat what we pleased. do what we pleased, and have a place in which to pass our leisure time without going to the saloons: so we picked up three or four more men, and, on last pay-day, moved in—seven of us in all—each man bringing his own chair, blankets and food. The latter, of course. was all put into common stock. and Miller had fixed everything else. Since then we have been getting along jolly."

"But who makes up your company?" inquired Alex.

"Oh, you know the whole outfit," answered Wright. "There is Miller. as I told you ; there are, besides, Tom Carlin. old man Brewster, Herbert Ashley. Sammy Harding. Barney Corrigan and myself."

"It is a good crowd ; but you are not all working in the same mine, are you?" said the Professor, inquiringly.

"Oh, no. Brewster is running a power-drill in the Bullion. He is a mechanic, you know, and not a real miner. Miller and Harding are in the Curry. Barney is in the Norcross. Carlin and Ashley are in the Imperial, and I in the Savage. But we all happen to be on the same shift, so. for this month at least, we have our evenings together."

"It must be splendid," enthusiastically remarked the Colonel.

"How do you spend your evenings?" asked Alex.

"We talk on all subjects except politics. That subject, we agreed at the start, should not be discussed. We read and compare notes on stocks."

"How do you manage about your cooking?" queried the Professor.

"We have a Chinaman, who is a daisy. He is cook, housekeeper, chambermaid, and would be companion and musician if we could stand it. You must come up and see us."

"I will come to-morrow evening," Alex replied, eagerly.

"So will I," said the Colonel, with a positiveness that was noticeable.

"And so will I," shouted the Professor.

Just then the eleven o'clock whistles sounded up and down the lead. "That is our signal for retiring," said Wright, and so good night."

"Let us go out and take a night cap, first," said the Colonel.

"Well, if I must," said Wright. "Though the rule of our Club is only a little for medicine."

The night caps were ordered and swallowed. Then the men separated, the Colonel, Professor and Wright going home, the journalist to his work.

Professor Stoneman was a character. Tall and spare, with such an outline as Abraham Lincoln had. He was fifty years of age, with grave and serene face when in repose, and with the mien of one of the faculty of a university. Still he had that nature which caused him when a boy to run away from his Indiana home to the Mexican war, and he fought through all that long day at Buena Vista, a lad of eighteen years. Of course he was with the first to reach California. He had tried mining and many other things, but the deeper side of his nature was to pursue the sciences—the lighter to mingle with good fellows. He would tell a story one moment and the next would combat a scientific theory with the most learned of the Eastern scientists, and carry away from the controversy the

2

full respect of his opponent. There was a great fund of merriment within him, and his generosity not only kept his bank account a minus number, but moreover, kept his heart aching that he had no more to give. When by himself he was an incessant student, and beside knowing all that the books taught, he had his own ideas of their correctness, especially those that deal with the formation of ore deposits. He was a learned writer, a gifted lecturer and an expert of mines. and, over all, the most genial of men.

Adrian Wright was of another stamp altogether. He was tall and strong, with large feet and hands, a massive man in all respects, and forty-five years of age.

He had a cool and brave gray eye, a firm, strong mouth, very light brown hair and carried always with him a something which first impressed those who saw him with his power, while a second look gave the thought that beside the power which was visible, he had unmeasured reserves of concealed force which he could call upon on demand.

He went an uncultured lad to California. He was at first a placer miner. Obtaining a good deal of money he became a mountain trader and the owner of a ditch, which supplied some hydraulic grounds. He was brusque in his address, said "whar" and "thar," but his head was large and firmly poised; his heart was warm as a child's, and he was loved for his clear, good sense and for the sterling manhood which was apparent in all his ways. Though uncultured in the schools, he had read a great deal, and, mixing much with men, his judgment had matured, until in his mountain hamlet his word had become an authority.

His friends persuaded him to become a candidate for the State Legislature. After he had consented to run he spent a good deal of money in the campaign. He was elected and went to Sacramento. There he was persuaded to buy largely of Comstock stocks. He bought on a margin. When it came time to put up more money he could not without borrowing. He would not do that through fear that he could not pay. He lost the stocks. He went home in the spring to find that his clerks had given large credits to miners; the hydraulic mines ceased to pay, which rendered his ditch property valueless, and a few days later his store burned down. When his debts were paid he had but a few hundred dollars left. He said nothing about his reverses, but went to Virginia City and for several years had been working in the mines.

As already said, a miners' mess had been formed. Seven miners on the Comstock might be picked out who would pretty nearly represent the whole world.

This band had been drawn together partly because of certain traits that they possessed in common, though they were each distinctly different from all the others.

We have read of Wright. Of the others, James Brewster, was the eldest of the company. He was fifty years of age, and from Massachusetts. He was not tall, but was large and powerful.

There were streaks of gray in his hair, but his eyes were clear, and black as midnight. He had a bold nose and invincible mouth; the expression of his whole face was that of a resolute, self-contained, but kindly nature. All his movements were quick and positive.

He was educated, and though of retiring ways, when he talked everybody near him listened. He was not a miner, but a mechanical engineer, and his work was the running of power drills in the mine. He never talked much of his own affairs, but it was understood that misfortune in business had caused him to seek the West somewhat late in life. The truth was he had never been rich. He possessed a moderately prosperous business until a long illness came to his wife. and when the depression which followed the reaction from the war and the contraction of the currency fell upon the North, he found he had little left, and so sought a new field.

He was the Nestor of the Club and was exceedingly loved by his companions.

Miller, who first proposed the Club, was a New Yorker by birth. a man forty-five years of age, medium height. keen gray eyes, a clear-cut, sharp face. slight of build, but all nerve and muscle, and lithe as a panther. He had been for a quarter of a century on the west coast, and knew it well from British Columbia to Mexico, and from the Rocky Mountains to the Pacific.

He was given a good education in his youth : he had mingled with all sorts of men and been engaged in all kinds of business. There was a perpetual flash to his eyes, and a restlessness upon him which made him uneasy if restrained at all. He had the reputation of being inclined to take desperate chances sometimes, but was honorable. thoroughly, and generous to a fault.

He had studied men closely, and of Nature's great book he was a constant reader. He knew the voices of the forests and of the streams; he had a theory that the world was but a huge animal; that if we were but wise enough to understand, we should hear from Nature's own voices the story of the world and hear revealed all her profound secrets.

He possessed a magnetism which drew friends to him everywhere. His hair was still unstreaked with gray, but his face was care-worn, like that of one who had been dissipated or who had suffered many disappointments.

Carlin was twenty-eight years of age, long of limb, angular, gruff, but hearty; quick, sharp and shrewd, but free-handed and generally in the best of humors. He was an Illinois man, and a good type of the men of the Old West.

His eyes were brown, his hair chestnut; erect, he was six feet in height, but seated, there seemed to be no place for his hands and hardly room enough for his feet. He was well-educated, and had been but three and a half years on the Comstock.

All the Californians in the Club insisted, of course, that there was no other place but that, but this Carlin always vehemently denied, for he came from the State of Lincoln and Douglas, and the State, moreover, that had Chicago in one corner of it, and he did not believe there was another such State in all the Republic.

Ashley was from Pennsylvania; a young man of twenty-five, above medium height, compact as a tiger in his make-up, and weighing, perhaps, one hundred and eighty pounds. His eyes were gray, his hair brown, his face almost classic in its outlines; his feet and hands were particularly small and finely formed, and there was a jollity and heartiness about his laugh which was contagious. He had an excellent education, and had seen a good deal of business in his early manhood.

Corrigan was a thorough Irishman, generous, warm-hearted, witty, sociable, brave to recklessness,

curly-haired, with laughing, blue eyes; the most open
and frank of faces that was ever smiling, powerfully
built and ready at a moment's notice to fight anyone
or give anyone his purse.

Everybody knew and liked him, and he liked
everybody that, as he expressed it, was worth the
liking.

He had come to America a lad of ten. He lived
for twelve years in New York City, attended the
schools, and was in his last year in the High School
when, for some wild freak, he had been expelled. He
worked two years in a Lake Superior copper mine,
then went to California and worked there until lured
to Nevada by the silver mines, and had been on the
Comstock five years when the Club was formed.

Harding was the boy of the company, only twenty-
two years of age. a native California lad. But he
was hardly a type of his State.

His eyes were that shade of gray which looks
black in the night; his hair was auburn. He had a
splendid form, though not quite filled out; his head
was a sovereign one.

But he was reticent almost to seriousness, and it
was in this respect that he did not seem quite like a
California boy. There was a reason for it. He was
the son of an Argonaut who had been reckless in
business and most indulgent to his boy. He had a
big farm near Los Angeles, and shares in mines all
over the coast. The boy had grown up half on the
farm and half in the city. He was an adept in his
studies; he was just as much an adept when it came
to riding a wild horse.

He had gained a good education and was just entering the senior class in college when his father

suddenly died. He mourned for him exceedingly, and when his affairs were investigated it was found there was a mortgage on the old home.

He believed there was a future for the land. So he made an arrangement to meet the interest on the mortgage annually, then went to San Francisco, obtained an order for employment on a Comstock superintendent, went at once to Virginia City and took up his regular labor as a miner. He had been thus employed for a year when the Club was formed.

This was the company that had formed a mess. Miller had worked up the scheme.

It had been left to Miller to prepare the house—to buy the necessary materials for beginning housekeeping, like procuring the dishes, knives and forks and spoons, and benches or cheap chairs, for the dining room, and it was agreed to begin on the next pay day.

CHAPTER II.

About four o'clock in the afternoon of the day appointed for commencing housekeeping, our miners gathered at this new home. The provisions, bedding and chairs had been sent in advance, in care of Miller, who had remained above ground that day, in order to have things in apple-pie shape. The chairs were typical of the men. Brewster's was a common, old-fashioned, flag-bottomed affair, worth about three dollars. Carlin and Wright each had comfortable arm-chairs; Ashley and Harding had neat office chairs, while Miller and Corrigan each had heavy upholstered armchairs, which cost sixty dollars each.

When all laughed at Brewster's chair, he merely answered that it would do, and when Miller and Corrigan were asked what on earth they had purchased such out-of-place furniture for, to put in a miner's cabin, Miller answered: "I got trusted and didn't want to make a bill for nothing," and Corrigan said: "To tell the truth, I was not over-much posted on this furniture business, I did not want to invest in too chape an article, so I ordered the best in the thavin' establishment, because you know a good article is always chape, no matter what the cost may be."

The next thing in order was to compare the bills for provisions. Brewster drew his bill from his pocket and read as follows: Twenty pounds bacon, $7.50; forty pounds potatoes, $1.60; ten pounds coffee, $3.75; one sack flour, $4.00; cream tartar and salaratus, $1.00; ten pounds sugar, $2.75; pepper, salt and mustard, $1.50; ten pounds prunes, $2.50; one bottle XXX for medicine, $2.00; total, $32.60.

The bill was receipted. The bills of Wright and Harding each comprised about the same list, and amounted to about the same sum. They, too, were receipted. The funny features were that each one had purchased nearly similar articles, and the last item on each of the bills was a charge of $2.00 for medicine. It had been agreed that no liquor should be bought except for medicine.

The bills of Carlin and Ashley were not different in variety, but each had purchased in larger quantities, so that those bills footed up about $45 each. On each of the bills, too, was an item of $4.75 for demijohn and "half gallon of whisky for medicine." All were receipted.

Corrigan's bill amounted to $73, including one-half gallon of whisky and one bottle of brandy "for medicine," and his too was receipted.

Miller read last. His bill had a little more variety, and amounted to $97.16. The last item was: "To demijohn and one gallon whisky for medicine, $8.00." On this bill was a credit for $30.00.

A general laugh followed the reading of these bills. The variety expected was hardly realized, as Corrigan remarked: "The bills lacked somewhat in versatility, but there was no doubt about there being plenty of food of the kind and no end to the medicine."

When the laugh had subsided, Brewster said: "Miller estimated that our provisions would not cost to exceed $15.00 per month apiece. I tried to be reasonable and bought about enough for two months, but here we have a ship load. Why did you buy out a store, Miller?"

"I had to make a bill and I did not want the grocery man to think we were paupers," retorted Miller.

"How much were the repairs on the house, Miller?" asked Carlin.

"There's the beggar's bill. It's a dead swindle, and I told him so. He ought to have been a plumber. He had by the Eternal. He has no more conscience than a police judge. Here's the scoundrel's bill," said Miller. excitedly, as he proceeded to read the following:

"'To repairing roof, $17.50; twenty battens, $4.00; to putting on battens, $3.00; hanging one door, $3.50; six lights glass, $3.00; setting same, $3.00; lumber, $4.80; putting up bunks, $27.50; total, $66.30.'

"The man is no better than a thief; if he is, I'm a sinner."

"You bought some dishes. did you not, Miller?" inquired Ashley. "How much did they amount to?"

"There's another scalper," answered Miller. warmly. "I told him we wanted a few dishes. knives, forks, etc.—just enough for seven men to cabin with —and here is the bill. It foots up $63.37. A bill for wood also amounts to $15.00; two extra chairs, $6.00."

Brewster, who had been making a memorandum, spoke up and said: "If I have made no error the account stands as follows:

Provisions	$357	56
Crockery, knives, forks, etc	53	37
Wood	19	00
Repairs	66	50
One month's rent	50	00
One month's water	7	00
Chairs	6	00
Making a total of	$559	43

Or, in round numbers, eighty dollars per captia for us

all.   I settled my account at the store, amounting to $32.60, which leaves $47.40 as my proportion of the balance. Here is the money."

This was like Brewster. Some of the others settled and a part begged off until next pay-day.

The next question was about the cooking. After a brief debate it was determined that all would join in getting up the first supper. So one rushed to a convenient butcher shop and soon returned with a basket full of porter house steaks, sweet-breads and lamb chops; another prepared the potatoes and put them in the oven; another attended to the fire; another to setting the table. Brewster was delegated to make the coffee. To Corrigan was ascribed the task of cooking the meats, while Miller volunteered to make some biscuits that would "touch their hearts."

He mixed the ingredients in the usual way and thoroughly kneaded the dough. He then, with the big portion of a whisky bottle for a rolling-pin, rolled the dough out about a fourth of an inch thick. He then touched it gently all over with half melted butter; rolled the thin sheet into a large roll; then with the bottle reduced this again to the required thickness for biscuits. and, with a tumbler, cut them out. His biscuit trick he had learned from an old Hungarian, who, for a couple of seasons, had been his mining partner. It is an art which many a fine lady would be glad to know. The result is a biscuit which melts like cream in the mouth—like a fair woman's smile on a hungry eye. Corrigan had his sweet-breads frying, and when the biscuits were put in the oven, the steak and chops were put on to broil. The steak had been salted and peppered—miner's fashion —and over it slices of bacon, cut thin as wafers, had been laid. The bacon, under the heat, shriveled up and rolled off into the fire, but not until the flavor had been given to the steak. One of the miners had opened a couple of cans of preserved pine-apples; the coffee was hot, the meats and the biscuits were ready, and so the simple supper was served. Harding had placed the chairs; Brewster's was at the head of the table.

Corrigan waited until all the others had taken their seats at the table; then, with a glass in his hand and a demijohn thrown over his right elbow, he stepped forward and said:

"To didicate the house, and also as a medicine, I prescribe for aitch patient forty drops."

Each took his medicine resignedly, and as the last one returned the glass, Corrigan added: "It appears to me I am not faling ony too well meself," and either as a remedy or preventive, he took some of the medicine.

The supper was ravenously swallowed by the men, who for months had eaten nothing but miners' boarding-house fare. With one voice they declared that it was the first real meal they had eaten for weeks, and over their coffee they drank long life to housekeeping and confusion to boarding-houses.

When the supper was over and the things put away, the pipes were lighted. By this time the shadow of Mount Davidson around them had melted into the gloom of the night, and for the first time in months these men settled themselves down to spend an evening at home. It was a new experience.

"It is just splendid," cried Wright. "No beer, no billiards, no painted nymphs, no chance for a row. We have been sorry fools for months—for years, for that matter—or we would have opened business at this stand long ago."

"We have, indeed," said Ashley. "To-night we make a new departure. What shall we call our mess?"

Many names were suggested, but finally "The Comstock Club" was proposed and nominated by acclamation.

THE COMSTOCK CLUB.

It was agreed, too, that no other members, except honorary members, should be admitted, and no politics talked. Then the conversation became general, and later, confidential : and each member of the Club uncovered a little his heart and his hopes.

Miller meant, so soon as he " made a little stake,"
to go down to San Francisco and assault the stock
sharps right in their Pine and California street dens.
He believed he had discovered the rule which could
reduce stock speculation to an exact science, and he
was anxious for the opportunity which a little capital
would afford, "to show those sharpers at the Bay a
trick or two, which they had never yet 'dropped on.'"
He added. patronizingly: "I will loan you all so
much money. by and by, that each of you will have
enough to start a bank."

" I shtarted a bank alridy, all be mesilf. night before last." said Corrigan.

" What kind of a bank was it, Barney?" asked
Harding.

" One of King Pharo's.   I put a twenty-dollar pace
upon the Quane ; that shtarted the bank.   The chap
on the other side of the table commenced to pay out
the pictures. and the Quane——"

" Well. what of the Queen, Barney?" asked Carlin.

" She fill down be the side of the sardane box, and
the chap raked in me double agle."

"How do you like that style of banking. Barney?"
asked Ashley.

"Oh! Its mighty plisant and enthertainin', of
course ; the business sames to be thransacted with a
grate dale of promptness and dispatch ; the only
drawback seems to be that the rates of ixchange are
purty high."

Tom Carlin knew of a great farm, a store, a flour
mill, and a hazel-eyed girl back in Illinois.   He
coveted them all, but was determined to possess the
girl anyway.

After a little persuasion, he showed her picture to

the Club. They all praised it warmly, and Corrigan declared she was a daisy. In a neat hand on the bottom of the picture was written: "With love, Susie Richards." Carlin always referred to her as "Susie Dick."

Harding, upon being rallied, explained that his father came with the Argonauts to the West: that he was brilliant, but over-generous; that he had lived fast and with his purse open to every one, and had died while yet in his prime, leaving an encumbered estate, which must be cleared of its indebtedness, that no stain might rest upon the name of Harding. There was a gleam in the dark eyes, and a ring to the voice of the boy as he spoke, that kindled the admiration of the Club, and when he ceased speaking, Miller reached out and shook his hand, saying: "You should have the money, my boy!"

Back in Massachusetts, Brewster had met with a whole train of misfortunes; his property had become involved; his wife had died—his voice lowered and grew husky when mentioning this—he had two little girls, Mable and Mildred. He had kept his children at school and paid their way despite the iron fortune that had hedged him about, and he was working to shield them from all the sorrows possible, without the aid of the Saint who had gone to heaven. The Club was silent for a moment, when the strong man added, solemnly, and as if to himself: "Who knows that she does not help us still?"

In his youth, Brewster acquired the trade of an engineer. At this time, as we learned before, he was running a power drill in the Bullion. He was a great reader and was thorough on many subjects.

Wright had his eyes on a stock range in California, where the land was cheap, the pasturage fine, the water abundant, and where, with the land and a few head of stock for a beginning, a man would in a few years be too rich to count his money. He had been accustomed to stock, when a boy, in Missouri, and was sure that there was more fun in chasing a wild steer with a good mustang, than finding the biggest silver mine in America.

Ashley had gained some new ideas since coming West. He believed he knew a cheap farm back in Pennsylvania, that, with thorough cultivation, would yield bountifully. There were coal and iron mines there also, which he could open in a way to make old fogies in that country open their eyes. He knew, too, of a district there, where a man, if he behaved himself, might be elected to Congress. It was plain, from his talk, that he had some ambitious plans maturing in his mind.

Corrigan had an old mother in New York. He was going to have a few acres of land after awhile in California, where grapes and apricots would grow, and chickens and pigs would thrive and be happy. He was going to fix the place to his own notion, then was going to send for his mother, and when she came, every day thereafter he was going to look into the happiest old lady's eyes between the seas.

So they talked, and did not note how swiftly the night was speeding, until the deep whistle of the Norcross hoisting engine sounded for the eleven o'clock shift, and in an instant was followed by all the whistles up and down the great lode.

Then the good nights were said, and in ten minutes the lights were extinguished and the mantles of night and silence were wrapped around the house.

CHAPTER III.

An early breakfast was prepared by the whole Club, as the supper of the previous evening had been. The miners had to be at the mines, where they worked, promptly at 7 o'clock, to take the places of the men who had worked since eleven o'clock the previous night.

While at breakfast the door of the house was softly opened and a Chinaman showed his face. He explained that he was a "belly good cook," and would like to work for ten dollars a week.

Carlin was nearest the door, and in a bantering tone opened a conversation with the Mongolian.

"What is your name, John?"

"Yap Sing."

"Are you a good cook, sure, Yap?"

"Oh, yes, me belly good cook; me cookie bleef-steak, chickie, turkie, goosie; me makie bled, pie, ebbything; me belly good cook."

"Have you any cousins, Yap?"

"No cuzzie; no likie cuzzie."

"Do you get drunk, Yap?"

"No gettie glunk; no likie blandy."

"Do you smoke opium?"

"No likie smokie opium. You sabe, one man smokie opium, letee while he all same one fool; all same one d——d monkey."

"Suppose we were to hire you, Yap, how long would it take you to steal everything in the ranch?"

"Me no stealie: me no likie stealie."

"Now, Yap, suppose we hire you and we all go off to the mines and leave you here, and some one

comes and wants to buy bacon and beans and flour
and sugar, what would you do?"

"Me no sellie."

"Suppose some one comes and wants to steal
things, what then?"

"Me cuttie his ears off; me cuttie his d——d
throat."

At this Brewster interposed and said: "I believe
it would be a good idea to engage this Chinaman.
We are away and the place is unprotected all day;
besides, after a man has worked all day down in the
hot levels of the Comstock, he does not feel like cooking his own dinner. Let us give John a trial."

It was agreed to. Yap Sing was duly installed.
He was instructed to have supper promptly at six
o'clock: orders were given him on the markets for
fresh meat, vegetables, etc. From the remnants of
the breakfast the dinner buckets were filled and the
men went away to their work.

Yap Sing proved to be an artist in his way. When
the members of the Club met again at their home, a
splendid, hot supper was waiting for them. They
ate, as hungry miners do, congratulating themselves
that, as it were from the sky, an angel of a heathen
had dropped down upon them.

After supper, when the pipes were lighted, the
conversation of the previous evening was resumed.

The second night brought out something of the
history of each. They had nearly all lived in California; some had wandered the Golden Coast all
over; all had roughed it, and all had an experience
to relate. These evening visits soon became very
enjoyable to the members of the Club, and the friendship of the members for each other increased as they

the more thoroughly, knew the inner lives of each other.

On this night, Wright was the last to speak of himself. When he had concluded, Ashley said to him : "Wright, you have had some lively experiences. What is the most impressive scene that you ever witnessed ?"

"I hardly know." Wright replied. "I think maybe a mirage that was painted for me, one day, out on the desert, this side of the sink of the Humbolt, when I was crossing the plains, shook me up about as much as anything that ever overtook me. except the chills and fever. which I used to have when a boy, back in Missouri. For only a picture it was right worrisome."

The Club wanted to hear about it, and so Wright proceeded as follows: .

"We had been having rough times for a good while : thar had been sickness in the train ; some of the best animals had been poisoned with alkali : thar had been some Injun scares—it was in '57—and we all had been broken. more or less, of our rest, I in particular, was a good deal jolted up : was nervous and full of starts and shivers. I suspect thar was a little fever on me. We halted one morning on the desert, to rest the stock, and make some coffee. It was about eight o'clock. We had been traveling since sundown the night before, crossing the great desert. and hoped to reach Truckee River that afternoon.

"While resting, a mighty desire took possession of me to see the river, and to feel that the desert was crossed.

"I had a saddle mule that was still in good condition. I had petted him since he was three days old, had broken him, and he and myself were the best of friends. His mother was a thoroughbred Kentucky mare : from her he had inherited his courage and staying qualities, while he had also just enough of his father's stubbornness to be useful, for it held his heart up to the work when things got rough.

"I looked over the train ; it was all right : I was not needed ; would not be any more that day.

"The mule was brought up in the Osage hills, and I had named him Osage, which after awhile became contracted to Sage. I went to him and looked him over. He was quietly munching a bacon sack. I took a couple of quarts of wheaten flour, mixed it into a soft paste, with water from one of the kegs which had been brought along, and gave it to him. He drank it as a hungry boy drinks porridge, and licked the dish clean. The journey had ·impressed upon him the absolute need of exercising the closest economy.

"When he had finished his rather light breakfast, I whispered to him that if he would stand in with me, I would show him. before night, the prettiest stream of water—snow water—in the world. I think he understood me perfectly. Telling the people of the train that I would go ahead and look out a camping place, I took my shotgun, put a couple of biscuits in my pocket, and mounted Sage. He struck out at once on his long swinging walk.

"It was an August morning and had been hot ever since the sun rose. That is a feature out thar on the desert in the summer. The nights get cold, but so soon as the sun comes up. it is like going down into the Comstock. In fifteen minutes everything is steaming. Old Ben Allen, down on the borders of the Cherokee Nation, never of a morning, warmed up his niggers any livelier than the sun does the desert.

"I rode for a couple of hours. As I said, I was weak and nervous. In the sand, Sage's feet hardly made any sound, and the glare and the silence of the desert were around and upon me. · If you never experienced it you don't know what the silence of the desert means. Take a day when the winds are laid; when in all directions, as far as your vision extends, thar is not a moving thing; when all that you can see is the brazen sky overhead, and the scarred breast of the earth, as if smitten and transfixed by Thor's thunderbolts, lying prone and desolate like the face of a dead world, before you; and withal not one sound; absolute stillness; and strong nerves after awhile become strained. On me, that forenoon, my surroundings became almost intolerable. I had been on foot driving team all night; I had eaten nothing since midnight, and then had only forced down a small slice of bread and a cup of horrible black coffee, and was really not more than half myself. One moment I was chilly; the next was perspiring, and sometimes it seemed as though I should suffocate. With my nerves strung up as they were, I guess it would not have required much to give me a panic.

"Just then, out against the sun to the southward, and apparently a mile away, I saw something. Talk about being impressed! that was my time. I was sure I saw five hundred Indian warriors, all mounted. They were wheeling in black squadrons on the desert, wheeling and forming, as I thought. Horses and men were all black, and now and then as they wheeled or swung to and fro, I marked what I was sure was the gleam of steel. They evidently had seen me; I expected every moment to hear their yell and wondered that I did not feel the tremble of the earth beneath their horses' feet: I was too nearly paralyzed to try to escape. I slipped or fell, I don't know which, from my mule, and lay panting like a tired hound upon the sand. But I could not keep my eyes from the terrible sight before me. Still those tawny warriors kept wheeling and forming, and, as I believed, menacing me.

"At length I grew a little calmer, and remember that I explained to myself that the reason I did not hear the thunder of their horses' feet, was because of the sand, and from the fact that the ponies could not be shod. But I wondered more and more where an Indian tribe could get so many black horses.

"Once, when they seemed particularly furious, and just on the point of charging down upon me: I remember that I said to myself: 'If they eat me they will have to broil me in the sun, for thar is no fuel here.' All the time too, I was pitying Sage, and my own voice frightened me as I unconsiously said: 'Poor Sage, it is a hard fate to be faithful and suffer as you have and then fall into the hands of savages.'

"When a little more under my own control, I cautiously rose to my feet and looked at the mule. It was no use. On top of the fatigue of coming quite two thousand miles, he had, on that morning, been constantly traveling for fourteen hours, with only two rests of thirty minutes each. He never could get away from those fresh ponies. I looked back in the direction of the train: it was nowhar in sight and must have been back probably five miles.

"In this strait I looked up again toward my savages. At that very moment the charge commenced; the whole array was bearing down upon me. I took my gun from the horn of the saddle and sat down on the ground. I felt—but no matter how I felt: I only know that at that moment I would have given my note for a large sum to have been back in Missouri.

"On they swept, and I watched them coming. But somehow they began to grow smaller and smaller, and in an instant more the squadron vanished. Where the moment before an armed band, terrible with life and bristling with fury, had shone upon my eyes, now all that there was to be seen was a flock of perhaps twenty ravens, flying with short flights, and hopping and lighting around some little thing, which lay above the level of the desert. I mounted Sage and rode out to the spot, some four hundred yards away.

"I found another road, and strung along it, were the carcasses of a good many cattle that had died in emigrant trains. The ravens were hopping about these carcasses and flying from one to another. I had heard of the mirage of the desert, when a boy in school, and suddenly 'I dropped upon' the whole business. By some mighty refraction of the beams of light, these miserable scavengers of the desert had been magnified into formidable, mounted warriors, and the glint of steel that I had seen, was but the shimmer of sunbeams upon their black wings.

"Again I headed Sage for the river. In a little while he commenced to stretch out his nose; soon, of his own accord, he quickened his pace to a trot, a little later he took up his long lope and never relaxed his speed until he drove his nose into the delicious water of the Truckee. I dismounted and joined him. Right there we each took the biggest and longest drink of our lives; then I gave Sage one of my biscuits and ate the other myself, and we both felt immensely refreshed. I stripped the saddle and bridle from the mule and let him go. The river bank was green with grass and Sage was happy.

"Throwing myself upon the ground, and laying my head upon the saddle, I composed myself for a sleep.

"I was greatly in need of sleep, but the moment I closed my eyes, here came my black cavalry charging down upon me again, and I sprang up with a cry. Of all impressive scenes, that was my biggest one sure. I see it in my dreams still, at times, and I never, from this mountain side, look down to where the sand clouds are piling up their dunes over toward the Sink of the Carson, that I do not instinctively take one furtive glance in search of my savages."

"I had a livelier mirage than that once," said Miller with a laugh. "I was prospecting for quartz in the foothills of Rogue River Valley, Oregon, and looking up, I thought I saw four or five deer, lying under a tree, on a hill side, about three hundred yards away. I raised the sight on my gun, took as good aim as I could on horseback, and blazed away.

"In a second, four of those Rogue River Indians sprang from the ground and made for me. I had a good horse, but they ran me six miles before they gave up the chase. No more mirages like that for me, if you please."

"I had a worse one than either of yees," chimed in Corrigan. "It was in that tough winter of '69. I had been placer mining up by Pine Grove, in California, all summer. I had a fair surface claim, and by wurking half the time, I paid me way and had a few dollars besides. The other half of the time I was wurking upon a dape cut, through bid rock, to get a fall in which I could place heavy sluices, and calculated that with the spring I could put in a pipe, and hydraulic more ground in one sason than I could wurk in the ould way in tin. One day, late in the autumn, I went up to La Porte to buy supplies, and on the night that I made that camp it began to snow. When once it got shtarted, it just continued to snow, as it can up in those mountains, and niver "lit up" for four hours at a time for thray wakes. It began to look as though the glacial period had returned to the wurld.

"When I wint into town, I put up at Mrs. O'Kelly's boardin' and lodgin' house. Mrs. O'Kelly was a big woman, weighin' full two hundred pounds, and she was a business woman. She didn't pretind to be remainin' in La Porte jist for her hilth.

"But there was a beautiful girl waitin' on the table in Mrs. O'Kelly's home. Her name was Maggie Murphy, and she was as thrim and purty a girl as you would wish to mate. She had bright, cheery ways, and whin she wint up to a table and sung out 'SOUP'? all the crockery in the dinin' room would dance for joy.

"Of an avenin' I used, after a few days, to visit a bit with Maggie. Some one had told about the camp that I had a great mine, and was all solid, and I was willin' to have the delusion kipt up, anyway until the storm saised. Maggie, I have a suspicion, had hurd the same story, for she was exceedingly gracious loike to me. One avenin,' as I was sayin' 'good night'— we were growin' mighty familiar loike thin—I said 'Maggie,' says I, 'the last woman I iver kissed was my ould mother, may I not kiss you, for I love you, darlint?' 'Indade you shall not,' says she, but in spite of that, somethin' in her eyes made me bould loike, and I saised upon and hild her—but she did not hould so very hard—and I kissed her upon chake and lips and eyes, and me arms were around her, and her heart was throbbin' warm against mine, and me soul was in the siventh heaven.

"After awhile we quieted down a bit, and with me arms shtill around her, I asked, didn't she think Corrigan was a purtier name nor Murphy, and as I could not change my name fur her sake, wouldn't she change hers fur moine?

"Thin with the tears shinin' loike shtars in her beautiful eyes, she raised up her arms, let thim shtale round me neck, and layin' her chake against me breast, which was throbbin' loike a stone bruise, said, said she, 'Yis, Barney, darlint.'

"I had niver thought Barney was a very beautiful name before, but jist then it shtruck upon me ear swater thin marriage bells."

Here Miller interrupted with, "You felt pretty proud just then, did you not, Barney?"

"The Koohinoor would not hiv made a collar button fur me."

"Don't interrupt him, Miller," interposed Carlin; let Barney tell us the rest of the story."

"There was a sofay near by. I drew Maggie to it, sat down and hild her to me side. She was pale, and we were both sort of trembly loike.

"We did not talk much at first, but after awile Maggie said, suddent, said she: 'What a liar you are, Barney!'

"And I said 'for why?' And she said 'to say you had niver kissed a woman since you had lift your ould mother. You have had plinty of practice.'

"'And how do you know,' says I, and thin—but no matter, we had to begin all over again.

"After awhile I wint away to bid, and talk about your mirages; all that night there was a convoy of angels around me, and the batein' of their wings was swater than the echoes that float in whin soft music comes from afar over still wathers.

"One of the angels had just folded her wings and taken the form of Maggie, and was jist bendin' over me, whisperin' beautiful loike, whin, oh murther, I was wakened with a cry of: 'Are ye there now, ye blackguard?' I opened me eyes, and there stood Mrs. O'Kelly, with a broomstick over her head, and somethin' in her eye that looked moighty like a cloud-burst.

"'Ye thavin' villin,' said she, 'pertendin' to be a rich miner, and atin' up a poor woman all the time.' Thin she broke down intoirely and commi nced wailin..

"'Oh, Mr. Corrigan,' she howled through her sobs, 'How could yees come here and impose upon a unsuspectin' widdie; you know how hard I wurk; that I am up from early mornin' until the middle of the night, cookin' and shwapin' and makin' beds, and slavin' loike a black nigger, and——' by this time she recovered her timper and complated the sintence with: 'If yees don't pay me at once I'll—I'll, I'll—'

"I found breath enough after awhile to tell her to hould on. My pantaloons were on a chair within aisy rache; I snatched thim up, sayin' as I did so: 'How much is your bill, Mrs. O'Kelly?'

"'Thray wakes at iliven dollars is thray and thirty dollars, and one extra day is a dollar and five bits, or altogither, thirty-four dollars and five bits.'

"I shtill had siveral twinty-dollar paces; I plunged

me hand into the pocket of me pants. saized them all, thin let them drop upon aich other, all but two, and holdin' these out. said sharply. and still with the grand air of a millionaire: 'The change. if you plase, Mrs. O'Kelly.'

"She took the money, gazed upon it a moment with a dazed and surprised look; thin suddenly her face was wrathed in smiles, and as softly as a woman with her voice (it sounded loike a muffled threshing machine) could, said: 'Take back your money. Mr. Corrigan, and remain as long as you plase. I was only jist after playin' a bit of a trick upon yees. what do yees think I care for a few beggarly dollars?'

"But I could not see it: I remained firm. Again I said: 'The change, if you plase, Mrs. O'Kelly, and as soon too as convanient.'

"She brought me the change. sayin': 'I'll have your brikfast smokin' hot for yees, in five minutes, Mr. Corrigan.'

"I put on me clothes and looked out. The storm had worn itself out at last. I wint down stairs to the dinin' room door, and beckoned to Maggie. She came to me. and there ware the rale love-light in her beautiful eyes. I can see her now. She was straight as a pump rod; her head sat upon her nick like a picture; the nick itsilf was white loike snow—but niver mind. 'Come out in the hall a bit.' I whispered, and she come. I clasped her hand for a moment and said: 'It's goin' home I am, Maggie; I am goin' to fix me house a little: it will take me forty days to make me arrangements. If I come thin, will you take me name and go back with me?'

"'I will,' says she.

"This is the sivinteenth of the month, Maggie, the

sivinteenth of next month will be thirty days, and tin more will make it the twinty-sivinth. If I come thin, will yees go?' I asked.

"'I will, Barney, Dear,' was the answer.

"'Have yees thought it over, and will yees be satisfied, darlint?' I asked.

"'I have, Barney; I shall be satisfied, and I will be a good wife to yees, darlint,' was the answer.

MAGGIE.

"Thin I hild out me arms and she sprang into thim. There was an embrace and a kiss and thin—

"'Good bye, Maggie!'

"'Good bye, Barney!' and I wint away.

"I wint to a ristaurant and got a cup of coffee, and was jist startin' fer home, whin a frind come up and said: 'Barney,' said he; 'there's a man here you ought to go and punch the nose off of.'

"'What fur.' says I.

"'He's a slanderin' of yer,' says he.

"'Who is the man and what is he sayin?' says I.

"'It's Mike Dougherty, the blacksmith,' says he; and he is a sayin' as how your claim is no account, and that you are a bummer.'

"Me heart was too light to think of quarrelin'; on me lips the honey of Maggie's kiss was still warm, and what did I care what ony man said. I merely laughed, and said: 'Maybe he is right,' and wint upon me way."

With this Corrigan ceased speaking. After a moment or two of silence, Carlin said:

"Well, Barney, how was it in six weeks?"

"I had another mirage thin," said Barney. "I wint up to town; called at Mrs. O'Kelly's: she mit me, smilin' like, and said: 'Walk in, Mr. Corrigan!' I said: 'If you please, Mrs. O'Kelly, can I see Miss Murphy?' There was a vicious twinkle in her eye, as she answered, pointin' to a nate house upon the hillside, as she spoke.

"'You will find her there, but her name is changed now. She was married on Thursday wake, to Mr. Mike Dougherty, the blacksmith. A foine man, and man of property, is Mr. Dougherty.'

"Talk about shtrong impressions! For a moment I felt as though I was fallin' down a shaft. I——but don't mention it."

Barney was still for a moment, and then said, in a

voice almost husky: "As I came into town that day, all the great pines were noddin,' shmilin' and stretchin' out their mighty arms, as much as to say: 'We congratulate you. Mr. Corrigan.' As I turned away from Mrs. O'Kelly's, it samed to me that ivery one of thim had drawn in its branches and stood as the hoodlum does whin he pints his thumb to his nose and wriggles his fingers."

Just then the Potosi whistle rung out on the still night again, the others answered the call, and the Club. at the signal. retired.

CHAPTER IV.

As the pipes were lighted next evening, Carlin said to Barney: "Corrigan. does the ghost of your La Porte mirage haunt you as Wright's does him?"

"Not a bit of it," answered Corrigan sharply. "It hurt for awhile, I confess it, but a year and a half after Maggie was married, I passed her house one avenin' in the gloaming, and in a voice which I knew well, though all the swateness had been distilled out of it, this missage came out upon the air: 'Mike, if yees have got the brat to slape, yees had better lay him down and come out to your tay. I should loike to get these supper things put away sometime tonight.' Be dad, there was no mirage about that, no ravens about that, Wright; it was the charge of the rale Injun!'"

"Speaking of babies," said Miller nonchalantly,

"do you know that about the most touching scene I ever witnessed was over a baby? It was in Downieville, California, way back in '51 or '2. You know at that time babies were not very numerous in the Sierras. There were plenty of men there who had not seen a good woman, or a baby, for two years or more. You may not believe it, but you shut the presence of women and children all out of men's lives, for months at a time, and they contract a disease, which I call 'heart hunger,' and because of that I suspect that more whiskey has been drunk in this country, and more killings have grown out of trifling quarrels, than through all other causes combined. Without the eyes of women, good women, that he respects, upon a man, in a little while the wild beast, which is latent in all men's hearts, begins to assert itself. Because of this, men who were born to be good and true, have, to kill the unrest within their souls, taken to drink; the drink has led naturally up to a quarrel; they have got away with their first fight; the fools around them have praised them for their 'sand'; there has been no look of sorrow and reproach in any honest woman's eyes to bring them back to their senses; and after such a beginning, look for them in a year, and, in nine cases out of ten, you will find that they are lost men.

"But I commenced to tell you about the Downieville baby. It had been decided that we would have a Fourth of July celebration. There was no trouble about getting it up. We had a hundred men in camp, either one of whom could make as pretty a speech as you ever heard; everybody had plenty of money, and there was no trouble about fixing things to have a lively time. True, there was no chance for a triumphal car, with a Goddess of Liberty, and a young lady to represent each State. There was a good reason for it. There were not thirty young ladies within three hundred miles of us.

" But we had a big live eagle to represent Sovereignty, and a grizzly bear as a symbol of Power, which we hauled in the procession: we had some mounted men. including some Mexican packers on mule back: a vast variety of flags, and many citizens on foot in the procession. Of course we had a marshal and his staff. a president of the day, an orator, poet. reader and chaplain. and last, but not least, a brass band of a few months' training. There were flags enough for a grand army, and every anvil in town was kept red hot firing salutes.

"After the parade, the more sedate portion of the people repaired to the theatre, to hear the Declaration, poem. and oration. The prayer, Declaration and poem had been disposed of. and the president of the day was just about to introduce the orator, when a solitary baby but a few months old, set up a most energetic yell. and continued it for two or three minutes, the frightened mother not daring in that crowd to supply the soothing the youngster was evidently demanding. To cause a diversion, I suppose. the leader of the brass band nodded to the others, and they commenced to play the ' Star Spangled Banner.' The band had not had very much more practice than the baby, but the players were doing the best they could, when a tremendous, big-whiskered miner sprang upon a back seat, and waving his hat wildly, in a voice like a thunder-roll, shouted: 'Stop that ——d band and give the baby a chance!'

" Nothing like what followed during the next ten

minutes had ever been seen on this earth, since the confusion of tongues transpired among the builders of Babel's Tower. Men shouted and yelled like mad men, strangers shook each other by the hand and screamed 'hurrah,' and in the crowd I saw a dozen men crying like children.

"For a moment every heart was softened by the memories that baby's cries awakened.

"The next time you feel provoked because the children shout and shy rocks as they return from school, you may all remember that could the world be carried on without children, it would not require more than two generations to transform men into wild beasts."

When Miller ceased speaking, Ashley remarked: "Miller, you talk very wisely on the subject of babies, why have you none of your own?"

Miller waited a moment before answering, and then in an absent-minded manner said:

"Did you never hear a gilt-edged expert talk familiarly about a mine, as though he knew all about it, when he did not really know a streak of ore from east country porphyry?"

At this the others all laughed, and Miller joined in the merriment heartily, but nevertheless, something in the thoughts which the question awakened, had its effect upon him, for he was moody and pre-occupied for several minutes. Meanwhile, a spell seemed to be upon the whole Club, except Brewster, who was reading a pamphlet on "The Creation of Mineral Veins," and Carlin, who was absorbed in a daily paper.

"Whoever stops to think," proceeded Miller, speaking as much to himself as to the others, "upon what sorrows the foundations of new States are laid, how many hearts are broken, how many strong lives are worn out in the pitiless struggle?

"Where are the men who were the Argonauts of the golden days? The most of them are gone. Every hill side is marked with their graves. They were a strong, brave, generous race. They laid the wand of their power on the barbarism which met them; it melted away at their touch; they blazed the trails and smoothed the paths, that, unsoiled, the delicate sandals of civilization might draw near; they rifled the hills and ravines of their stores of gold, and poured it into the Nation's lap, until every sluggish artery of business was set bounding; they built temples to Religion, to Learning, to Justice and to Industry; as they moved on, cities sprung up in their wake; following them came the enchantments of home and the songs of children: but for them, what was their portion? They were to work, to struggle, to be misjudged in the land whence they came; to learn to receive any blows which outrageous fortune might hurl at them, without plaint; to watch while States grew into place around them, and while the frown on the face of the desert relaxed into a smile at their toil, that toil was simply to be accepted as a matter of course by the world, and in the severe and self-satisfied civilization of older States, only pity was to be felt for their ignorance, and only horror for their rough ways. They were to be path-finders, the sappers and miners to storm the strong-holds of barbarism; through summer's heat, and winter's cold, to continue their march, until the final night should come, and then to sink to a dreamless bivouac under the stars. What wonder if some became over-wearied! if others grew reckless?"

He had risen and was walking the floor, to and fro, like a caged lion, as he talked. Going now to the kitchen door, he cried: "Yap, bring some hot water, some sugar, a nutmeg and some limes, if you have them."

The heathen obeyed, and Miller made seven big, hot whiskey punches. Then lifting his glass he offered this toast:

"Here's to the Old Boys; to those who worked and suffered and died, but never complained!"

All rose and drank in silence.

CHAPTER V.

At the next meeting, when the pipes were all lighted, Ashley, turning to Miller, said:

"You took too gloomy a view of things last night. What you said, or rather something in your tone, has haunted me ever since. But you were wrong. The Argonauts will not be forgotten.

"The names of the kings who compelled the building of the pyramids are mostly matters of conjecture now, but no man who ever gazed upon those piles of stone that have borne unscarred the desert storms that have been breaking upon and around them through the centuries, has failed to think of the tremendous energy of the race that reared those monuments above the sand; reared them so that the abrasion of the ages avails not against them.

"One loves to dream of how that race must have looked, there under that sky, while yet the world was young. and while the energy and beauty of youth was upon it.   There was no steam power to assist, no power drills, there were only rude, untempered tools. The plain wedge, and the lever in its more effective form, were about all that was known of mechanics; still from the quarries of Syene. far up the Nile, those blocks were wrested. hewed, transported, lifted up and laid in place, and with such mathematical precision was the work performed, that the ebb and flow of the centuries have no effect upon the work. While this material work was going on, in the same realm wise men were putting into a language the alphabet of the sky, tracing out the procession of the stars and solving the mystery of the seasons.   When we think of Ancient Egypt. it is not of her kings, but what was wrought out there by brain and hand.

   " To-day I was at work on the twenty-four hundred-foot level of the mine.   Around me power drills were working. cars were rattling, cages were running: three hundred men were stoping. timbering and rolling cars to and from the chutes and ore-breasts, and in the spectral light I thought it was a scene for a painter.   But while so thinking, for some reason, there came to me the thought of the one hundred times three hundred men, who, for a generation. worked on a single pyramid; worked without pay days, without so much as a kind word, and on poorer fare than one gets at a fourth-rate miners' boarding house; and, as I reflected over that. our little work here seemed small indeed.

   " So, in estimating Greece, we do not pick out a few men or women to remember, but we think of the race that made Thermopylæ and Marathon possibilities, of the men who followed Xenophon, of the

women who closed their hearts and left their deformed offspring to perish in the woods that Greece
should rear no woman who could not bear soldiers,
no man who could not bear arms: of the race
so finely strung that poetry was born of it; that
sculpture and eloquence were so perfected in, that
to copy is impossible; that was so susceptible to
beauty that it turned justice aside, and yet that was
so valiant that it mastered the world.

"So of Rome! It is not that the great Julius
lived that we call it 'The Imperial Nation.' We
stand in awe of it still, not because out of its millions a few superb figures shine. Rather, we think
of the valor that from a little nucleus widened until
it subdued the world; of the ten thousand fields on
which Romans fought and conquered. We think how
they marshaled their armies, and taught the nations
how to lay out camps; how they built roads and aque-
ducts, that their land might be defended and the Imperial City sustained; how they carved out an archi-
tecture of their own which the world still clings to in
its most stately edifices; how, from barbarism, they
progressed until they framed a code which is still
respected; how, in literature and the arts, they ex-
celled, and how, for a thousand years, they were the
concernment of the world.

"So of England. Which merits the greater glory,
King John or the stern, half barbarous barons who,
with an instinct generations in advance of their age,
circled around their sullen king and compelled him
to give to them 'the great charter?' Through the
thousand years that have succeeded that act, how
many individual names can we rescue from the hosts
that on that little isle have lived and died? Not

many. But the grand career of the nation is in the mind forever. How, through struggle after struggle, the advance has been made; struggles that, though full of errors, knew no faltering or despair, until at last, for the world, she became the center and the bulwark of civilization; until in material strength she had no equal; until the sheen of her sails gave light to all the seas, and under her flag signal stations were upreared the world around. We do not remember many men, but there is ever in the mind the thought of English valor and persistence, and the clear judgment which backed the valor by land and sea.

"But we need not go abroad; our own land has examples enough. Not many can call over the names of those who came in the 'Mayflower,' or those who made up the colonies up and down the Atlantic coast. But the spectacle of the 'Mayflower' band kneeling, on their arrival, in the snow and singing a triumphal song, is a picture the tints of which will deepen in splendor with the ages. We need not call over the names of our statesmen and warriors; they give but a slight impression of our race. But when we think how, from the Atlantic to the Mississippi, the woods were made to give place to gardens, fruitful fields and smiling homes: when we think that the majority of those families had each of them less to start with than any one of us gets for a month's labor and yet how they subdued the land, pressed back the savage, reared and educated and created a literature for their children, until over all the vast expanse there was peace, prosperity, enlightenment and joy, then it is that we begin to grow proud.

"If the Argonauts of the Golden Coast can show

that they have wrought as well, they will not be forgotten. Those who succeed them will know that they were preceded by a race that was strong and brave and true, and their memory in the West will be embalmed with the memory of those in the East who, starting under the spray that is tossed from the white surf of the eastern sea, with no capital but pluck, hewed out and embellished the Republic.

"Of course, there have been sorrows: of course, hearts have broken: but there has been much of triumph also. It is something to have a home in this Far West; there is something in the hills, the trees, the free air and action of this region which brings to men thoughts that they would never have had in other lands. It is not bad sometimes for men to leave their books and turn to Nature for instruction. Here of all the world some of the brightest pages of Nature's book are spread open for the reader. And many a man that others pity because they think his heart must be heavy, does not ask that pity; does not feel its need. Those hearts have gathered to themselves delights, which, if not, perhaps, of the highest order, still are very sweet. Let me give an instance.

"Last year I went to look at a mine down in Tuolumne county, California. I was the guest of a miner who had lived in the same cabin for more than twenty years. He was his own cook and housekeeper and seldom had any company except his books—a fine collection—his daily papers, his gun and some domestic animals. He had a little orchard and garden. Around his garden tame rabbits played with his dogs. In explanation, he said: 'They were all babies at the same time and have grown up together.' While walking with him in his garden, he asked me if I had ever seen a mountain quail on her nest. At the same moment he parted the limbs of a shrub, and there, within six inches of his hand, sat a bird, her bright eyes looking up in perfect confidence into his.

"The place was in the high foothills; there was a space in front of his cabin. From that point the hills, in steadily increasing waves, swelled into the great ridges of the higher Sierras, and far away to the east the blue crest of Mount Bodie stood out clear against the sky.

"It was not strange to me that he loved the place. When within doors he talked upon every subject with a peculiar terse shrewdness all his own. He had had many bouts with the world; he knew men thoroughly; he had in a measure withdrawn himself from them, and found a serener comfort in his pets, his hills and trees. He had acquired that faculty which men often do when a great deal alone in the mountains. He did not reason his way up through the proof of a proposition, but with a clear sagacity reached the truth at a bound, and left the reasoning for others. He had his theory of how fissures were originally formed and filled; he had his opinion of ancient and modern authors; he understood politics well, and gave brief and true reasons for his belief. In short, he was a self-appointed ambassador to the court of the hills, to represent all the world.

"My admiration for him increased the longer I remained with him, for he knew much of interest to me; but he spoke always in a tone as though he was revealing only a little of what he knew. I suspect that was the real state of the case. There was a charm, too, about his manner. Though I knew that he had suffered many disappointments, if not sorrows, there was no bitterness. Whatever he did or said, was with a gentle grace of his own. He was free, alike, from either harshness, egotism or diffidence. Something of the great calm of the hills around him had entered into his soul.

"But the greatest surprise was reserved for me to the last. I had to get up at three o'clock in the morning and walk over a dim trail two or three miles to a little village, in order to take the stage which passed the village at five o'clock. When I was ready, my friend said: 'There are so many trails through the hills you might take the wrong one in the uncertain light. I will pilot you.'

"When we set out it was yet dark. There was an absolute hush upon the world. Up through the branches of the great pines, God's lanterns were swinging as though but just trimmed and lighted, and under the august roof where they swung, they shone with rays more pure than vestal lamps. But at length up the east some shafts of light were shot, and soon the miracle of the dawn began to unfold. It was a June morning and entirely cloudless Soon the warm rays of approaching day began to bend over the hills from the east; the foliage which had been black began to grow green; the scarlet of the hills shone out where the light touched it; the sentinel fires above began to grow dim. A little later the hills began to grow resonant with the manifold voices which they held, and which commenced to awaken to hail the approaching day.

"Then my sententious companion, as though kindled by the same influences, opened his lips. He seemed to have forgotten that I was near; he was answering the greetings of his friends in the woods. I can only give the faintest idea of what he said, and I grieve over it, for it was sweeter than music. His words ran something like this:

"'Chirp, chirp; O, my martin, (the swallow's grandmother); as usual you are up first, to say good morning, the first to hail the beautiful coming day. Ah, there you are, whistling, my lovely quail, you charming cockaded glory; and now, my mocking bird, you brown splendor with a flat nose, where do you get all your voices? Heigh, O! you are up, Mr. Jacob (woodpecker) up to see if Mrs. Jacob is gathering acorns this morning, you old miser of the woods, with your black and white clothes and your thrift worse than a Chinaman's; and now, my morning dove has commenced its daily drone, growling because breakfast is not ready, I suppose. At last you have opened your eyes, Mrs. Lark; a nice bird you are to claim to be an early riser, but you have a cheery voice, nevertheless. Now, my wren and my oreole, you are making some genuine music, if both of you together are not as big as one note of an organ. Hist! that was a curlew's cry from away down on the river's bank, and now you are all awake and singing, you noisy chatterers, as though your hearts would burst for joy. Finally, old night-raiding owl, you are saying 'good night' this morning, you old burglar of the woods.'

"Meanwhile the banners of the dawn had grown more and more bright in the sky, and as he ceased speaking, the full disc of the sun, lighted with omnipotent fires, shone full above the hills, with a splendor too severe for human eyes.

"I had not interrupted my friend during the half

hour that he, striding before me on the trail, had been talking. I half suspected that he had forgotten that I was near, absorbed as he was in greeting his warblers. Of course I have not named the birds in their order: nor have I named half that he greeted: I might as well try to repeat to you all the scientific terms in one of Professor Stewart's earthquake lectures. But all that day, and for many days afterwards, his words were ringing in my ears: and often have I wondered, if, with his thoughts and his surroundings, he was not with more reason and more peace, passing down life's trail, than as though he were out in the pitiless world of men, striving for wealth and for power. Never since have I seen a lonely man in town, with shy face which revealed that he was unused to the crowds of the city, purchasing some few little necessaries, and, apparently, hurrying to get away, that I have not said to myself: 'He has a cabin somewhere with books and dogs, and with a garden outside, and he knows every bird in the forest by its morning call.'"

While Ashley was talking, he had unconsciously fixed his eyes upon the light which shone from a reflector, up through the window from the hoisting works down the hill, and seemed to forget the presence of any one near.

As he ceased and looked around, he discovered that all his auditors had fallen asleep in their chairs, except Yap Sing, who had stolen into the room. He looked up knowingly, smiled and said:

"You talkie belly nice. Me heap sabbie, clail, chickie, duckie, goosie. Me cookie lem flirst late, you bettie."

"You be—" said Ashley, and went to bed. The rest, awakened by the whistles, started up in surprise, and

Corrigan said: "I was dramin' of agles and pacocks and swans and hummin' birds. I must have been afther atin too much supper."

CHAPTER VI.

The next evening as the club gathered around the hearth, Brewster, who, next to Harding, was the most reticent member of the party, said apologetically to Ashley:

"It was shabby of us not to give more heed to your story last night, but the truth with me was, I was very tired. We were cutting out a station on the 2,300 level of the mine, yesterday; the work was hard, the ventilation bad, and it was hot and prostrating work. But, I heard most of your story, nevertheless. While I know nothing of your miner who lives with his books and birds and dogs and flowers; and hence know nothing of what storms he has breasted and what heart-aches he has borne; and, therefore, cannot, in my own mind, fix his place, still, on general principles, it is man's duty never to accept any rebuff of unkind fortune as a reason for ceasing to try; but rather he should struggle on and do the best he can; if needs be dying with the harness on his back. Moreover, as a rule, it is the easier way. It is in harmony with nature's first great law, and man seldom errs when he follows the laws that were framed before the world's foundations were laid. When man was given his two feet to stand upon; his arms to cleave out for himself a path and a career, and his brain to be his guide: then with the rich earth for a field, in the opinion of the Infinite Goodness, he has all the capital that he required. The opportunities of this land, especially this free West, with a capacity to plan and work, are enough for any man. The trouble is, men falter too soon. On that last night of anxiety, before the New World rose out of the sea to greet the eyes of Columbus; when his sullen and fear-stricken crews were on the point of mutiny, suddenly there came to the senses of the great commander, the perfume of earthly flowers. Soon after the veil of the ocean was rent asunder, and upon his thrilled eyes there burst a light. Columbus was not the only man who ever discovered a new world. They are being found daily. I meet men often on the street and know by something in their faces, that, at that very moment, the perfume of the flowers of some glory to come is upon them, and that the first rays of the dawn of a divine light are commencing to fill with splendor their eyes.

"When the idea of the Alexandrian, after having been transmitted from mortal to mortal, for more than fifty generations, at last materialized, and the care worn man who was watching, heard the first sob of artificial life come from a steam engine, to him was the perfume and the light.

"When, after generations of turmoil and war, in the deadly double struggle to assimilate various peoples, and at the same time out of barbarism to construct a stable and enlightened government; when the stern old English barons caught the right inspiration, and gathering around their sovereign, asked him to recognize the rights of the men on whose valor his throne leaned for safety and to sign Magna Charta; to them came the perfume and the light.

"When the desire of the colonies, voiceless before, at lenth through the pen of Jefferson, found expression in the words: 'We hold these truths to be self-evident—that all men are created equal; that they are endowed by their Creater with certain unalienable rights;' then to a whole nation, yes to the world, came the perfume and the light.

"In public life these emotions are marked, and the world applauds. In humble life they are generally unnoticed, but they are frequent, and the enchantment of the perfume becomes like incense, and it is a softer light that dawns. When the poor man, who lays aside daily but a pittance from his earnings, finds at last, after months and years, that the sum has increased until it is certain that he can build a little home for his wife—a home which is to be all his own—and that he can educate his children; then the perfume and lights of a new world entrance him, and in his sphere he is as great as was the dark-eyed Italian.

"In the Bible we read that all the prophets were given to fasting and to labor, in order to bring the body under subjection to the soul. This is but typical of what a great soul must submit to, if it would catch the perfume and the light. The world's wealth rests on labor. Whether a man tills a garden or writes a book, the harvest will be worth gathering just in proportion to the soil, and to the energy and intelligence of the work performed. Columbus could never have discovered a new world by standing on the sea shore and straining his eyes to the West. The tempests had to be met; the raging seas outrode; the mutinous crew controlled. There are tempests, waves and mutineers in every man's path, and it is only over and beyond them that there comes the perfume and the light. The lesson taught at Eden's gate is the one that must still be learned. All that man can gain is by labor, and the sword that guards the gate flames just as fiercely as of old.

"To the Argonauts was given a duty. They were appointed to redeem a wild and create a sovereign state. I believe they were a brave, true race. The proof is, that without the restraint of pure women and without law, they enforced order. Their energy, also, was something tremendous. After building up California, they, in great part, made a nucleus for civilization to gather to in each of half-a-dozen neighboring Territories. But they had advantages which the men who settled the Eastern States—the region beyond the Mississippi River, I mean—never possessed. They had better food to eat, a better climate to live in. If they did not have capital, they knew a living, at least, could be had from the nearest gravel bank or ravine, and if they lacked the encircling love of wife and children, they were spared the sorrow of seeing dear women wear out lives of hardship and poverty, as has been seen on all other frontiers in America.

"If some fell by the wayside, it was natural, for human nature is weak and Death is everywhere: if some in the pitiless struggle failed, they had no right to cease to try, for when men do that the hope that to them will come the perfume or that upon their eyes will ever shine the light, is forever closed."

"All that is good," said Carlin, "but the rule does not always hold true. There is sometimes a limit to man's capacity to suffer, and his heart breaks: and still after that his face gives no sign, and there is no abatement of his energies. In such cases, however, men generally lose the capacity to reason calmly and chase impossibilities. I saw a case yesterday. I met a man mounted on a cheap mustang, and leading another on which was packed a little coarse food, a pick, shovel, pan, coffee-pot and frying pan. As he moved slowly up C. street, a friend—himself an Argonaut—clutched me by the arm with one hand, and with the other pointing to the man on horseback, asked me if I knew him. Replying that I did not, he said: 'Why, that is "Prospecting Joe;" I thought everybody knew him.' I told him I had never heard of him, when he related his story, almost word for word, as follows:

"He came to the far West from some Eastern state in the old, old days. He was not then more than twenty-three or twenty-four years old. Physically he was a splendid specimen of a man, I am told. He was, moreover, genial and generous, and drew friends around him wherever he went. He secured a claim in the hills above Placerville. One who knew him at that time told me, that, calling at his cabin one night, he surprised him poring over a letter written in a fair hand, while beside him on his rude table lay the picture of a beautiful girl. His heart must have been warmed at the time, for picking up the picture and handing it to my friend, he said. 'Look at her! She is my Nora, *my* Nora. She, beautiful as she is, would in her divinity have bent and married a coarse mold of clay like myself, and poor, too, as I was; but her father said: 'Not yet, Joe. Go out into the world, make a struggle for two years, then come back, and if by that time you have established that you are man enough to be a husband to a true woman, and you and Nora still hold to the thought that is in your hearts now, I will help you all

I can. And, mind you, I don't expect you to make a fortune in two years; I only want you to show that the manhood which I think you have within you is true.' 'That was square and sensible talk, and it was not unkind. So I came away.' Then he took the picture and looked fondly at it for a long time, and said: 'I see the delicious girl as she looked on that summer's day, when she waved me her last good by. I shall see her all my life, if I live a thousand years.'

"Well, Joe worked on week days; on Sundays, as miners did in those days, he went to camp to get his mail and supplies. His claim paid him only fairly well, but he was saving some money. In eight months he had been able to deposit twelve hundred dollars in the local bank. One Sunday he did not receive the expected letter from his Nora, and during the next hour or two he drank two or three times with friends. He was about to leave for home, when three men whom he slightly knew, and who had all been drinking too much, met him and importuned him to drink with them. He declined with thanks, when one of the three caught him by the arm and said he must drink.

"At any other time he would have extricated himself without trouble and gone on his way. But on that day he was not in good humor, so he shook the man off roughly and shortly told him to go about his own affairs.

"The others were just sufficiently sprung with liquor to take offense at this, and the result was a terrific street fight. Joe was badly bruised but he whipped all three of the others. Then he was arrested and ordered to appear next morning to answer a charge of fighting. He was of course cleared without difficulty, but it took one-fourth of his deposit to pay his lawyer. Then the miners gathered around him and called him a hero and he went on his first spree.

"Next morning when he awoke and thought of as much as he could remember of the previous day's events, he was thoroughly ashamed. As he went down to the office of the hotel, in response to an inquiry as to how he felt, he answered: 'Full of repentance and beer.' A friend showed him the morning paper with a full account of the Sunday fight and his trial and acquittal. This was embellished with taking head-lines, as is the custom with reporters. It cut him to the heart. He knew that if the news reached his old home of his being in a street fight on Sunday, all his hopes would be ended. His first thought was to draw his money and take the first steamer for Panama and New York. He went to the bank and asked how his account stood, for he remembered to have drawn something the previous day. He was answered that there was still to his credit $150. The steamer fare was $275. Utterly crushed, he returned to his claim. The fear that the news of his disgrace would reach home, haunted him perpetually and made him afraid to write. He continued to work, but not with the old hope.

"After some weeks, a rumor came that rich ground had been 'struck' away to the north, somewhere in Siskiyou county. He drew what money he had, bought a couple of ponies, one to ride and one to pack, and started for the new field. Before starting, he confided to a friend that the previous night he had dreamed of a mountain, the crest of which glittered all over with gold, and he was going to find it.

"The friend told him it was but a painted devil of

the brain, the child of a distempered imagination, but he merely shook his head and went away.

"He has pursued that dream ever since. His eyes have been ever strained to catch the reflection from those shining heights. When he began the search, his early home and the loving arms which were there stretched out to him, began to recede in the distance. In a few years they disappeared altogether. Then his hopes one by one deserted him, until all had fled except the one false one which was, and still is, driving him on. Youth died and was buried by the trail, but so absorbed was he that he hardly grieved. As Time served notice after notice upon him; as his hair blanched, his form bent and the old sprightliness went out of his limbs, he retired more and more from the haunts of men; more and more he drew the mantle of the mountains around him. But his eyes, now bright with an unnatural splendor, were still strained upon the shining height. There were but a few intervening hills and some forests that obstructed his view. A little further on and the goal would be reached. Last night he was in his cups and he told my friend that this time he would 'strike it sure,' that the old man would make his showing yet, that he would yet go back to the old home and be a Providence to those he loved when a boy.

"Poor wretch. There is an open grave stretched directly across his trail. On this journey or some other soon, he will, while his eyes are still straining towards his heights of gold, drop into that grave and disappear forever.

"Some morning as he awakens, amid the hills or out upon the desert, there will be such a weariness upon him that he will say, 'I will sleep a little longer,' and from that sleep he will never waken.

" Heaven grant that his vision will then become a reality and that he may mount the shining heights at last.

"Of course it is easy to say that he was originally weak, but that is no argument, for human nature is prone to be weak. His was a high-strung, sensitive, generous nature. He never sought gold for the joy it would give him, but for the happiness he dreamed it would give to those he loved. His Nora was a queen in his eyes and he wanted to give her, every day, the surroundings of a queen. He made one mistake and never rallied from it. Had the letter come that fatal Sunday from Nora, as he was expecting it, or had he left for home half an hour earlier, or had he been of coarser clay, that day's performance would have been avoided, or would have been passed as an incident not to be repeated, but not to be seriously minded. But he was of different mold, and then that was a blow from Fate. It is easy enough to say that there is nothing in that thing called luck. Such talk will not do here on the Comstock. There is no luck when a money lender charges five dollars for the use of a hundred for a month and exacts good security. He gets his one hundred and five dollars, and that is business.

" But in this lead where ore bodies lie like melons on a vine, when ore is reported in the Belcher and in the Savage, when Brown buys stock in the Belcher and Rogers buys in the Savage; when the streak of ore in the Belcher runs into a bonanza and Brown wakes up rich some morning, and when the streak of ore in the Savage runs into a Niagara of hot water which floods the mine and Rogers's stock is sold out to meet an assessment, it will not do to call Brown a shrewd fellow and Rogers an idiot.

"Still, I do not object to the theory that a man should always keep trying, even if the luck is against him, because luck may change sometime, and if it does not, he sleeps better when he knows that with the lights before him he has done the best he could. A man can stand almost anything when his soul does not reproach him as he tries to go to sleep.

"Then, too, man is notoriously a lazy animal, and unless he has the nerve to spur himself to work, even when unfortunate, he is liable to fail and get the dry rot, which is worse than death.

"But my heart goes out in sympathy when I think of the glorified spirits, which on this coast have failed and are failing every day, because from the first an iron fortune has hedged them round and baffled their every effort, struggle as they would."

Carlin ceased speaking. and the silence which prevailed in the Club for a moment was broken by Miller, who said: "Don't worry about them, Carlin. If they do fail they have lots of fun in trying."

"I would grave more for your mon Joe," interposed Corrigan, "did I not remember Mrs. Dougherty, who married the gintleman of propherthy, and thin your Joe war a fraud onyway. What war there in a bit of a scrap to make a mon grave himself into craziness over it?"

"Your stock-buying illustration is not fair, Carlin, for that is only a form of gambling at best," suggested Brewster.

The club winced under this a little, for every member dabbled in stocks sometimes, except Brewster and Harding.

For two evenings Harding had been scribbling away behind the table, and during a lull in the conversation Ashley asked him what he had been writing. " Letters?" suggested Ashley.

" No, not letters," answered Harding, sententiously.

" What is it, then," asked Miller; "won't you read it to us?"

" Yes, rade it, rade it," said Corrigan, and the rest all joined in the request.

" You won't laugh?" said Harding, inquiringly.

They all promised, and Harding read as follows:

THE PROSPECTOR.

How strangely to-night my memory flings
From the face of the past its shadowy wings,
And I see far back through the mist and tears
Which make the record of twenty years;
From the beautiful days in the Golden State,
When life seemed sure by long leases from Fate;
From the wondrous visions of "long ago"
To the naked shade that we call " now."

Those halcyon days! There were four with me then—
Ernest and Ned, Wild Tom and Ben.
Now all are gone; Tom was first to die.
I held his hands, closed his glazed eye;
And many a tear o'er his grave we shed
As we tenderly pillowed his curly head
In the shadows deep of the pines, that stand
Forever solemn, forever fanned
By the winds that steal through the Golden Gate
And spread their balm o'er the Golden State.

And the others, too, they all are dead.
By the turbid Gila perished Ned;
Brave, noble Ernest, he was lost
Amid Montana's ice and frost;
And out upon a desert trail
Our Bennie met the spectre pale.

And I am left—the last of all—
And as to-night the white snows fall,
As barbarous winds around me roar,
I think the long past o'er and o'er—
What I have hoped and suffered, all,
From twenty years rolls back the pall,
From the dusty, thorny, weary track,
As the tortuous path I follow back.

In my childhood's home they think me, there,
A failure, or lost, till my name in the prayer
At eve is forgot. Well, they cannot know
That my toil through heat, through tempest and snow,
While it seemed for naught but a struggle for pelf,
Was more for them, far more, than myself.

Ah, well! As my hair turns slowly to snow
The places of childhood more distantly grow;
And my dreams are changing. 'Tis home no more,
For shadowy hands from the other shore
Stretch nightly down, and it seems as when
I lived with Tom, Ned, Ernest and Ben.

And the mountains of Earth seem dwindling down,
And the hills of Eden, with golden crown,
Rise up, and I think, in the last great day,
Will my claim above bear a fire assay?
From the slag of earth, and the baser strains,
Will the crucible show of precious grains
Enough to give me a standing above,
Where in temples of Peace rock the cradles of Love?

"That is good, but it is too serious by half," Miller said, critically. "What is a young fellow like you doing with such a melancholy view of things?"

"It's a heap better to write such things for pleasure in boyhood than to have to feel them for a fact in old age," said Wright.

"I say, Harding, have you measured all the faet in that poem?" remarked Corrigan, good-naturedly.

"We have been talking too seriously for two or three evenings and it is influencing Harding," was Miller's comment.

Brewster thought it was a good way for Sammie to spend his evenings. It would give him discipline, which would help him in writing all his life.

CHAPTER VII.

The next evening Wright had business down town.

"Carlin was right last night," began Miller, "when he said that all men were naturally lazy. Laziness is a fixed principle in this world. I can prove it by my friend Wand down at Pioche.

"When he was not so old as he has been these last few years, he made a visit to San Francisco, and one day, passing a building on Fourth street, saw within several hives of bees, evidently placed there to be sold. Some whim led him within the building and, from the man in charge, he learned that in California, because of the softer climate, bees worked quite nine months in the year; that a good swarm of bees would gather a certain number of pounds of honey in a season, which sold readily at a certain price, making a tremendous percentage on the cost of the bees, which was, if I remember correctly, one hundred dollars per hive. The idea seemed to strike Wand. He had fifteen-hundred dollars, and all that day he was mentally estimating how much money could be made out of fifteen swarms of bees in a year. The figures looked exceedingly encouraging. They always do, you know, when your mind is fixed upon a certain business which you want to engage in.

"That evening Wand happened to meet a friend who had just come in from Honolulu. This friend was enthusiastic over the Hawaiian Islands. There was perpetual summer there and ever-blooming flowers. Before one flower cast its leaves, others on the same tree were budding. Their glory was ever before the eyes and their incense ever upon the air.

"Wand fell asleep that night trying to estimate how much money a swarm of bees would make a year in a land of perpetual summer. The conclusion was that next morning Wand bought twelve hives of bees, and that afternoon sailed with them for Honolulu

"He found a lovely place for his bees, and saw with kindling pleasure that they readily assimilated with the new country and went to work with apparent enthusiasm.

"The bees worked steadily until, in their judgment, it was time for winter to come. Then they ceased to work, remained in their hives until they ate up their hoarded wealth, and then, as Wand expresses it, 'took to the woods.'

"He borrowed the money necessary to pay his passage to San Francisco, and ever since has sworn that bees are like men, 'natural loafers,' that will not work unless they are forced to. He believes that the much lauded ant would be the same way if it were not urged on to work perpetually by the miser's fear of starvation."

Carlin suggested that the question be tested nearer home, and called out, "Yap Sing!"

The Mongolian came in from the kitchen and Carlin interrogated him.

"Yap, do you like to work?"

"Yes, me heap likee workee."

"How many hours a day do you like to work, Yap?"

"Maybe eight hour, maybe ten hour, maybe slixteen hour."

"We give you forty dollars a month. Would you work harder if we paid you fifty dollars?"

"No. Me thinkee not," answered Yap, adroitly. "You sabbie, you hire me, me sellee you my time. Me workee all the slame, forty doll's, fifty doll's, one hundred doll's. No diffelence."

"Yap, suppose you were to get $3,000, would you, work then?"

"Oh, yes. Me workee all the slame, now."

"Suppose, Yap, you had $5,000—what then?"

"Me workee all the slame."

"Do you ever buy stocks?"

"Slum time buy lettle; not muchee."

"Suppose, Yap, that some time stocks would go up and make you $20,000, would you work then?"

The Chinaman, with eyes blazing, replied vehemently: "Not one d——d bittee."

The Club agreed that Carlin had pretty well settled a vexed question, that conditions which would make both the bee and the Chinaman idlers, would be apt to very soon cause the Caucasian to lie in the shade.

"And yet," mused Brewster, "there are mighty works going on everywhere. This Nation to-day makes a showing such as this world never saw before. From sea to sea, for three thousand miles, the chariot wheels of toil are rolling and roaring as they never did in any other land. The energy that is exhausted daily amounts to more than all the world's working forces did a hundred years ago. The thing to grieve about is not that there is not enough work being performed, but that in this intensely practical and material age, the gentler graces in the hearts of men are being neglected. In the race for wealth the higher aspirations are being smothered. If from the 'tongueless past' there could be awakened the silent voices, the cry which would be heard over all others would be: 'I had some golden thoughts; I meant to have given them expression, but the swiftly moving years with their cares were too much for me, and I died and made no sign.'

"If there is such a thing as a ghost of memory, all the aisles of the past are full of wailing voices, wailing over facts unspoken, over eloquence that died in passionate hearts unuttered, over divine poems that never were set to earthly music. Aside from native indolence, most men are struggling for bread, and when the day's work is completed, brain and hand are too weary for further effort. So the years drift by until the zeal of young ambition loses its electric thrill; until cares multiply; until infirmities of body keep the chords of the soul out of tune, and the night follows, and the long sleep. There were great soldiers before Achilles or Hector, but there were no Homers, or if there were, they were dissipated fellows, or they were absorbed in business, or, under the clear Grecian sky, it was their wont to dream the beautiful days away, and so, no sounds were uttered, of the kind which, booming through space, strike at last on the immortal heights, and there make echoes which thrill the earth with celestial music ever after. If fortune

had not made an actor of Shakespeare, and if his
matchless spirit, working in the line of his daily duties,
had not felt that all the plays offered were mean and
poor, as wanting in dramatic power as they were false
to human nature, and so was roused to fill a business
need, the chances are a thousand to one that he 'would
have died with all his music in him,' and would, to-
day, have been as entirely lost in oblivion as are the
boors who were his neighbors. Just now there is not
much hope for our own country, and probably will
not be for another century. Present efforts are all for
wealth and power and are almost all earthly. Everything is calculated from a basis of coin. Before that,
brains are cowed, and for it Beauty reserves her sweetest smiles. The men who are pursuing grand ideas
with no motive more selfish than to make the masses
of the world nobler, braver and better, or to give new
symphonies to life, are wondrously few. There are
splendid triumphs wrought, but they are almost every
one material and practical.

"The men who created the science of chemistry
dreamed of finding the elixir of life; the modern
chemist pursues the study until he invents a patent
medicine or a baking powder, and then all his energies are devoted to selling his discovery.

"In its youthful vitality the Nation has performed
wonders, and from the masses individuals have solved
many of nature's mysteries and bridled many ele-
mental forces.

"The winds have been forced to swing open the
doors to their caves and show where they are brewed;
the lightnings have submitted to curb and rein; the
ship goes out against the tempest, carried forward on
its own iron arms; the secret of the sunlight has been

fathomed and a counterfeit light created; the laws which govern sound have been mastered until the human voice now thrills a wire and is caught with perfect distinctness sixty miles away, and a thousand other such triumphs have been achieved.

"But no deathless poem has been written, no immortal picture has been called to life on canvas; no master hand has touched the cold stone and transfigured it into something which seems ready, like the fabled statue of the old master, to warm into life and smiles.

"Souls surcharged at first with celestial fire have waited for the work of the bodies to be finished, that they might materialize into words of form and splendor, waited until the tenement around them fell away and left them unvoiced, to seek a purer sphere, and a generation, three generations have died with their deepest tints unpainted, their sweetest music unsung.

"This is one of the penalties attached to the laying of the foundations of new States. There is too much to be accomplished, too many purely material struggles to be made, and so hearts are stifled and souls, glowing with celestial fervor, are forbidden an altar on which to kindle their sacred flame.

"England struggled a thousand years before a man appeared to shame wealth, power and titles with the majesty of a divine mind. Perhaps it will be as long in the United States before some glorified spirit will appear to show by example that the things which this generation is struggling most for are mere dust, which, when obtained, are but Dead Sea apples to the lips of hope."

"But Brewster," said Harding, "do you not think

that a good miner is of more use to the world than a bad sculptor?"

"Suppose," said Carlin, "we were all to stop this four dollars a day business of ours and go to writing poetry, who would pay the Chinaman and settle the grocery bills at the end of the month?"

"Were not the Argonauts making pretty good use of their time," asked Miller, "when in twelve years they dug up and gave to the world nearly a thousand millions of dollars and caused such a change in the business of the country as comes to the fainting man's circulation through a transfusion of healthy blood into his veins?"

"Did you not tell us last evening," said Ashley, "that when a poor man earned a home for his wife and babies, that to him came the perfume and the light?"

"I carved out some beautiful stories and shpoke any amount of illegint poethry to Maggie Murphy, but it would not do," said Corrigan.

"There is a mirage before Brewster's eyes to-night," said Miller; "the business of most men is to earn bread."

Then Brewster, bristling up, responded:

"My answer to all of you is this: Man's first duty is to provide for himself, and for those dependent upon him, by honest toil, either of hand or brain, or both. For a long time you have each worked eight hours out of the twenty-four; perhaps eight hours more have been absorbed in eating and sleeping. What have you done with the other eight hours? You are miners. You can set timbers in line, you can lie on your backs and hit a drill above you with perfect precision; but could you make a draught of a mine, or clothe a description of one in good language on paper? You look upon a piece of ore, but can you test it and tell how much it is worth? These are all legitimate parts of your business as miners, and I refer to them merely to illustrate that in the excitements of this city, and the dream of getting rich in stock speculations, you have not only neglected your better natures, but have failed to thoroughly accomplish yourselves in your real business. You can see what you have actually lost, but you cannot estimate the pleasure you have been denying yourselves. Then when you are too old to work, what amusements and diversions are you preparing for old age?"

"For that matter," said Miller, "ask the man who fell down the Alta shaft last week, 800 feet to the sump, and the pieces of whose body, that could be found, were sewed up in canvas to be brought to the surface."

Then there was a silence for several minutes until a freight train, with two locomotives (a double header), came up the heavy grade from Gold Hill and, when opposite the house of the Club, both locomotives whistled. At this Corrigan said:

"Hear those black horses neigh! What a hail they give to the night! What a power they have under their black skins! I wonder if they don't think sometimes, the off-colored monsters."

"If the steam engine has not reflective faculties it ought to have," said Harding. "The highest pleasures which a man, in his normal state, can have are the approving whispers of his own soul. If in the iron frame of the steam engine there could be hidden a soul, what whispers would thrill it in these days! Methinks they would be something like this:

"'When I was born Invention gave to Progress a child which was to be to the modern world what the Genii were to the ancient world, except that I am real, while the Genii were but dreams. In me man finds the materialization of a dream which haunted mortals through the centuries, while the world was slowly pressing onward to a better state. At my birth men were glad to give to me their burdens, because I could carry them without fatigue. They thought me but a dumb slave to do their bidding; they saw that I could add greatly to their achievements by enabling them to overcome heavy matter, and with tireless feet to chase the swift hours. I cannot add to man's actual years, but I can make one hour for him equal to a day in the olden time. At first my work was confined to the closely peopled regions. But at length I was pushed out beyond the settlements of men, and then something of the divinity within me began to assert itself. Savage man and the wild beast retired before me; when the path was made for me into the immemorial hills, before my scream the scream of the eagle died away. The lordly bird spread his wings to seek more impenetrable crags. Following in my wake, civilization came; homes sprang up, temples to art and to learning were upreared, and on the air, which but a year before was startled only by barbarous cries, there fell the benediction of children's voices, as with swinging satchels in their hands, they sang their songs going to and returning from schools. Then man began to discover that there was more to me than polished iron and brass; more than a heart of fire and a breath of steam. In my headlight they began to discover a faint reflection of the Infinite light, and in whispers began to say: "It is not a dumb slave; rather it is to Progress an evangel." As my power increased, it was seen that as the wild man and wild beast fled before me, old bigotries and old superstitions likewise fled, snarling like wolves, from my path; man moved up to a higher plane, and as he comprehended himself better, his thoughts were led upward; with enlarged ideas and deeper reverence, he turned to the contemplation of the First Great Cause who thrilled the dull matter of the universe with His own celestial light and order, and established that nothing was made in vain. And now a path is to be made down where the terrible Spaniard wrested an empire from the Aztecs; where, with the sword, he hewed down the altars on which human sacrifices were made, and built up new altars consecrated to Christianity. The people there will gather around me and rejoice. They think only of material things; how I will carry their burdens, take from them the fatigue of travel and increase their trade. They do not know that mine is a higher mission; that as I do their work there is to gradually fade from the faith that holds them, the superstitions which for centuries have environed their better selves and benumbed their grander energies. They will not realize, what is true, that angels still walk with men; that it is the near presence of the angels of Progress, Truth, Free Thought, Mercy and Eternal Justice, all rejoicing, which will give the thrill to their hearts. As yet my work has hardly commenced. It is not yet fifty years since I became a power in the world. Wait until I am better understood, until the smooth paths are made for me through all the wilderness, over all the rivers and hills, and I am given dominion over all the deep seas, that I may swiftly bring together the children of men, till gradually the nations will take on common thoughts and return to that tongue which was universal when the world was young, and, as yet, man walked in the clear image of his Creator. Then armies will melt away before me as savage tribes now do; then no more cannons will be cast, no more swords fashioned. Then, through my example, labor in the walks of peace will become exalted; then the thirst for gold will cease, because I will till the field, drive the loom, and take from man all that is servile or gross in toil; and gradually the wild beast in men's souls will be bred out, and in the peace of perfect brotherhood men will possess the earth, and I will be the good angel that will take away the burdens.'"

As if in response to the words of Harding, just as he finished, the whistles all up and down the great lode sounded for the eleven o'clock change of shift, and the Club retired with this remark from Corrigan:

"Harding, they heard what yez was remarkin' upon, and now hear the whole row of them cheerin' your spache."

CHAPTER VIII.

Just after the lamps were lighted the next evening the door opened and the Professor, Colonel Savage and Alex Strong came in. The greetings were warm all around, and at once conversation turned upon stocks. The Professor insisted that the first great showing was to be made in the south end mines, Alex still believed in Overman, the Colonel was sanguine over Utah. Ashley asked the opinion of the others on Sierra Nevada. The general sentiment was that if Skae had any real indication there the Bonanza firm would gobble it up before any outsider could realize.

Wright still inclined to the belief that the water must be conquered pretty soon in the Savage and that there would be a showing that would make every servant girl and hostler on the coast want some Savage.

So the conversation ran on for an hour, until something was said which turned the conversation upon the strange characters which had been met on the western coast. At length the Colonel settled down for a talk, and the others became willing listeners.

"I have met many royal people on this coast," began the Colonel. "Royal, though they never wore crowns, at least crowns not visible in the dim light of this world. The emblems of their royalty were hidden from most mortal eyes. In narrow spheres they lived and died, and only a few, besides God, knew of their sovereignty. One of these was

OLD ZACK TAYLOR.

"His last years were passed in Plumas and Lassen counties, California. When he came there his hair was already silvered; he must have been fifty years of age.

"No one knew his antecedents. In the excitements and free-heartedness of those days not many questions were asked. Besides the young and hopeful there were many who had sought the new land as a balm for domestic troubles; as a spot where former misfortunes might be forgotten, where early mistakes might, in earnest lives, be buried out of sight. With the rest came Zack Taylor. From the first that region seemed to possess a charm for him. No person can imagine the splendor in natural scenery of Plumas county. It must be seen to be comprehended. The mountains are tremendous; the valleys are so fair that they seem like pictures in their mountain frames. And so they are. They are the work of a Master's hand, whose work never fades. His signet is upon them as it was indented, when, in the long ago, it was decided that at last the earth was fitted to be a habitation for man.

"The forests are such forests as are no where seen in this world, except in the Pacific States of the United States. There is no exaggeration in this. Ordinary pines will make ten thousand feet of lumber, and they stand very near together, those mighty pines of the Sierras.

"The panoramas that are unrolled there when nature is in the picture-making mood are most gorgeous. Some that I saw there linger fresh upon my mind still. They come to me sometimes when I am down in the depths of the mine, and for a moment I forget the heat and the gloom.

"As a rule, all the summer long, the skies are of a crystal clearness; the green of the hill tops melts into the everlasting incandescent white beyond, and there is no change for days and weeks at a time, except as the green of the day fades into the shadows of the night. and the gold of the sunlight gives place to the silver of the stars.

" It was to this region that Zack Taylor came and made his abode. About him was an air of perfect contentment. Besides his blanching hair, there were deep lines about his face, which were an alphabet from which could be spelled out stories of past excitements and trials, but if sorrows and sufferings were included, the firm lips gave no sign, and the bright. black eyes were ever kindly. There were rumors that he had been a soldier, but the general impression was. that from childhood, he had been tossed about on the frontier. He had the moods. the gestures and dialect of the frontier. He liked wild game cooked upon a camp fire, and, in frontier phrase, he could ·punish a heap of whisky.'

"He was at home everywhere: in the saloons his coming was always welcome: when he met a lady on the street, no matter whether she was young or old, fair or ugly, he always doffed his hat, and the few children of those early days looked upon him as a father—or an angel. He had a cheery. hearty, winsome way about him which drew all hearts to him.

" When I saw him last the gray hair had turned to snowy white; the scars of time had grooved deeper furrows on cheek and brow, the old elastic. merry way had grown sedate, but the black eyes were still kindly and bright. At that time he lived. a welcome pauper, on the citizens of Susanville, in Lassen county.

" When hungry he went where he pleased and got food; when he needed clothes they were forthcoming in any store where he applied for them. When, sometimes, merchants would in jest banter him for money on account of what he owed, his way was to softly suggest to them that if the patronage of the place did not, in their judgments, justify them in remaining, there was no constitutional objection that he was aware of to prevent their making an auction.

"One fearfully cold winter's night a few of us were sitting around the stove in the Stewart House, in Susanville, when old Zack came in. The circle was widened for him, and as he drew up to the fire, some one said: 'Zack, tell us about that night's work when you tended bar for the poker players?'

"'It was down on Noth Fok (North Fork) of Feather River, 'bout '52 or '53, I disremember which,' began Zack. 'It wus in the winter, and it being too cold for mining, ther boys wus all in camp. Thar wus no women thar, least ways, no ladies, and women as isn't ladies —but we dun no who thar mothers wus, nor how much they has suffered, and we haint got no business to talk about 'em. But, as I wus sayin', the boys wus all in camp, and thar wus lots of beans and whisky and sich things, and we hed good times, you bet!

"'Jake Clark kept a saloon thar, which wus sort of headquarters, and sometimes when the boys got warmed up on Jake's whisky thar wus lively times. Well, I *should* remark. It wussent much wonder, neither, for Jake made his whisky in the back room, made it out of old boots, akerfortis and sich things, and if you believe me, a fire assay of that beverage would have shown 93 per cent. of cl'ar hell. Thar wus three or four copies of Shakespeare in camp, and everbody got a Sacermento *Union* every week when the express came in; so we kept posted solid. Speakin' of that, if folks only jest stick to Shakespeare and then paternize one first-class paper, sich as the old *Union* wus, and read 'em, in the long run they'd have a heap more sense.

"'Of course the boys would play poker sometimes. Men will always do that when the reproach in honest women's eyes is taken away, and I have heard, now and then, of one who would play in spite of good influences. At least thar is rumors to that effect.

"'Well, they wus playin' one night, five or six of them, inter Jake's saloon. It got to be about ten o'clock, and Jake says to me, says he, "Zack, them fellers is playin' and will most likely run it all night. By mornin' Tom D. will have the hul pile, and Tom never pays nuthin'. I'm goin' home. You run the ranch, Zack, and when they call for it you give 'em whisky outer this 'ere keg, so if they never pay we won't lose too much." This he told me in a low voice behind the bar, in confidence like.

"'Jake started for home and I went on watch. Thar wus lots of coin and dust on the table and the boys wus playin' high. I stood behind the bar and watched 'em, and as I watched I said to myself, says I, "The doggoned cusses! They come here and bum Jake's fuel and lights, and drink his whisky, and don't pay nuthin'. It's too bad."

"'Then an idea struck me. I had a log of fat pine in the back yard. It wus fuller of pitch than Bill Pardee is of religion in revival times, and I thought of somethin'. I went out, got a lot of the pitch, warmed it in the candle down behind the bar and rubbed it all along the bottom of my hands, so, and then I waited developments.

"'Pretty soon thar wus a call for whisky. I

started out with a bottle in one hand and a glass in the other, and, setting down the glass first, I said, "'Ere's your glass," and settin' down the bottle, said, "'Ere's your whisky."

"'They drank all 'round, when Harlow Porter said: "This is mine, Zack." I argued the pint with him and asked him how a man could furnish a house, lights, fires and whisky, and keep it up if nobody paid? They told me to "hire a hall," and all laughed. It wus only old Zack, you know.

"'But I did tolerable well after all. When I sat down the glass half a dollar stuck to my hand, and when I sat down the whisky the other hand caught up a two and a half piece.

"'The playin' went on, and I warmed my hands. By and by more whisky wus called for. I responded. Once more I said, "'Ere's your glass," and "'Ere's your whisky." They drank, and then Henry Moore said to Hugh Richmond: "Why don't you ante?" "I have," wus Hugh's reply; "I jist put up five dollars." "No you didn't," said Henry. "Yes I did," said Hugh, hotly. "You're a liar," said Miller, and then biff! biff! biff! came the blows.

"'I got down behind the bar, for some of them cusses would shoot if half a chance wus given them. The truth wus, I had picked up the five with my pitch when I said "'Ere's your whisky."

"'The boys got hold and stopped the row and the players proceeded. The oftener they drank the wus bookkeepers they became, and all the time I wus doin' reasonably well.

"'Durin' the night I took in eighty-three dollars and seen a beautiful fight.

"'I didn't tell of it, though, for nigh onto three

year, 'cept to Jake. It nearly killed me to keep it to myself. But Lord! wouldn't they have made it tropic for me if they'd ever dropped on the business! Well, I should remark!'

"When Zack finished his story I asked if he would not take something.

"He remarked that he was not particularly proud and, besides, the weather was 'powerful sarchin';' he believed he would.

"He swallowed a stiff drink, returned to the stove, resumed his seat, began and told the whole story over, except that the whisky was having its effect, and as he drew towards the close he commenced to exaggerate, and wound up by the assertion that he took in one hundred and sixty dollars and saw two tremendous fights.

"Some one else asked him to drink. He accepted, then returned to his chair and apparently fell into a doze. After a few minutes, however, he aroused himself and began again, as follows:

"'It wus down on North Fok of Feather River, in '52 or '53, I disremember which. It was in the winter, and it bein' too cold for minin' ther boys wus all in camp. Thar wus no women thar, leastways no ladies, and women as is no ladies—but we dun no.'

"Here I arose and slipped out of the room. Returning about fifteen minutes later, I found old Zack gesticulating wildly and in a high key exclaiming:

"'I everlastingly broke the boys with my pitch. I took in *three hundred and forty-three dollars* and seen three the *dod-durndest fights in the world*.'

"But it was not this that I began to tell. Three or four years before Zack's death, a courier announced to the people of Susanville that three days before, out near Deep Hole, on the desert eighty miles east of Susanville, a man had been killed by renegade Pi Ute Indians. The announcement made only a temporary impression, for such news was often brought to Susanville in those days. In a very few years eighty Lassen county men were murdered by Indians.

" A few days after the news of this particular murder was brought in, Susanville began to be vexed by the evident presence of a mysterious thief. If a hunter brought in a brace of grouse or rabbits and left them exposed for a little while they disappeared.

" If a string of trout were caught from the river and were left anywhere for a few minutes they were lost. Gardens were robbed of fruit and vegetables; blankets, flannels and groceries disappeared from stores. The losses became unbearable at length. everybody was aroused and on the alert, but no thief could be discovered, though the depredations still went on. This continued for days and weeks, until the people became desperate, and many a threat was made that when the thief should finally be caught, in disposing of him the grim satisfaction of the frontier should be fully enjoyed. Old Zack was especially fierce in his denunciations.

" One morning a horseman dashed into town. his mustang coming in on a dead run. Reining up in front of the main hotel, he sprang down from his horse and to the people who came running to see what was the matter, he explained that half a mile from town. around the bend of the hill, in the old deserted cabin. he had found the widow of the man killed weeks before by the Indians; had found her and a nest of babies, and none of them with sufficient food or clothing.

"When the story was finished. men and women—half the population of the village—made a rush for the cabin. It was nearly concealed from view from the road by thick bushes, but they found the woman there and four little children. The woman seemed like one half dazed by sorrow and despair, but when questioned. she replied that she had been there five weeks. 'But how have you lived?' asked half a dozen voices in concert. Then the woman explained that she and her children would have starved, had it not been for a kind old gentleman who brought her everything that she required.

"'Indeed.' she added. 'he brought me many things that I did not need. and which I felt that I ought not to accept. but he over-persuaded me, telling me that I did not know how rich he was, that his supplies were simply inexhaustible.

"When asked to describe this man. she began to say: 'He is a heavy-set old gentleman: wears blue clothes: his hair is white as snow. but his eyes are black, and—' but she was not allowed to go any farther. for twenty voices, between weeping and laughing. cried 'Old Zack!'

"The widow and her children were taken to the village, a house with its comforts provided for them. and there was. thenceforth. no more trouble from the ubiquitous thief.

"Living on charity himself. with the wreck of a life behind him and nothing before him but the grave. which he was swiftly nearing, this great-hearted, old heavenly bummer and Christian thief, had taken care of this helpless family, and had done it because despite the dry rot and the whisky which had benumbed his energies. his soul, deep down, was royal to the core.

"It is true that he had robbed the town to minister to the woman and her babies, but in the books of the angels, though it was written that he was a thief, in the same sentence it was also added, 'and God bless him.' and these words turned to gold even as they were being written.

"When Old Zack was asked why he did not make the facts about, the family known, after waiting a moment he replied:

"'You see I've been tossed about a powerful sight in my time: have drank heaps of bad whisky; have done a great many no-account things and not a great many good ones. Since I wus a boy I have never had chick or kin of my own. I met the woman and her babies up by the cabin; they wus as pitiful a sight as ever you seen; and besides, the woman wus jist about to go stark mad with grief and hunger and anxiety and weariness. I seen she must have quiet and that anxiety about her children must be soothed some way. Then I did some of the best lyin' you ever heard. I got her to eat some supper and waited until the whole outfit wus fast asleep. I watched 'em a little while and then I got curis to know what kind of a provider I would have made for a family had I started out in life different, and that wus all there wus about it.'

"Is it a wonder, then, that when the old man died his body was dressed in soft raiment, placed in a costly casket, and that, preceded by a martial band playing a requiem, all the people followed sorrowingly to the grave: and that, as they gently heaped the sods above his breast. they sent after him into the Beyond heartfelt 'all-hails and farewells?'"

"You see your man through colored spectacles,

Colonel," spoke up Brewster. "From your description, I think there was more of the border deviltry in the old man than there was true royalty. Life had been a joke to him always; he played it as a joke to the end. One such a man was entertainment to the village: had there been a dozen more like him they would have become intolerable nuisances?"

"That," said the Colonel, "only shows how miserable are my descriptive powers. There are not a dozen other such men as old Zack Taylor was among all the fourteen hundred millions of people on this sorrowful earth."

"No," interposed Miller, "you told the story well enough, but it was only descriptive of a good-humored bummer at best—of one who was warm-hearted without a conscience, of one who was more willing to work to perpetrate a joke on others than to honorably earn the bread that he ate.

"I will tell you of a royal fellow that I knew. It was Billie Smith. He lived in Eureka that first hard winter of '70-71. He was not a miner as we are, receiving four dollars per day. He and his partner, a surly old fellow, had a claim which they were developing, hoping that it would amount to something in the spring. That was before smelting had been made a success. The ores were all base and of too low a grade to ship away. These men had a little supply of flour, bacon and coffee, and that was about all, and it was all they expected until spring.

"It was early in January and the weather was exceedingly cold. Their cabin was but a rude hut, open on every side to the winds. I was there and I know how things were. One day I was waiting in a tent, which by courtesy was called a store, when Billie came in. He had a cheery smile and hearty, welcome words for every one. He had been there but a few minutes when his partner came in. The old man was fairly boiling with rage. So angry was he that he could hardly articulate distinctly. Finally he explained that some thief had stolen their mattress, a pair of their best blankets and a sack of flour. He wanted an officer dispatched with a search warrant. Then I overheard the following conversation between the two men:

"'O, never mind.' said Billie; 'some poor devil needed the things or he would not have taken them.'

"'Yes, but we need them, too; need them more than anything else,' was the response.

"'O, we will get along; we have plenty.'

"'Yes,' retorted the partner, 'but what are we going to do for a bed? Our hair mattress and best pair of blankets are gone, and the cabin is cold.'

"'We can sew up some sacks into a mattress, and fill it with soft brush and leaves, and use our coats for blankets,' replied Billie. 'We'll get along all right. The truth is we have been sleeping too warm of late.'

"'Too warm!' said the partner, bitterly; 'I should think so. A polar bear would freeze in that cabin without a bed.'

"'Do you think so?' asked Billie, smiling. 'Well, that is the way to keep it, and so if any wild animal comes that way we can freeze him out. Brace up, partner! Why should a man make a fuss about the loss of a trifle like that?'

"Later I found out the facts. A little below Billie's cabin was another cabin, into which a family of emigrants had moved. They were dreadfully poor.

Going to and returning from town Billie had noticed how things were. One night as he passed, going home in the dark, he heard a child crying in the cabin and heard it say to its mother that it was hungry and cold.

"Next morning he waited until his partner had gone away, then rolled the mattress around a sack of flour, then rolled the mattress and flour up in his best pair of blankets, swung the bundle on his shoulder, carried it down the trail to the other cabin, where, opening the door, he flung it inside; then with finger on his lip he said in a hoarse whisper to the woman: 'Don't mention it! Not a word. I stole the bundle, and if you ever speak of it you will get me sent to prison,' and in a moment was swinging down the trail singing joyously:

> "If I had but a thousand a year, Robin Ruff,
> If I had but a thousand a year."

"Last winter, after the fire, there was one man in this city, John W. Mackay, who gave $150,000 to the poor. It was a magnificent act, and was as grandly and gently performed as such an act could be. No one would ever have known it, had not the good priest who distributed the most of it, one day, mentioned the splendid fact. That man will receive his reward here, and hereafter, for it was a royal charity. But he has $30,000,000 to draw against, while, when Billie in the wilderness gave up his bed and his food, he not only had not a cent to draw against, but he had not a reasonably well-defined hope.

"When at last the roll-call of the real royal men of this world shall be sounded, if any of you chance to be there, you will hear, close up to the head of the list, the name of Billie Smith, and when it shall be pronounced, if you listen, you will hear a very soft but dulcet refrain trembling along the harps and a murmur among the emerald arches that will sound like the beating of the wings of innumerable doves."

"That was a good mon, surely. Did he do well with his mine?" asked Corrigan.

"No," answered Miller. "It was but a little deposit, and was quickly worked out. He scuffled along until the purchase of the Eureka Con. in the spring, then went to work there for a few months, then came here, and a day or two after arriving, was shot dead by the ruffian Perkins.

"He was shot through the brain, and people tell me he was so quickly transfixed that in his coffin the old sunny smile was still upon his face. I don't believe that, though. I believe the smile came when, as the light went out here, he saw the dawn and felt the hand clasps on the other side.

"By the way, there was a man here who knew him, and who wrote something with the thought of poor Billie in his mind while he was writing."

At this Miller arose and went to his carpet-sack, opened it and drew out a paper. Then handing it to Harding, he said: "Harding, you read better than I do, read it for us all."

Harding took the paper and read as follows:

ERNEST FAITHFUL.

"Twas the soul of Ernest Faithful
  Loosed from its home of clay—
Its mission on earth completed,
  To the judgment passed away.

"Twas the soul of Ernest Faithful
  Stood at the bar above,
Where the deeds of men are passed upon
  In justice, but in love.

And an angel questioned Faithful
  Of the life just passed on earth!
What could he plead of virtue,
  What could he count of worth.

And the soul of Ernest Faithful
  Trembled in sore dismay:
And from the judgment angel's gaze
  Shuddering, turned away.

For memory came and whispered
  How worldly was that life;
Unfairly plotting, sometimes,
  In anger and in strife;

For a selfish end essaying
  To treasures win or fame.
And the soul of Ernest cowered 'neath
  The angel's eye of flame.

Then from a book the angel drew
  A leaf with name and date,
A record of this Ernest's life
  Wove in the looms of Fate.

And said: "O, Faithful, answer me.
  Here is a midnight scroll,
What didst thou 'neath the stars that night?
  Didst linger o'er the bowl?

"Filling the night with revelry
  With cards and wine and dice,
And adding music's ecstacy,
  To give more charms to vice?"

Then the soul of Faithful answered,
  "By the bedside of a friend
I watched the long hours through; that night
  His life drew near its end."

"Here's another date at midnight,
  Where was't thou this night, say?"
"I was waiting by the dust of one
  Whose soul had passed that day."

"These dollar marks," the angel said;
  "What mean they, Ernest, tell?"
"It was a trifle that I gave
  To one whom want befell."

"Here's thine own picture, illy dressed;
  What means this scant attire?"
"I know not," answered Faithful, "save
  That once midst tempest dire,

"I found a fellow-man benumbed,
  And lost amid the storm
And so around him wrapped my vest,
  His stiffening limbs to warm."

"Here is a woman's face, a girl's.
  O, Ernest, is this well?
Knowst thou how often women's arms
  Have drawn men's souls to hell?"

Then Ernest answered: "This poor girl
  An orphan was. I gave
A trifle of my ample store
  The child from want to save."

"Next are some words. What mean they here?"
  Then Ernest answered low:
"A fellow-man approached me once
  Whose life was full of woe,

"When I had naught to give, except
  Some words of hope and trust;
I bade him still have faith, for God
  Who rules above is just."

Then the grave angel smiled and moved
  Ajar the pearly gate
And said: "O, soul! we welcome thee
  Unto this new estate.

"Enter! Nor sorrow more is thine,
  Nor grief; we know thy creed—
Thou who hast soothed thy fellowmen
  In hour of sorest need.

"Thou who hast watched thy brother's dust,
  When the wrung soul had fled;
And to the stranger gave thy cloak,
  And to the orphan, bread.

"And when all else was gone, had still
  A word of kindly cheer
For one more wretched than thyself,
  Thou, soul, art welcome here.

" Put on the robe thou gav'st away
    'Tis stainless now and white;
And all thy words and deeds are gems;
    Wear them, it is thy right!"

And then from choir and harp awoke
    A joyous, welcome strain,
Which other harps and choirs took up,
    In jubilant refrain,

Till all the aisles of Summer Land
    Grew resonant, as beat
The measures of that mighty song
    Of welcome, full and sweet.

"That is purty. I hope there were no mistake about the gintleman making the showing up above," said Corrigan.

"What lots of music there must be up in that country," chimed in Carlin. "I wonder if there are any buildings any where on the back streets where new beginners practice."

"That represents the Hebrew idea of Heaven," said Alex. "I like that of the savage better, with hills and streams and glorious old woods. There is a dearer feeling of rest attached to it, and rest is what a life craves most after a buffet of three score years in this world."

"Rest is a pretty good thing after an eight-hours' wrestle with the gnomes down on a 2,300 level of the Comstock," said Miller; "suppose we say good night."

"Withdraw the motion for a moment, Miller," said Wright. "First, I move that our friends here be made honorary members of the Club."

It was carried by acclamation, and thereafter, for several nights, the three were present nightly.

CHAPTER IX.

When the Club reassembled Carlin, addressing the Colonel, said: "You told us of a royal old bummer last night, and Miller told us of an angel in miner's garb. Your stories reminded me of something which happened in Hamilton, in Eastern Nevada, in the early times, when the thermometer was at zero, when homes were homes and food was food. There was a royal fellow there, too, only he was not a miner, and though he lived upon the earnings of others, he never accepted charity. By profession he was a gambler, and not a very 'high-toned' gambler at that. He was known as 'Andy Flinn,' though it was said, for family reasons, he did not pass under his real name.

"Well, Andy had, in sporting parlance, been 'playing in the worst kind of luck' for a good while. One afternoon his whole estate was reduced to the sum of fifteen dollars. He counted it over in his room, slipped it back into his pocket and started up town. A little way from the lodging where he roomed he was met by a man who begged him to step into a house near by and see how destitute the inmates were.

"Andy mechanically followed the man, who led the way to a cabin, threw open the door and ushered Andy in. There was a man, the husband and father, ill in bed, while the wife and mother, a delicate woman, and two little children, were, in scanty garments, hovering around the ghost of a fire.

"Andy took one look, then rushed out of doors, the man who had led him into the cabin following.

Andy walked rapidly away until out of hearing of the wretched people in the house, then swinging on his heel, for full two minutes hurled the most appalling anathemas at the man for leading him, as Andy expressed it, 'into the presence of those advance agents of a famine.'

"When he paused for breath the man said, quietly: 'I like that; I like to see you fellows, that take the world so carelessly and easily, stirred up occasionally.'

"'Easy!' said Andy; 'you had better try it. You think our work is easy; you are a mere child. We don't get half credit. I tell you to make a man an accomplished gambler requires more study than to acquire a learned profession; more labor than is needed to become a deft artisan. You talk like a fool. Easy, indeed!'

"'I don't care to discuss that point with you, Andy,' said the man. 'I expect you are right, but that is not the question. What are you, a big, strong, healthy fellow, going to do to help those poor wretches in the cabin yonder?'

"Andy plunged his hand into his pocket, drew out the fifteen dollars and was just going to pass it over to the man when a thought struck him. 'Hold on,' he said; 'a man is an idiot that throws away his capital and then has to take his chances with the thieves that fill this camp. You come with me. I am going to try to take up a collection. By the way,' he said, shortly, 'do you ever pray?'

"The man answered that he did sometimes. 'Then," said Andy, 'you put in your very biggest licks when I start my collection.'

"Not another word was said until they reached

and entered a then famous saloon on Main street.

"Going to the rear where a faro game was in progress, Andy exchanged his fifteen dollars for chips and began to play. He never ceased; hardly looked up from the table for two hours. Sometimes he won and sometimes he lost, but the balance was on the winning side. Finally he ceased playing, gathered up his last stakes, and beckoning to the man who had come with him to the saloon, and who had watched his playing with lively interest, he led the way into the billiard room.

"Andy went to a window on one side of the room and began to search his pockets, piling all the money he could find on the sill of the window. The money was all in gold and silver.

"When his pockets were emptied, with the quickness of men of his class, he ran the amount over. Then taking from a billiard table a bit of chalk he, with labored strokes, wrote on the window sill the following:

```
hul sum . . . . . . . . . . . . . . . . . . . . . . $263 50
starter . . . . . . . . . . . . . . . . . . . . . . .   15 00
                                                       _____
doo ter god . . . . . . . . . . . . . . . . . . . . $248 50
```

"He picked up a ten-dollar piece and a five-dollar piece from the amount, then pushing the rest along the sill away from the figures, asked the man to count it. He did so and said:

"'I make altogether $248.50, Andy.'

"'I suspect you are correct,' said Andy, 'and now you take that money and go and fix up those people as comfortably as you can. Tell 'em we took up a collection among the boys; don't say a word about it on the outside; and see here. If you ever again show me as horrible a sight as that crowd makes in that accursed den down the street, I'll break every bone in your body.'

"'But,' said the man, 'this is not right, Andy. It is too much. Fifty dollars would be a most generous contribution from you. Give me fifty dollars and you take back the rest.'

"'What do you take me for?' was Andy's reply. 'Don't you think I have any honor about me? When I went into that saloon I promised God that if He would stand in with me, His poor should have every cent that I could make in a two hours' deal. I would simply be a liar and a thief if I took a cent of that money. You praying cusses have not very clear ideas of right and wrong after all.'

"The man went on his errand of mercy, and Andy returned and invested his money in the bank again, as he said, 'to try to turn an honest penny.'"

"That was a right ginerous man," remarked Corrigan.

"May be and may be not," was the remark of the Colonel. "It is possible that he had been 'playing in bad luck,' as they say, for a good while and did it to change that luck. Confirmed gamesters never reason clearly on ordinary subjects. They are either up in the clouds or down in the depths; they are perpetually studying the doctrine of chances, and are as full of superstitions as so many fortune tellers."

"That class of men are proverbially generous, though," said Harding; "but the way they get their money, I suspect, has something to do with the matter. Had the man earned the money at four dollars a day, running a car down in a hot mine, he would hardly have given up the whole sum."

Here Miller took up the conversation. "I knew

a man down in Amador county, California," said he, "who worked in a mine as we are working here, except that wages were $3.50 instead of $4.00 per day. He came there in the fall of the year and worked eight months. His clothes were always poor. He lived in a cabin by himself, and such miners as happened into his cabin at meal time declared their belief that his food did not cost half a dollar a day. He never joined the miners down town; was never known to treat to as much as a glass of beer. We all hated him cordially and looked upon him as a miner so avaricious that he was denying himself the common comforts of life. He was the talk of the mine, and many were the scornful words which he was made to hear and to know that they were uttered at his expense. Still he was quiet and resented nothing that was said, and there was no dispute about his being a most capable and faithful miner. At last one morning as the morning shift were waiting at the shaft to be lowered into the mine, Baxter (that was his name) appeared, and, after begging our attention for a moment, said:

"'Gentlemen, there is the dead body of an old man up in the cabin across from the trail. It will cost sixty dollars to bury it in a decent coffin. The undertaker will not trust me, but if twenty of you will put in three dollars each, I will pay you all when pay-day comes.'

"Then we questioned him, and it came out at last that Baxter had found the old man sick a few days after he came to work, and of his $3.50 per day had spent $3.00 in food, medicine and medical attendance upon the man, all through the long winter, and had moreover often watched with him twelve hours out of the twenty-four. It was not a child that something might be hoped for; there was no beautiful young girl about the place to be in love with. It was simply a death watch over a worn-out pauper. I thought then, I think still, it was as fine a thing as ever I saw.

"There were sixty of us on the mine. We put in ten dollars apiece, went to Baxter in a body, and, begging his pardon, asked him to accept it.

"With a smile, he answered: 'I thank you, but I cannot take it. I have wasted much money in my time. Now I feel as though I had a little on interest, and I shall get along first rate.'

"Talk about royalty, our Baxter was an Emperor."

"He did have something on interest," said Brewster. "Something for this world and the world to come."

"Did you ever hear about Jack Marshall's attempt to pay his debts by clerking in a store?" asked Savage. "Jack brought a good deal of coin here and opened a store. He did first rate for several months, and after awhile branched out into a larger business, which required a good many men. When everything was promising well a fire came and swept away the store and a flood destroyed the other property. There was just enough saved out of the wreck to pay the laborers.

"When all was settled up Jack had but forty-three dollars left and an orphan boy to take care of. Just then a man that Jack had known for a good while as a miner, came into town, and hearing of Jack's misfortunes, hunted him up and told him that he had given up mining and settled down to farming, and begged Jack to come and make his home with him until he had time to think over what was best to do.

He further said that he had twelve acres of land cleared and under fence, with ditches all dug for irrigating the crop; that he had a yoke of oxen to plough the land; that his intention was to plant the whole twelve acres to potatoes; that a fair crop would yield him sixty tons, which, as potatoes then were four cents a pound, would bring him nearly $5,000 for the season. But he explained that he could not drive oxen, and more than that, it required two men to do the work, and as he had not much money and did not want to run in debt, his business in town was to find some steady man who could drive oxen, who would go with him and help him plant, tend, harvest and sell the crop on shares. The ranch was down on Carson River, not far from Fort Churchill.

"When the man had finished his story, Jack said to him: 'How would I do for a steady man and a bovine manipulator?'

"'My God, Mr. Marshall! you would not undertake to drive oxen and plant potatoes, would you?' said the man.

"'That's just what I would,' said Jack, 'if you think you can endure me for a partner. I will become a horny-handed tender of the vine—the potato vine. What say you?'

"Well, that evening both men started for the farm. No friend of Jack knew his real circumstances. They knew he had been unfortunate, but did not know that it was a case of 'total wreck.' He bade a few of them good-bye, with the careless remark that he was going for a few days' hunt down toward the sink of the Carson.

"Well, he ploughed the land, the two men planted the crop and irrigated it until the potatoes were splendidly advanced and just ready to blossom. It got to be the last of June and the promise for a bountiful crop was encouraging. They had worked steadily since the middle of March. But just then a thief, who had some money, made a false affidavit, got from a court an injunction against the men and shut off the water. It was just at the critical time when the life of the crop depended upon water. In two weeks the whole crop was ruined. In the meantime for seed and provisions, clothes, etc., a debt of one hundred and fifty dollars had been contracted at the store of a Hebrew named Isaacs. News of the injunction reached the merchant, and one morning he put in an appearance.

" 'Meester Marshall, hous dings?' asked Isaacs.

"Pointing to the blackened and withering crop, Jack answered: 'They look a little bilious, don't you think so?'

" 'Mine Gott! Mine Gott!' was the wailing exclamation. Then, after a pause. 'Ven does you suppose you might pay me. Meester Marshall?'

" 'As things have been going of late. I think in about seven years. It is said that bad luck changes about every seven years.'

" 'Mine Gott! Meester Marshall.' cried Isaacs; 'haven't you got nodings vot you can pay? I vill discount de bill—say ten per cent.'.

" 'Nothing that I can think of, except a dog. I have a dog that is worth two hundred dollars, but to you I will discount the dog twenty-five per cent.'

" 'O, mine Gott! vot you dinks I could do mit a dog?' said the despairing merchant.

" 'Why keep him for his society, Mr. Isaacs,' was the bantering answer. 'With him salary is not so

much an object as a comfortable and respectable
home. There's too much alkali on the soil to en-
courage fleas to remain, so there's no difficulty on
that score: and he's an awfully good dog, Isaacs; no
bad habits, and the most regular boarder you ever
saw; he has never been late to a meal since we have
been here. You had better take him; twenty-five
per cent is an immense discount.'

"By this time the Hebrew was nearly frantic.

"'Meester Marshall.' he said, hesitatingly, 'did
you clerk ever in a store?'

"'Oh, yes.'

"'Vould you clerk for me?'

"'Yes; that is, until that bill shall be settled.'

"'Ven could you come?'

"'Whenever you wish.'

"'Vould you come next Monday—von of mine
clerks, Henery, goes avay Monday?'

"'Yes, I will be on hand Monday. Let us see; it
is seven miles to walk. I will be there about nine
o'clock in the morning.'

"'Vell, I danks you, Meester Marshall; danks you
very much.'

"He turned away and rode off a few steps, then
stopped and called back: 'Meester Marshall, if you
dinks vot de society of de dog is essential to your
comfort, bring him.'

"'Thanks, Isaacs.' cried Jack, cheerfully; 'considering where I am going to work. and the company I
am going to keep, it will not be necessary.'

"Jack went as he had promised. Isaacs, who was
a thoroughly good man, was delighted to see him,
shook hands cordially, and then suddenly, with a
mysterious look, led him to the extreme rear end of

the store, and when there, placing his lips close to
Jack's ear, in a hoarse whisper, said:

"'Meester Marshall, de vater here is·——— bad;
it is poison, horrible. You drinks nodings but vine
until you gets used to de vater.'

"Marshall went to work at once. It was in 1863.
The war was at its height, and Jack was intensely
Union, while Isaacs, his employer, was a furious Dem-
ocrat. Nothing of especial interest transpired for a
couple of weeks, when one day an emigrant woman,
just across the plains, leading two little children,
came into the store.

"She was an exceedingly poor woman, evidently.
All her clothes were not worth three dollars, while
her children were pitiful looking beyond description.

"Isaacs was in the front of the store; Jack was
putting up goods in the rear, but in hearing, while
another clerk was in the warehouse outside of the
main store. Isaacs went to wait on the woman. She
picked out some needed articles of clothing for her
children, amounting to some six or eight dollars, then
unrolling a dilapidated kerchief, from its inner folds
drew out a Confederate twenty-dollar note and ten-
dered it in payment.

"Isaacs, who had been all smiles, drew back in
horror, exclaiming: 'I cannot take dot; dot is not
monish, madam.'

"Jack overheard what Isaacs said and the woman's
reply, as follows:

"'It is all that I have; it is all the money that we
have had in Arkansas since the war commenced.
Everybody takes it in Arkansas.'

"This conversation continued for two or three
minutes, and the woman was just about turning away

without the goods when Jack, unable to longer bear it, stepped forward and said:

"'Mr. Isaacs, Mr. Smith would like to see you in the warehouse; please permit me to wait upon the lady.'

"'All right,' said Isaacs, 'only (in a whisper) remember dot ish not money.'

"Isaacs passed out of the store and Jack then said: 'If you please, madam, let me see your money.'

"The woman, with a trembling hand, presented the Confederate note. Jack glanced at it and said:

"'Why, this is first-class money, madam. It is just a prejudice that that infernal old Abolitionist has. I will discharge him to-night. They would hang him in two hours in Arkansas, and they ought to hang him here. Buy all the goods you want, madam.'

"With eyes full of gratitude the woman increased the bill, until it amounted to eleven dollars and a half. Jack tied up the goods, took the Confederate note, handed the woman a five-dollar gold piece and three dollars and fifty cents in silver, and she went on her way holding the precious coin, the first she had seen in years, closely clasped in her hand.

"Jack charged goods to cash twenty dollars, charged himself to cash twenty dollars, and went back to putting up goods, humming to himself.

"'Half the world never knows how the other half lives.' Jack's salary was one hundred and fifty dollars a month. He owed one hundred and fifty dollars when he went to work. It took him four months to pay off his indebtedness. but when he gave up his place he had all his pockets full of Confederate money."

As the story was finished, Miller said: "A real pleasant but characteristic thing happened right here in this city when Bishop W—— first came here.

"He wanted to establish a church, and his first work was to select men who would act and be a help to him as trustees.

"It is nothing to get trustees for a mining company here, but a church is a different thing. In a church, you know, a man has to die to fill his shorts, and then, somehow, in these late years men have doubts about the formation, so that when a man starts a company on that lead any more he finds it mighty hard to place any working capital.

"At the time I was speaking of it was just about impossible to get a full staff of trustees that would exactly answer the orthodox requirements. But the Bishop is a man of expedients. It was sinners that he came to call to repentance, and it did not take him long to discover that right here was a big field. He went to work at once with an energy that has never abated for a moment since. He selected all his trustees but one, and looking around for him, with a clear instinct he determined that Abe E—— should be that one if he would accept the place.

"Now Abe was the best and truest of men, but he would swear sometimes. Indeed when he got started on that stratum he was a holy terror. But the Bishop put him down as a trustee, and, meeting Abe on the street, informed him that he was trying to organize a church; had taken the liberty to name him as a trustee, and asked Abe to do him the honor of attending a trustees' meeting at 1 o'clock the next afternoon.

"'I would be glad to help you, Bishop,' said Abe, 'but —— it —— —— I don't know. I can run a mine or a quartz mill, but I don't know any more than a Chinaman about running a church.'

" But the Bishop plead his case so ably that Abe at length surrendered, promised to attend the meeting, and, having promised, like the sterling business man that he was, promptly put in an appearance.

" Besides Abe and the Bishop, there were six others. When all had assembled the Bishop explained that he desired to build a church; that he had plans, specifications and estimates for a church to cost $9,000, with lot included; that he believed $1,500 might be raised by subscription, leaving the church but $7,500 in debt, which amount would run at low interest and which in a growing place like Virginia City the Bishop thought might be paid up in four or five years, leaving the church free. He closed by asking the sense of the trustees as to the wisdom and practicability of making the attempt.

"There was a general approval of the plan expressed by all present except Abe, who was silent until his opinion was directly asked by the Bishop.

"'Why —— it, Bishop,' said he, 'I told you that I knew nothing about church business, but I don't like the plan. If you were to get money at fifteen per cent per annum, which is only half the regular banking rate, your interest would amount to nearly $1,200 a year, or almost as much as you hope to raise for a commencement. I am afraid, Bishop, you would never live long enough to get out of debt. You want a church, why —— it, why don't you work the business as though you believed it would pay? That is the only way you can get up any confidence in the scheme.'

" Abe sat down and the Bishop's heart sank with him. 8

" With a smile, one of the other gentlemen asked Abe what his plan for getting a church would be.

" 'I will tell you,' said Abe, 'I move that an assessment of one thousand dollars be levied upon each of the trustees. payable immediately.'

" It was a startling proposition to the Bishop, who was just from the East and who had not become accustomed to Comstock ways. With a faltering voice he said:

" 'Mr. E., I fear that I cannot at present raise $1,000.'

" 'Never mind. Bishop,' said Abe, 'we will take yours out in preaching; but there is no rebate for any of the rest of you. If you are going to serve the Lord, you have got to be respectable about it. Your checks if you please. gentlemen.'

" All were wealthy men. the checks were laughingly furnished. with joking remarks that it was the first company ever formed in Virginia City where the officers really invested any money.

" Abe took the checks, added his own to the number. begged the Bishop to excuse him, remarking as he went out that while he had every faith in the others still he was anxious to reach the bank a little in advance of them. and started up town.

" He met this man and that and demanded of each a check for from $50 to $250, as he thought they could respectively afford to pay.

" When asked how long he would want the money his reply was: 'I want it for keeps, —— it. I am building a church.' In forty minutes he had the whole sum. He took the checks to the bank and for them received a certificate of deposit in the Bishop's name. Carrying this to the Bishop's house he rang the bell.

"The Bishop had seen his coming and answered the summons in person. Handing him the certificate Abe said:

"'Take that for a starter, Bishop. It won't be enough, for a church is like an old quartz mill. The cost always exceeds the estimates a good deal, but go ahead, and when you need more money we will levy another assessment on the infernal sinners.'"

Strong, who had been listening attentively said: "I heard the Bishop preach and pray over Abe's dead body three years ago, and watched him as he took a last, long look at Abe's still, clear-cut splendid face as it was composed in death. Abe never joined the church, and I am told that he swore a little to the last. His part in building the church was simply one of his whims, but for years he was a Providence here to scores of people. No one knew half his acts of bountiful, delicate charity, or in how many homes bitter tears were shed when he died.

"But the Bishop knew enough to know and feel as he was praying over his remains, that while it was well as a matter of form, it was quite unnecessary; that, so far as Abe was concerned, he was safe; that in the Beyond where the mansions are and where the light is born; where, over all, are forever stretched out the brooding wings of celestial peace, Abe had been received, and that, upon his coming, while the welcomes were sounding and the greetings were being made to him, flowers burst through the golden floor and blossomed at his feet.

"Among the royal ones of the earth, the soul of Abe E—— bore the sceptre of perfect sovereignty."

"I knew him," said Corrigan, "may his soul rest in peace, for he was a noble man."

"I knew him," interposed Carlin, "no words give
an idea of how sterling and true a man he was."

"I knew him," added Wright. "When he died
Virginia City did not realize the loss which his death
entailed."

"I knew him," concluded Strong. "His heart was
a banyan tree, its limbs were perpetually bending
down and taking root, till it made shade for the poor
of the city."

Then Carlin, opening the door to the kitchen,
called Yap Sing to bring glasses. A night-cap toddy
was made and as it was drank the good nights were
spoken.

CHAPTER X.

With the lighting of the pipes the next night
Miller said:

"All your royal people so far, though not perfect
men, have had redeeming traits. I once knew one
who had not a single characteristic, except, perhaps,
some pluck. My man was simply a royal liar. In
Western parlance, 'he was a boss.' His name was
Colonel Jensen.

"Now, in my judgment, lying is the very grossest
of human evils. A common liar is a perpetual proof
of the truth of the doctrine of original sin. By that
vice more friendships are broken and more real
misery is perpetrated and perpetuated in the world
than comes through any other channel.

"But as genius excites admiration even when exerted for sinister purposes, so when the art of lying is reduced to an absolute science there is something almost fine about it.

"My liar, when I first knew him, seemed to be between fifty and sixty years of age; but no one ever knew what his real age was.

"But he was quite an old man, for his hair was perfectly white, and that, with a singularly striking face and fine faculty of expressing his ideas, gave him an appearance at once venerable and engaging. It was hard to look into his almost classical face and to think that if he had told the truth within twenty years, it must have been an accident; but such was the fact, nevertheless.

"He was indeed a colossal prevaricator. He was at home, too, on every theme, and there was the charm of freshness to every new falsehood, for he spoke as one who was on the spot—an actor. If it was an event that he was describing, he was a participant; if a landscape or a structure, it was from actual observation; if it chanced to be a scientific theme, he invariably reported the words of some great scientist 'just as they fell from his lips.'

"He knew and had dined with all the great men of his generation—that is, he said so. He always spoke with particularly affectionate remembrance of Henry Clay and Daniel Webster, always referring to them as 'Hank' and 'Dan,' so intimate had he been with them.

"My introduction to him was on a stormy winter night, in the early years of the Washoe excitement. A few of us were conversing in a hotel. One gentleman was describing something that he had witnessed in his boyhood, in Columbus, Ohio.

"As he finished his story, a venerable gentleman, who was a stranger in Washoe, and who had, for several minutes, been slowly pacing up and down the room, suddenly stopped and inquired of the gentleman who had been talking if he was from Columbus? When answered in the affirmative, the stranger extended his hand, dropped into a convenient seat as he spoke, and expressed his pleasure at meeting a gentleman from Columbus, at the same time introducing himself as Colonel Jensen and remarking that one of the happiest recollections of his life was of a day in Columbus, on which day all his prospects in life were changed and wonderfully brightened.

"With such an exordium, the rest could do no less than to press the old gentleman to favor the company with a rehearsal of what had transpired.

"The story was as follows:

"'I had just returned with the remnant of my regiment from Mexico, and had received the unanimous thanks of the Legislature of Ohio for—so the resolution was worded—"the magnificent ability and steadfast and desperate courage displayed by Colonel Jensen for twelve consecutive hours on the field of Buena Vista." I was young at the time and had not got over caring for such things. The day after this resolution of thanks was passed the Governor of the State ordered a grand review, at the capital, of the militia of the State in honor of the soldiers who had survived the war. As a mark of especial honor I was appointed Adjutant-General on the Governor's staff. My place at the review was beside the Governor— who was, of course, Commander-in-Chief—except when my particular regiment was passing.

" 'There are a few things which I have never out-grown a weakness for. One is a real Kentucky blood horse. I had sent to Kentucky and paid four thousand dollars for a son of old Gray Eagle. I bought him cheap, too, because of his color. He was a dappled gray. The Boston stock of horses was just then becoming the rage, and gray was beginning to be an off color for thoroughbreds. My horse was a real beauty. He had been trained on the track, and from a dead stand would spring twenty-two feet the first bound. But he was thoroughly broken and tractable, though he had more style than a peacock, and when prancing and careering, though not pulling five pounds on the bit, he looked as though in a moment he would imitate Elijah's chariot and take to the clouds.

" 'As the hour for the review approached I mounted my horse and took my position, as as-signed, beside the Governor.

" 'I was quietly conversing with him and with our Brigadier-General, when a runaway team, at-tached to an open carriage in which were two ladies, dashed past us.

" 'What followed was instinct. I gave Gray Eagle both rein and spur. In a few seconds he was beside the running horses. I sprang from his back upon the back of the near carriage horse, gathered the inside reins of the team, drew the heads of the two horses together and brought them to a standstill only a few feet from the bluffs, which any one from that city will remember, and over which the team would have dashed in a moment more.

" 'People gathered around instantly, took the horses in hand and helped the ladies from the vehicle.

Being relieved, I caught and remounted my horse, took my place and the review proceeded.

"'After the review, I received a note from the Governor asking me to dine with him that evening.

"'I accepted, supposing the invitation was due to my Mexican record. Judge my surprise, then, when going to the Governor's mansion, I was shown into the parlor, and, on being presented to the Governor's wife and her beautiful unmarried sister, in a moment found myself being overwhelmed by the grateful thanks of the two ladies, learning for the first time, from their lips, that they were the ladies I had rescued.

"'Of course, after that, I was a frequent visitor at the house, and in a few months the young lady became my wife.'

"His story was told with an air of such modest candor and at the same time with such dramatic effect, that what might have seem improbable or singular about it, had it been differently related, was not thought of at the time. The old man was a real hero for a brief moment at least.

"When, later, we knew the Colonel had never been in the Mexican war or any other war; that he had never been married; that if he had ever witnessed a military review it was from a perch on a fence or tree; that he had never possessed four thousand or four hundred dollars with which to buy a horse, and that his oldest acquaintances did not believe that he had ever been on a horse's back, still, while the admiration for the man was somewhat chilled, there was no difference of opinion as to the main fact, which was that as a gigantic and dramatic liar, on merit, he was entitled to the post of honor on a day when the Ananiases of all the world were passing in review.

"Old and middle-aged men in the West will remember the delightful letters, which Lieut. B., under the *nom de plume* of 'Ching Foo,' used to write to the Sacramento *Union*. Once in the presence of Colonel Jensen these letters were referred to as masterpieces. The Colonel smiled significantly and said:

"'They were delicious letters, truly. Take him all in all, Ching Foo was the most intelligent Chinaman I ever saw. He cooked for me three years in California. I taught him reading and writing. I reckon he would have been with me still, but the early floods in '54 washed out my bed-rock flume in American River and I had to break up my establishment. I had a ton of gold in sight in the river bed, but next morning the works were all gone and with them $125,000 which I had used in turning the river.'

"One day an Ohio man and a Tennessee man engaged in a warm dispute over the relative excellencies of the respective State houses in Ohio and Tennessee. Finally they appealed to Colonel Jensen for an opinion. The Colonel, with his sovereign air, said to the Ohio man:

"'You are wrong, Tom. I had just completed the State house at Columbus, when I was sent for to go and make the plans and superintend the construction of the State house at Nashville. It would have been strange if I had not made a great many improvements over the Ohio structure, in preparing plans for the one to be erected in Tennessee.'

"The Colonel was a bungling carpenter by trade, and never built anything more complicated or imposing than a miner's cabin.

"One more anecdote and I will positively stop. Two neighbors had a law suit in Washoe City. One was an honest man, the other a scoundrel. As is the rule in Nevada, both the plaintiff and defendant testified. The defendant denied point blank the testimony of the plaintiff. It was plain that one or the other had committed terrible perjury. Some other witnesses were called, the case was closed and the jury retired to consider upon a verdict. But how to decide was the question. Which was the honest man and which the scoundrel?

"At last one juror hit upon a happy thought. He said:

"'Gentlemen. did you notice closely the last witness for the defendant? His hair was white as snow, his body bent, his steps were feeble and tottering. That man has already one foot in the grave: he will not survive another month. Surely a man in his condition would tell the truth.' The argument seemed logical and the reasoning sound. The verdict was unanimous for the defendant.

"No case ever showed clearer the 'infallibility' of a jury. The witness was Colonel Jensen. The defendant was the perjurer, and all the Colonel knew of the case was what the defendant had, that morning, out behind a hay corral, drilled him to know and to swear to, for a five-dollar piece.

"The Colonel has gone now to join his ancestors on the other side. In the old orthodox days there would not have been the slightest doubt as to who his original ancestor was, or of the temperature of his present quarters, but who knows?

"I only know that, while upon the earth. he was one of the few men whom I have known that I believed was a native genius; a very Shakespeare (or Bacon) in language; a Michael Angelo in coloring; a colossal, all-embracing, magnificent, measureless liar."

"He was a good one, sure," said Carlin.

"He was a bad one, sure," remarked Ashley.

Then Brewster, taking up the theme, said: "He had a chronic disease, that was all. He was as much of an inebriate in his way as ever was drunkard a slave to alcohol. He had great vanity and self-esteem and a flowery imagination. These were chastened or disciplined by no moral attributes. He could no more help being what he was than can the raven avoid being black."

"There was bad stock in the mon," said Corrigan. "He should have been strangled in his cradle; for sich a mon is forever making bitterness in a neighborhood, and is not fit to live."

"Boys," asked the Colonel, "do you believe that lying is ever justifiable?"

Brewster, Harding and Ashley simultaneously answered "No."

"It depends," said Carlin.

"Hardly iver," said Corrigan.

Miller thought it might be necessary.

"For one's self. no ; for another, perhaps yes," said the Professor.

"That is just the point," remarked the Colonel. "Let me tell you about a case which transpired right here in this city. There were two men whose first names were the same, while their surnames were similar. Their given names were Frank and their surnames were, we will say, Cady and Carey, respectively. Cady was a young married man. He had a beautiful wife, a lovely little girl three years of age and a baby boy a year old at the time I am speaking of. Carey was five or six years younger and single. They were great friends, notwithstanding that Cady was pretty fast while Carey was as pure-hearted a young man as ever came here. More, he was devotedly attached to a young lady who was a close friend of the wife of Cady. The young couple were expecting to be married in a few weeks at the time the incident happened which I am going to relate.

"Cady was wealthy, while Carey was poor and a clerk in a mercantile establishment. One day Cady said to his friend: 'Carey, I bought some Con. Virginia stock to-day at $55. I have set aside eighty shares for you. Some people think it is going to advance before long. If it does and there is anything made on the eighty shares it shall be yours.' Sixty days later the stock struck $463, when it was sold and the bank notified Carey that there was a deposit of $32,000 to his credit. When this stroke of good fortune came the youth hastened to tell the good news to the girl of his heart, and before they separated their troth was plighted and the marriage day fixed.

"During this delicious period, one morning Carey stepped into the outer office of Cady and was horrified to hear from behind the glass screen which separated the inner office from the main office the wife of Cady upbraiding her husband in a most violent manner. Her back was to the front of the building. She was holding a letter in her hand, and as Carey entered the building she began and read the letter through, and wound up by crying: 'Who is this Marie who is writing to you and directing the letters simply to Frank, Postoffice box 409? You are keeping a private box, are you? But you are too careless by half; you left this letter in your overcoat pocket, and when I went to sew a button on the coat this morning it fell out, so I could not help but see it.'

"Just then Cady looked up and saw Carey through the glass petition. The latter with a swift motion touched a finger to his lips and shook his head, which in perfect pantomime said: 'Don't give yourself away.' then in a flash slipped noiselessly from the building.

"Once outside, he hastily, on a leaf of his memorandum book, wrote to the postmaster that if he called with a lady and asked what his postoffice box was to answer 409; to at once take out anything that might be in the box, and if he had time to seal and stamp an envelope, direct it to him and put it in 409, and he added: 'Don't delay a moment.'

"Calling a bootblack who was standing near, he gave him the note and a silver dollar, bade him run with the letter to the postoffice and to be sure to deliver the note only to some of the responsible men there, to the postmaster himself if possible.

"Then, with a good deal of noise, he rushed into his friend's place of business again.

"As he entered he heard his friend's wife, through her sobs, saying: 'Oh, Frank! I should have thought that respect for our children would have prevented this, even if you have no more love for me.'

"Carey dashed through the sash door, seemed taken all aback at seeing Cady's wife in the office. In great apparent confusion he advanced and said: 'Excuse me, Cady, but I am in a little trouble this morning. I was expecting a letter last night directed simply to my first name and my postoffice box. It has not come, and as you and myself have the same first name, I did not know but the mistake might have been made at the postoffice.' He was apparently greatly agitated and unstrung and seemed particularly anxious about the letter.

"Cady replied: 'With my mail last night a letter came directed as you say. I opened and glanced over it, thought it was some joke, put it in my pocket and thought no more about it until my wife brought it in this morning. Somehow she does not seem satisfied at my explanation.'

" At this the lady sprang up, and, confronting the young man, said: 'Frank Carey, what is the number of your box in the postoffice?'

"With steady eyes and voice he answered, '409.' The woman was dumfounded for a moment, but she quickly rallied.

" ' Come with me,' she said. The young man obeyed. She took her way directly to the postoffice. Arriving, she tapped at the delivery window and asked if she could see the postmaster in person. The boy delivered the message and in a moment the door opened and the pair were ushered into the private office of the postmaster. Hardly were they seated when the lady said abruptly: 'We have come, Judge, on a serious business. Will you be kind enough to tell me the number of this gentleman's postoffice box?'

" The postmaster looked inquiringly at Carey, who nodded assent. Then in response to the lady, he replied: 'I do not exactly remember. I will have to look at the books.'

" He passed into the main office, but returned in a moment with a petty ledger containing an alphabetical index. He opened at the 'C's' and read: ' Frank Carey, box 409; paid for one quarter from Jan——' Continuing, he said: 'I remember now, Frank, you hired the box about the time you realized on Con. Virginia, and the quarter has about a month more to run.'

"This he said with an imperturbable and incorruptible face, and with an air of mingled candor and business which it was charming to behold.

"The lady was nearly paralyzed, but she made one more effort.

"'There can be no possible mistake in what you have told me, Judge?' she asked.

"'I think not the least in the world,' was the reply, and, rising, he continued: 'Please step this way.' He led the way to the boxes, and there over 409 was the name of Frank Carey. More, there was a sprinkle of dust over it, showing that it had been there for some time.

"'By the way,' said the postmaster, 'you have a letter, Frank. It must be a drop letter, as no mail has been received this morning.' He took the letter from the box in a manner so awkward that the lady could not help seeing that it had evidently been directed in a disguised female hand, and that the superscription was simply 'Frank, P. O. Box 409.'

"Arrived again in the private office, the lady said to the young man, in a latitude 78-degree north tone, 'I see, sir, you have a very extensive, and I have no doubt, very *select* correspondence.'

"At the same time she caught up her skirts—the ladies wore long skirts that year—and, with a 'I thank you, Judge; good morning.' started toward the door. As she passed Carey she drew close to the wall, as though for her robes to touch the hem of his garments would be contamination, and passed haughtily into the street.

"When she had disappeared Carey sank into a chair and drew a long breath of relief, while the grave face of the ancient 'Nasby' unlimbered and warmed into a smile which shone like virtue's own reward.

"'Lord! Lord!' he said, 'but it was a close shave. I had just got things fixed when you came. And was not she mad though? She looked like the prospectus of a cyclone. But tell me. Carey. am I not rather an impressive liar, when, in the best interests of domestic peace. my duty leads me into that channel?"

"Frank answered, 'As Mark Twain told those wild friends of his who perpetrated the bogus robbery upon him, "You did a marvelous sight too well for a mere amateur." But now. Judge. mum is the word about this business.'

"'Mum is the word,' was the reply.

"That evening Carey called at the home of his betrothed. A servant showed him into the parlor, but for the first time the young lady did not put in an appearance. In her stead her mother came. The elder lady, without sitting. in a severe tone said: 'Mr. Carey, my daughter has heard something to-day from Mrs. Cady. Until you explain that matter to my satisfaction my daughter will beg to decline to see you.'

"Carey replied: 'Since your daughter has heard of the matter, it does concern *her*, and I shall very gladly explain to her; but I cannot to any one else, not even to you.'

"'You could easily impose upon a silly girl who is in love, but I am no silly girl, and am not in love, especially not with *you*, and you will have to explain to *me*,' said the lady.

"'My dear madam,' said Carey, mildly, 'in one sense there is nothing in all that gossip. In another sense so much is involved that I would not under the rack whisper a word of it to any soul on earth save she who has promised to give her happiness into my keeping. When your daughter becomes my wife your authority as mother in our home shall never be questioned by me. Until then my business is not with you.'

"'It is not worth while to prolong this discussion,' said the old lady, excitedly. 'If you have nothing more to say, I will bid you good evening.'

"'Good evening, madam,' said Carey, and went out into the night.

" A year later the young lady married the wildest rake on the Comstock, but Carey never married, and died last year.

" When Cady saw how things were going, he went to Carey and said: 'Carey, let me go and explain to those ladies. It kills me to see you as your are.'

"'It will never do,' was the reply. 'They would not keep the secret, especially the elder one never would. It would kill her not to get even with your wife. It worried me a little at first, for I feared that —— might grieve some and be disappointed; but she is all right. I watched her covertly at the play last night. She will forget me in a month. She will be married within the year. We will take no chance of having your home made unhappy. Dear friend, it is all just as I would have it.'"

" It was too bad," said Harding.

"That Carey was a right noble fellow," was Wright's comment.

Miller thought if he had been right game he would have seen that girl, old woman or no old woman.

" He was punished for his falsehood. He had to

9

atone for his own and his friend's sins," was Brewster's conclusion.

"O, murther! I think he had a happy deliverance from the whole family intoirely," said Corrigan.

Carlin, addressing Brewster, said: "You say he was punished for the sins of himself and his friend; how do you dispose of the wickedness of the postmaster?"

"Possibly," was the response, "he is wicked by habit, and it may be he is being reserved for some particular judgment."

"All that I see remarkable about Carey's case," said Ashley, "is that he made the money in the first place. Had that stock been carried for me, the mine would have been flooded the next week and my work would have been mortgaged for a year to come to make good the loss."

"It was a hard case, no doubt," said Strong, "but I think with Corrigan, that the punishment was not without its compensations."

"He had his mirage and it was worse than wild Injuns, was it not, Wright?" asked Corrigan.

"Or worse, Barney," said Wright, "than a blacksmith, a foine mon and a mon of property."

"O, murther, Wright," said Corrigan; "stop that. There go the whistles. Let us say good night."

CHAPTER XI.

About this time Virginia City was visited one day by a heavy rain storm accompanied with thunder. But as the sun was disappearing behind Mount Davidson, the clouds broke and rolled away from the west, while at the same time a faint rainbow appeared in the East, making one of those beautiful spectacles common to mountainous regions.

At the same time the flag on Mount Davidson caught the beams from the setting sun and stood out a banner of fire. This, too, is not an unfrequent spectacle in Virginia City, and long ago inspired a most gifted lady to write a very beautiful poem, "The Flag on Fire."

The storm and the sunset turned the minds of the Club to other beautiful displays of nature which they had seen. Said Miller, "I never saw anything finer than a sunset which I witnessed once at sea down off the Mexican coast.

"We were in a tub of a steamship, the old "Jonathan." We had been in a storm for four days, three of which the steamer had been thrown up into the wind, the machinery working slowly, just sufficient to keep steerageway on the ship.

"There were 600 passengers on board, with an unusual number of women and children, and we had been miserable past expression. But at last, with the coming of the dawn, the wind ceased; as soon as the waves ran down so that it was safe to swing the ship, she was turned about and put upon her course.

"In a few hours the sea grew comparatively smooth, and the passengers by hundreds sought the deck.

"All the afternoon the Mexican coast was in full view, blue and rock-bound and not many miles away.

"Just before the sun set its bended rays struck those blue head-lands and transfigured them. They took on the forms of walls and battlements and shone like a city of gold rising out of the sea in the crimson East, and looked as perhaps the swinging gardens of Semiramis did from within the walls of Babylon. In the West the disc of the sun, unnaturally large, blazed in insufferable splendor, while in glory this seeming city shone in the East. Between the two pictures the ship was plunging on her course and we could feel the pulses of the deep sea as they throbbed beneath us. The multitude upon the deck hardly made a sound; all that broke the stillness was the heavy respirations of the engines and the beating of the paddles upon the water. The spell lasted but a few minutes, for when the sun plunged beneath the sea, the darkness all at once began as is common in those latitudes, but while it lasted it was sublime.

"Speaking of Nature's pictures, in my judgment about the most impressive sight that is made in this world, is a storm at sea. I mean a real storm in which a three thousand ton ship is tossed about like a cork, when the roar of the storm makes human voices of no avail. and when the billows give notice that 'deep is answering unto deep.'

"When a boy I often went down under the overhanging rock over which the current of Niagara pours. As I listened to the roar and tried to compute the energy which had kept those thunders booming for, heaven only knows how many thousands of years, it used to make me feel small enough; but it never influenced me as does an ocean storm. When all the world that is in sight goes into the business of making Niagaras, and turns out a hundred of them every minute, I tell you about all an ordinary landsman can do is to sit still and watch the display.

"A real ocean storm--a shore shaker--is about the biggest free show that this world has yet invented."

Corrigan spoke next; said he: "Spakin' of storms, did you iver watch the phenomenon of a ragin' snow storm high up in the Sierras? When it is approaching there is a roar in the forest such as comes up a headland when the sea is bating upon its base. This will last for hours, the pines rocking like auld women at a wake, and thin comes the snow. Its no quiet, respectable snow such as you see in civilized countries, but it just piles down as though a new glacial period had descinded upon the worreld. As it falls all the voices of the smaller streams grow still and the wind itself grows muffled as though it had a could in the head. The trees up there are no shrubs you know. They grow three hundred feet high and have branches in proportion, and whin they git to roarin' and rockin', it is as though all the armies of the mountains were presentin' arms.

"When the storm dies away, thin it is you see a picture, if the weather is not too cold. The snow masses itself upon the branches, and thin you stand in a temple miles in extent, the floor of which is white like alabaster while the columns that support it are wrought in a lace-work of emerald and of frost more lofty and dilicate than iver was traced out by the patient hand of mortal in grand cathadrals."

Here Carlin interrupted.

"Say, Barney, is there not a great deal of frieze to one of those Sierra temples?"

"It might same so, lookin' from the standpoint of the nave," was Barney's quick reply.

Groans followed this outbreak, from various members of the Club. They were the first puns that had been fired into that peaceful company and they were hailed as omens of approaching trouble.

The gentle voice of Brewster next broke the silence.

"I saw," he said, "in Salt Lake City, three years ago on a summer evening, a sunset scene which I thought was very beautiful. The electric conditions had been strangely disturbed for several days; there had been clouds and a good deal of thunder and lightning. You know Salt Lake City lies at the western base of the Wasatch range. On this day toward evening the sky to the west had grown of a sapphire clearness, but in the east beyond the first high hills of the range a great electric storm was raging. The clouds of inky blackness which shrouded the more distant heights, and through which the lightnings were incessantly zigzaging, were in full view from the city, though the thunders were caught and tied in the deep caverns of the intervening hills. To the southeast the range with its imposing peaks was snowcrowned and under a clear sky. In the southwest the Oquirrh range was blue and beautiful. Just then from beyond the great lake the setting sun threw out his shafts of fire, and the whole firmament turned to glory. The sun blazed from beyond the waters in the west, the lightnings blazed beyond the nearer hills in the east, the snowy heights in the southeast were turned to purple, while in the city every spire, every pane of glass which faced the west, every speck of metal on house and temple in a moment grew radiant as burnished gold, and there was a shimmer of splendor in all the air. Then suddenly over the great range to the east and apparently against the black clouds in which the lightnings were blazing the glorious arch of a magnificent rainbow was upreared. All the colors were deep-dyed and perfectly distinct. There was neither break nor dimness in all the mighty arch. There it stood, poised in indescribable splendor for quite five minutes. So wonderful was the display that houses were deserted; men and women came out into the open air and watched the spectacle in silence and with uncovered heads.

"No one stopped to think that the glory which shone on high was made merely by sunlight shining through falling water: the cold explanation made by science was forgotten, and hundreds of eyes furtively watched, half expecting to catch glimpses of a divine hand and brush, for the pictures were rare enough to be the perfect work of celestial beings sent to sketch for mortals a splendor which should kindle within them dim conceptions of the glories which fill the spheres where light is born.

"Salt Lake City is famous for its sunsets, but to this one was added new and unusual enchantments by the storm which was wheeling its sable squadrons in the adjacent mountains.

"As I watched that display I realized for the first time how it was that before books were made men learned to be devout and to pray; for the picture was as I fancy Sinai must have appeared, when all the elements combined to make a spectacle to awe the multitude before the mountain; and when they were told that the terrible cloud on the mountain's crest was the robe which the infinite God had drawn around

Himself in mercy, lest at a glimpse of His unapproachable brightness they should perish, it was not strange if they believed it."

It was not often that Brewster talked, but when he did there was about him a grave and earnest manner which impressed all who heard him with the perfect sincerity of the man.

After he ceased speaking the room was still for several seconds. At length the Colonel broke the silence:

"Brewster, you spoke of Sinai. What think you of that story; of the Red Sea affair; of the Sinai incident, and the golden calf business?"

"Believed literally." Brewster continued, "it is the most impressive of earthly literature; looked upon allegorically, still it is sublime. Its lesson is, that when in bondage to sorrow and to care, if we but bravely and patiently struggle on. the sea of trouble around us will at length roll back its waves into walls and leave for us a path. Unless we keep straining onward and upward. no voice of Hope, which is the voice of God, will descend to comfort us. If we are thirsty we must smite the rock for water; that is, for what we have we must work, and if we cease our struggle and go into camp. we not only will not hold our own, but in a little while we will be bestowing our jewels upon some idol of our own creation. If we toil and never falter, before we die we shall climb Pisgah and behold the Promised Land; that is, we shall be disciplined until we can look every fate calmly in the face and turn a smiling brow to the inevitable.

"I found a man once, living upon almost nothing. in a hut that had not one comfort. He had graded out a sharp hillside, set some rude poles up against the bank, covered them with brush, and in that den on a bleak mountain's crest he had lived through a rough winter. I asked him how he managed to exist without becoming an idiot or a lunatic. His answer was worthy of an old Roman. 'Because,' said he, 'I at last am superior to distress.'

"He had reached the point that Moses reached when he gained the last mountain crest. After that the Promised Land was forever in sight."

"Suppose," asked Savage, "you buy stocks when they are high and sell them, or have them sold for you, when they are low, where does the Promised Land come in?"

"What becomes of the 'superior to distress' theory," asked Carlin, "when a man in his fight against fate gets along just as the men do in the Bullion shaft, finding nothing but barren rock, and all the time the air grows hotter and there is more and more hot water?"

"Oh, bother the stocks and the hot water," said Strong. "Professor, we have heard about the Wasatch Range and Mount Sinai, shake up your memory and tell us about old Mount Shasta! I heard you describe it once. It is a grand mountain, is it not?"

"The grandest in America, so far as I have seen," was the reply. "It is said that Whitney is higher, but Whitney has for its base the Sierras, and the peaks around it dwarf its own tremendous height. But Shasta rises from the plain a single mountain, and while all the year around the lambs gambol at its base, its crown is eternal snow. Men of the North tell me that it is rivaled by Tacoma, but I never saw Tacoma. In the hot summer days as the farmers at Shasta's base gather their harvests, they can see where the wild wind is heaping the snow drifts about his crest. The mountain is one of Winter's stations, and from his forts of snow upon its top he never withdraws his garrison. There are the bastions of ice, the frosty battlements; there his old bugler, the wind, is daily sounding the advance and the retreat of the storm. The mountain holds all latitudes and all seasons at the same time in its grasp. Flowers bloom at its base, further up the forest trees wave their ample arms; further still the brown of autumn is upon the slopes and over all hangs the white mantle of eternal winter.

"Standing close to its base, the human mind fails to grasp the immensity of the butte. But as one from a distance looks back upon it, or from some height twenty miles away views it, he discovers how magnificent are its proportions.

"For days will the mountain fold the mist about its crest like a vail and remain hidden from mortal sight, and then suddenly as if in deference to a rising or setting sun, the vapors will be rolled back and the watcher in the valley below will behold gems of topaz and of ruby made of sunbeams, set in the diadem of white, and towards the sentinel mountain, from a hundred miles around, men will turn their eyes in admiration. In its presence one feels the near presence of God, and as before Babel the tongues of the people became confused, so before this infinitely more august tower man's littleness oppresses him, and he can no more give fitting expression to his thoughts.

"It frowns and smiles alternately through the years; it hails the outgoing and the incoming centuries, changeless amid the mutations of ages, forever austere, forever cold and pure. The mountain eagle strains hopelessly toward its crest; the storms and the sunbeams beat upon it in vain; the rolling years cannot inscribe their numbers on its naked breast.

"Of all the mountains that I have seen it has the most sovereign look; it leans on no other height: it associates with no other mountain; it builds its own pedestal in the valley and never doffs its icy crown.

"The savage in the long ago, with awe and trembling, strained his eyes to the height and his clouded imagination pictured it as the throne of a Deity who issued the snow, the hoar frost and the wild winds from their brewing place on the mountain's top.

"The white man, with equal awe, strains his eye upward to where the sunlight points with ruby silver and gold the mimic glaciers of the butte, and is not much wiser than the unlettered savage in trying to comprehend how and why the mighty mass was up-reared.

"It is a blessing as well as a splendor. With its cold it seizes the clouds and compresses them until their contents are rained upon the thirsty fields beneath; from its base the Sacramento starts, babbling on its way to the sea; despite its frowns it is a merciful agent to mankind, and on the minds of those who see it in all its splendor and power a picture is painted, the sheen and the enchantment of which will linger while memory and the gift to admire magnificence is left."

"That is good, Professor," said Corrigan: "but to me there is insupportable loneliness about an isolated mountain. It sames always to me like a gravestone set up above the grave of a dead worreld. But spakin' of beautiful things, did yees iver sae Lake Tahoe in her glory?

"I was up there last fall, and one day, in antici-pation of the winter, I suppose, she wint to her wardrobe, took out all her winter white caps and tied them on; and she was a daisy.

"Her natural face is bluer than that of a stock sharp in a falling market; but whin the wind 'comes a wooin' and she dons her foamy lace, powders her face with spray and fastens upon her swellin' breast a thousand diamonds of sunlight, O, but she is a win-some looking beauty, to be sure. Thin, too, she sings her old sintimintal song to her shores, and the great overhanging pines sway their mighty arms as though keeping time, joining with hers their deep murmurs to make a refrain; and thus the lake sings to the shore and the shore answers back to the song all the day long. Tahoe, in her frame of blue and grane, is a fairer picture than iver glittered on cathadral wall; older, fairer and fresher than ancient master iver painted tints immortal upon. There in the strong arms of the mountains it is rocked, and whin the winds ruffle the azure plumage of the beautiful wathers, upon wather and upon shore a splendor rists such as might come were an angel to descend to earth and sketch for mortals a sane from Summer Land."

"You are right, Corrigan," said Ashley. "If the thirst for money does not denude the shores of their trees, and thus spoil the frame of your wonderful picture, Lake Tahoe will be a growing object of in-terest until its fame will be as wide as the world.

"But while on grand themes, have you ever seen the Columbia River? To me it is the glory of the earth. It is a great river fourteen hundred miles above its mouth, and from thence on it rolls to the sea with increasing grandeur all the way. Where it hews its way through the Cascades a new and gorgeous picture is every moment painted, and when the mountain walls are pierced, with perfect purity and with mighty volume it sweeps on toward the ocean. It is, through its last one hundred and fifty miles, watched over by great forests and magnificent mountains. There are Hood and St. Helens and the rest, and where, upon the furious bar, the river joins the sea, there is an everlasting war of waters as beautiful as it is terrible.

"It makes a man a better American to go up the Columbia to the Cascades and look about him. He is not only impressed with the majesty of the scene, but thoughts of empire, of dominion and of the glory of the land over which his country's flag bears sovereignty, take possession of him. He looks down upon the rolling river and up at Mount Hood, and to both he whispers, 'We are in accord; I have an interest in you,' and the great pines nod approvingly, and the waterfalls babble more loud.

"The Mississippi has greater volume than the Oregon, the Hudson makes rival pictures which perhaps are as beautiful as any painted in the Cascades; but there is a power, a beauty, a purity and a wildness about the river of the West which is all its own and which is unapproachable in its charms.

"More than that. To me the river is the emblem of a perfect life. Through all the morning of its career it fights its way, blazing an azure trail through the desert. There is no green upon its banks, hardly does a bird sing as it struggles on. But it bears right on, and so austere is its face that the desert is impotent to soil it. Then it meets a rocky wall and breaks through it, roaring on its way. Then it takes the Willamette to its own ample breast, and it bears it on until it meets the inevitable, and then undaunted goes down to its grave.

"It fights its way, it bears its burdens, it remains pure and brave to the last. That is all the best man that ever lived could do."

As Ashley concluded Strong said: "Why, Ashley! that is good. Why do you not give up mining and devote yourself to writing?"

Ashley laughed low, and said: "Because I have had what repentant sinners are said to have had, my experience. Let me tell you about it.

"It was in Belmont in Eastern Nevada, during that winter when the small pox was bad. It took an epidemic form in Belmont, and a good many died.

"Among the victims was Harlow Reed. Harlow was a young and handsome fellow, a generous, happy-hearted fellow, too, and when he was stricken down, a 'soiled dove,' hearing of his illness, went and watched over him until he died.

"The morning after his death, Billy S. came to me, and handing me a slip of paper on which was Reed's name, age. etc., asked me to prepare a notice for publication. I fixed it as nearly as I could, as I had seen such things in newspapers. It read:

DIED -In Belmont, Dec. 17, Harlow Reed, a native of New Jersey aged twenty-three years.

"Billie glanced at the paper and then said: 'Harlow was a good fellow and a good friend of ours, can you not add something to this notice?'

"In response I sat down and wrote a brief eulogy of the boy, and closed the article in these words:

And for her, the poor woman, who braving the dangers of the pestilence, went and sat at the feet of the man she loved, until he died; for her, though before her garments were soiled, we know that this morning, in the Recording Angel's book it is written "her robes are white as snow."

"Billie took the paper to the publisher, and as he went away, I had a secret thought that, all things being considered, the notice was not bad.

"Next morning I went into a restaurant for breakfast and took a seat at a small table on one side of the narrow room. Directly opposite me were two short-card sharps. One was eating his breakfast, while the other, leaning back to catch the light, was reading the morning paper. Suddenly he stopped, and peering over his paper, though with chair still tilted back, said to his companion: 'Did you see this notice about that woman who took care of Harlow Reed while he was sick?'

"'No,' was the reply. 'What is it?' asked the companion.

"'It's away up,' said the first speaker. 'But what is it?' asked the other.

"The first speaker then threw down the paper, leaned forward, and, seizing his knife and fork, said shortly:

"'Oh, it's no great shakes after all. It says the woman while taking care of Harlow got her clothes dirty, but after he died she changed her clothes and she's all right now.'

"Since then I have never thought that I had better undertake a literary career so long as I could get four honest dollars a day for swinging a hammer in a mine; but I have always been about half sorry that I did not kill that fellow, notwithstanding the lesson that he taught me."

There was a hearty laugh at Ashley's expense, and then Strong roused himself and said:

"The Columbia is very grand, but you must follow it up to its chief tributary if you would find perfect glory—follow it into the very desert. You have heard of the lava beds of Idaho. They were once a river of molten fire from 300 feet to 900 feet in depth, which burned its way through the desert for hundreds of miles. To the east of the source of this lava flow, the Snake River bursts out of the hills, becoming almost at once a sovereign river, and flowing at first south-westerly, and then bending westerly, cuts its way through this lava bed, and, continuing its way with many bends, finally, far to the north merges with the Columbia. On this river are several falls. First, the American Falls, are very beautiful. Sixty miles below are the Twin Falls, where the river, divided into two nearly equal parts, falls one hundred and eighty feet. They are magnificent. Three miles below are the Shoshone Falls, and a few miles lower down the Salmon Falls. It was of the Shoshone Falls that I began to speak.

" They are real rivals of Niagara. Never anywhere else was there such a scene; never anywhere else was so beautiful a picture hung in so rude a frame; never anywhere else on a background so forbidding and weird were so many glories clustered.

" Around and beyond there is nothing but the desert, sere, silent, lifeless, as though Desolation had builded there everlasting thrones to Sorrow and Despair.

" Away back in remote ages, over the withered breast of the desert, a river of fire one hundred miles wide and four hundred miles long, was turned. As the fiery mass cooled, its red waves became transfixed and turned black, giving to the double desert an indescribably blasted and forbidding face.

" But while this river of fire was in flow, a river of

water was fighting its way across it, or has since made
the war and forged out for itself a channel through
the mass This channel looks like the grave of a
volcano that has been robbed of its dead.

"But right between its crumbling and repellant
walls a transfiguration appears. And such a picture!
A river as lordly as the Hudson or the Ohio, springing
from the distant snow-crested Tetons, with waters
transparent as glass, but green as emerald, with ma-
jestic flow and ever-increasing volume, sweeps on until
it reaches this point where the august display begins.

"Suddenly, in different places in the river bed,
jagged, rocky reefs are upraised, dividing the current
into four rivers, and these, in a mighty plunge of
eighty feet downward, dash on their way. Of course,
the waters are churned into foam and roll over the
precipice white as are the garments of the morning
when no cloud obscures the sun. The loveliest of
these falls is called "The Bridal Veil," because it is
made of the lace which is woven with a warp of falling waters and a woof of sunlight. Above this and
near the right bank is a long trail of foam, and this is
called "The Bridal Train." The other channels are
not so fair as the one called "The Bridal Veil," but
they are more fierce and wild, and carry in their
furious sweep more power.

"One of the reefs which divides the river in mid-
channel runs up to a peak, and on this a family of
eagles have, through the years, may be through the
centuries, made their home and reared their young,
on the very verge of the abyss and amid the full
echoes of the resounding boom of the falls. Surely
the eagle is a fitting symbol of perfect fearlessness
and of that exultation which comes with battle
clamors.   10

"But these first falls are but a beginning. The greater splendor succeeds. With swifter flow the startled waters dash on and within a few feet take their second plunge in a solid crescent, over a sheer precipice, two hundred and ten feet to the abyss below. On the brink there is a rolling crest of white, dotted here and there, in sharp contrast, with shining eddies of green, as might a necklace of emerald shimmer on a throat of snow, and then the leap and fall.

" Here more than foam is made. Here the waters are shivered into fleecy spray, whiter and finer than any miracle that ever fell from India loom, while from the depths below an everlasting vapor rises—the incense of the waters to the water's God. Finally, through the long, unclouded days, the sun sends down his beams, and to give the startling scene its crowning splendor, wreaths the terror and the glory in a rainbow halo. On either sullen bank the extremities of its arc are anchored, and there in its many-colored robes of light it stands outstretched above the abyss like wreaths of flowers above a sepulcher. Up through the glory and the terror an everlasting roar ascends, deep-toned as is the voice of Fate, a diapason like that the rolling ocean chants when his eager surges come rushing in to greet and fiercely woo an irresponsive promontory.

"But to feel all the awe and to mark all the splendor and power that comes of the mighty display, one must climb down the steep descent to the river's brink below, and, pressing up as nearly as possible to the falls, contemplate the tremendous picture. There something of the energy that creates that endless panorama is comprehended; all the deep throbbings of the mighty river's pulses are felt; all the magnificence is seen.

"In the reverberations that come of the war of waters one hears something like God's voice; something like the splendor of God is before his eyes; something akin to God's power is manifesting itself before him, and his soul shrinks within itself, conscious as never before of its own littleness and helplessness in the presence of the workings of Nature's immeasurable forces.

"Not quite so massive is the picture as is Niagara, but it has more lights and shades and loveliness, as though a hand more divinely skilled had mixed the tints, and with more delicate art had transfixed them upon that picture suspended there in its rugged and sombre frame.

"As one watches it is not difficult to fancy that away back in the immemorial and unrecorded past, the Angel of Love bewailed the fact that mortals were to be given existence in a spot so forbidding, a spot that apparently was never to be warmed with God's smile, which was never to make a sign through which God's mercy was to be discerned; that then Omnipotence was touched, that with His hand He smote the hills and started the great river in its flow; that with His finger He traced out the channel across the corpse of that other river that had been fire, mingled the sunbeams with the raging waters and made it possible in that fire-blasted frame of scoria to swing a picture which should be, first to the red man and later to the pale races, a certain sign of the existence, the power and the unapproachable splendor of the Great First Cause.

"And as the red man through the centuries watched the spectacle, comprehending nothing except that an infinite voice was smiting his ears, and insufferable glories were blazing before his eyes; so through the centuries to come the pale races will stand upon the shuddering shore and watch, experiencing a mighty impulse to put off the sandals from their feet, under an overmastering consciousness that the spot on which they are standing is holy ground.

" There is nothing elsewhere like it: nothing half so weird, so wild, so beautiful, so clothed in majesty. so draped with terror; nothing else that awakens impressions at once so startling, so winsome, so profound. While journeying through the desert to come suddenly upon it, the spectacle gives one something of the emotions that would be experienced to behold a resurrection from the dead. In the midst of what seems like a dead world, suddenly there springs into irrepressible life something so marvelous, so grand, so caparisoned with loveliness and irresistible might, that the head is bowed, the strained heart throbs tumultuously and the awed soul sinks to its knees."

The whistles had sounded while Strong was speaking, and as he finished the good nights were spoken and the lights put out.

CHAPTER XII.

With the lighting of the pipes one evening, the conversation of the Club turned upon what constituted courage and a high sense of honor; whether they were native or acquired gifts. A good deal of talk ensued, until at last Wright's opinion was asked:

" You are all right," said he, " and all wrong. Some men are born insensible to fear, and some have a high sense of honor through instinct. But this, I take it, is not the rule and comes, I think, mostly as an hereditary gift, through long generations of proud ancestors. In my judgment, no gift to mortals is as noble as a lofty, honest pride. I do not mean that spurious article which we see so much of, but the pride which will not permit a man or woman to have an unworthy thought, because of the sense of degradation which it brings to the breast that entertains it. This, I believe, is more common in women than in men, and I suppose that it was this divine trait, manifesting itself in a brutal age, which gave birth to the chivalry of the Middle Ages.

"I have known a few men who, I believe, were born without the instinct of fear. Charley Fairfax was one of these. He was a dead shot with a pistol. He had some words with a man one day on the street in Sacramento, and the man being very threatening, Fairfax drew and cocked his Derringer. At the same moment the man drove the blade of a sword cane through one of the lungs of Fairfax, making a wound which eventually proved fatal. Fairfax raised his Derringer and took a quick aim at the heart of the murderer, but suddenly dropped the weapon and said: 'You have killed me, but you have a wife and children; for their sakes I give you your life,' and sank fainting and, as he thought, dying, into the arms of a friend who caught him as he was falling.

"There are other men as generous as Fairfax was, but to do what he did, when smarting under a fatal wound, requires the coolness and the nerve of absolute self-possession.

"Not one man in a million under such circumstances could command himself enough to think to

be generous. Many a man has, for his courage, had
a statue raised to his memory who never did and
never could have given any such proof of a manhood
absolutely self-contained as did Fairfax on that occasion.

"But, as a rule, we are all mere creatures of education. A friend of mine came 'round the Horn in a
clipper ship. He told me that when off the cape they
encountered a gale which drove the ship far to the
southward; that the weather was so dreadfully cold
that the ship's rigging was sheeted with ice from sleet
and frozen spray.

"One evening the gale slackened a little and some
sails were bent on, but toward the turn of the night
the wind came on again and the sails had to be taken
in. Said my friend: 'The men went up those sway-
ing masts and out upon those icy yards apparently
without a thought of danger, while I stood upon the
deck fairly trembling with terror merely watching
them.' After awhile the storm was weathered, the
cape was rounded and the ship put into Valparaiso
for fresh supplies.

"The sailors were given a holiday. They went
ashore and hired saddle horses to visit some resort a
few miles out of town. They mounted and started
away, but within three minutes half of them returned
leading their horses, and one spoke for all when he
said: 'The brute is crank; I am afraid he will
broach to and capsize.'

"The men who rode the icy spars off Cape Horn
on that inky midnight were afraid to ride those gentle mustangs.

"There are, I suppose, in this city to-night one
hundred men who, with knife or pistol, would fight

anybody and not think much about it. But what would they do were they placed where I saw Corrigan unconcernedly working to-day?

"He was sitting on a narrow plank which had been laid across a shaft at the eight hundred-foot level, repairing a pump column. He was eight. hundred feet from the surface, and there was only that plank between him and the bottom of that shaft nine hundred feet below. Put the ordinary ruffian who cuts and shoots on that plank and he would faint and fall off through sheer fright."

"I guess you are right," interposed Carlin. "There is the Mexican who lives across the street from us. If I were to take a revolver and go over there in the morning and attack him, the chances are I would scare him to death; were I to try the same experiment with a bowie knife the chances are more than even that he would give me more of a game than I would want, and simply because he is accustomed to a knife and not to a pistol.

"So the mountain trapper will attack a grizzly bear with perfect coolness, or cross the swiftest stream in a canoe without any fear, but bring the same man for the first time here to the mine and ask him to get on a cage with you and go down a shaft, and he will grow pale and tremble like a girl."

"An Indian," suggested the Professor, "at the side of a white man will go into a desperate battle and never flinch; so long as the white man lives he will fight even unto death. But let a white man engage in a hand to hand fight with two or three Indians, and if he has the nerve to hold him up to the fight for two or three minutes he will conquer, because an hereditary fear. overcomes the savage that the

pale face will conquer in the end. That is really
the cowardice which Falstaff assumed to feel, the
cowardice of instinct in the presence of the true
prince, and is the mark which the Indian mothers
have impressed upon their babes for ten generations.

"The rule is that we follow our trades!"

"Then some men are brave at one time and cow-
ardly at another," said the Colonel. " Men who will
fight without shrinking, by day, are often completely
demoralized by a night attack. With such men the
trouble is, they cannot see to estimate their danger,
and their imaginations multiply and magnify it a
hundred fold. I know a man in this city who has
been in a hundred fights, many of them most desperate encounters. He told me once that he believed
it would frighten him to death to be awakened at
night by a burglar in his room.

" This is the fear, too. which paralyzes men in the
presence of an earthquake. The sky may be clear
and the air still. but the thought that in a moment
chaos may come is too much for the ordinary nerves
of mortals."

" The bravest act I ever witnessed was on C street
in this city." responded Strong. " It was a little Hebrew dunning a desperado for the balance due on a
pair of pantaloons. The amount was six dollars and
fifty cents. I would not have asked the fighter for
the money for six times the sum. but the little chap
not only asked for it, but when the fighter tried to
evade him. he seized him by the arm with one hand
and putting the forefinger of his other hand along-
side his own nose, in the most insulting tone possible
said: 'You docs not get avay. Der man vot does not
bay for his glose is, vots yer call him? one d——d
loafer. I vants my monish.'

"The fighter could no more escape from that eye than a chicken hawk can from the spell of the eye of the black snake, and so he settled.

"That was the courage which it required the hardships and persecutions of one hundred generations of suffering men to acquire, and I tell you there was something thrilling in the way it was manifested."

"So, too, men's ideas of honor are often warped strangely by education," Miller said. "Do you remember there was a Frenchman hanged in this city a few years ago? On the scaffold, with a grandiloquent air, just before the cap was drawn over his face, he said: 'Zey can hang me, but zey cannot hang Frawnce.' He had from childhood entertained the belief that there was but one entirely invincible nation on this earth, and that was France; and the thought that to the last France must be honored possessed him.

"That man had murdered a poor woman of the town for her money."

"I should say there were some queer ideas of honor in this country," chipped in the Colonel. "I believe the rule among some or all sporting men is, that it is entirely legitimate to practice any advantage on an opponent in a game, so long as the same idea controls the opponent. Still those men have most tenacious ideas of honor. Indeed they have a code of their own. If one borrows money of another he pays it if he has to rob someone to do it. If one stakes another—that is gives him money to play—and a winning is made, the profits are scrupulously divided. If one loses more at night than he has money to pay, he must have it early next morning or go into disgrace.

"A friend of mine who lived on Treasure Hill during that first fearful winter, told me that during that season a faro game was running, and the owners of the bank had won some thirty-five hundred dollars. The dealer's habit was to lock up his place in the forenoon and not return until evening. The interval was his only time for sleep, as the game frequently ran all night.

"Three or four 'sports' who lived together in a house, had lost heavily at this game. One morning, one of them said that if he could only get that dealer's cards for half an hour he believed he could 'fix' them so that the luck of the boys would change.

"They had for a cook and servant a young man who had confessed that he left the East without any extensive or extended preparations, and that he did it to avoid paying a penalty for picking a lock and robbing a till.

"He was called up, it was explained to him what was wanted and for what reason, and asked if it was not possible for him to procure those cards.

"The youth took kindly to the proposition, went away, and in a few minutes returned—not with the cards—but with the dealer's sack of coin, saying as he laid down the sack: 'As I picked the lock of the drawer I found the sack and the cards lying side by side. I thought it would be easier to take the coin than to fool with the cards, and here it is.'

"Instantly there was a commotion, and a perfect storm of imprecations was poured out upon the thief. On every side were shouts of: 'Take back that money! you miserable New York thief! What do you take us for? Take back that sack or we will sell you for headcheese before night!'

"The youth carried back the coin and brought the cards. They were found to be 'fixed'; they were 'fixed' over and returned, and that night 'on the dead square,' the bank was broken. The boys had the sack for the second time, but this time the transaction, according to their code, was entirely legitimate.

"By the operation the professional thief obtained new ideas of the nice distinctions which are made in the gamblers' code of honor."

"I once in Idaho knew a most conscientious judge," said Miller. "In his court a suit involving the title of some mining ground was pending between two companies. In another part of the district the Judge had some claims which were looked upon as mere 'wild cat.'

"He had for a year been trying to raise money to open his claims, but without avail. He had incorporated with 40,000 shares and held his shares at one dollar, with the understanding that twenty per cent. of the stock should be set aside as a working capital. But no one could see the ground with the sanguine eyes of the Judge. so he still had all his stock.

"But one night quite late the Judge heard a soft knock on the door. In answer to his 'come in,' the president of the company that was plaintiff in the mining suit entered, when this conversation ensued:

"'I was looking at your claims over on the east side to-day,' said the President, 'and I believe they are good and would like some of the stock.'

"'There is some of it for sale at one dollar,' was the reply.

"'I will take ten thousand shares,' said the President. 'If you please, have the stock ready and I will call at nine o'clock to-morrow morning with the money.'

" 'I suppose this transaction had better be kept secret at present,' suggested the Judge.

" 'Oh, yes. It is a private speculation of my own and I would rather my company would not hear of it.'

" 'Very well, the stock will be ready.'

"The money was promptly paid and the stock delivered.

"The day of trial drew near, when one day the Judge met the superintendent of the company which was defendant in the suit. The Judge told the superintendent that he had some promising claims, and added impressively that if he could afford to purchase about 10,000 shares he felt sure that he would do well. The superintendent admitted that he had examined the claims with considerable care, and believed with the Judge, that there was promise in them. The result was that the next day another ten thousand dollars was paid to the Judge and ten thousand more shares delivered. The Judge deposited sixteen thousand dollars to his own account and four thousand dollars to the credit of the company. With the four thousand dollars he let a contract for work on the mine.

"In due time the case in court came on and was decided in favor of the plaintiff and an appeal provided for. The plaintiff kept still about the stock transaction, but the superintendent of the defendant company did not hesitate to declare that the Judge was a thief. So matters ran along for some months, when one day the aforesaid president and superintendent each received a note asking them to call at the office of the Judge at a certain hour. Both responded, and each was greatly surprised to see the other.

"The Judge opened the business by saying that a

grand deposit of ore had been struck on one of the claims from which enough ore had already been taken to enable the company to pay a dollar per share dividend on the capital stock, upon which he pushed a check for ten thousand dollars to each of the men. He then went on to say that he had that morning received an offer of two hundred thousand dollars for the property, which he thought was a fair price, and asked the opinion of the others. They thought so too, and in a few days the money was paid over and each of the two received fifty thousand dollars.

" ' Now,' said the Judge, ' let me give you some advice. Settle up that foolish lawsuit outside of court. The claim is not worth what either one of you will pay out in attorneys' fees if you fight it out in the courts.'

" By this time the three men had grown familiar, so the superintendent ventured to say:

"'Judge, will you tell me what caused you to urge me to buy those shares?'

" ' I thought it was a good investment,' was the reply.

"'But was not there something else?' asked the superintendent.

" ' To tell you the truth,' replied the Judge, ' I had received ten thousand dollars from the President here, and I was afraid if the matter went that way into the court I might be prejudiced, so I sold you a like amount that I might go upon the bench, to try the case, *entirely unbiased.*' "

" He was a good judge, no doubt, but he ividently had a leaning toward the east side," said Corrigan.

" That was one case where the only justification was success," said Brewster.

"He took his chances, that was all," Miller remarked, "and that is the corner-stone on which every fortune on the coast has been builded. I mean every fortune in mining."

"That is so," chimed in Carlin. "Mining is simply a grand lottery and is about as much of a game of chance as poker or faro."

"Oh. no. Carlin." said Strong. "You have picked up the idea that is popular, but there is nothing to it. I am not referring to mining on paper, that mining which is done on Pine and California streets. That is not only gambling. but it is, nine times out of ten. pure stealing. But what I mean is where a man, or a few men, from the unsightly rock. by honest labor, wrest something, which all men, barbarous and civilized alike, hold as precious; something which was not before, but which when found, the whole world accepts as a measure of values, and the production of which makes an addition to the world's accumulated wealth, and not only injures none. but quickens the arteries of trade everywhere; that is not gambling. Of course there are mistakes, of course worlds of unnecessary work have been performed, of course hopes have been blasted and hearts broken through the business, but in this world men have to pay for their educations. Twenty years ago there was not a man in America who could work Comstock ores up to seventy-five per cent. of their money value; only a scholarly few knew anything about the formations in which ore veins are liable to be found; processes to work ores and economical methods to open and work mines had to be invented; so far as the West was concerned the business of mining and reducing ores had to be created. The results do not justify any man in calling mining a lottery. In my judgment, it is the most legitimate business in the world; the only one in which there can be no overproduction, and the one which, above all others, advances every other industry of the country.

"When the steam engine was first invented steam boilers blew up every day. This was no argument against the engine, but was a notice to men to build better boilers. For the same reason the sixty-pound steel rail has been substituted for the old wooden rail with an iron strap on top on railways, and the sixteen ton Pullman car for the old rattle trap that the slightest collision would smash. The Westinghouse air brake and the Miller platform are part of the same education.

"By and by men will learn to know the rocks, and when their marks and signs are reduced to a perfect alphabet the crude work of mining as carried on now will take on the dignity of a science, and mining will become what it deserves to be, the most honored of industries."

CHAPTER XIII.

At length the first sorrow fell upon the Club. The mail brought to Corrigan one day the news of the death of his mother in New York. It was a terrible blow to him. It had been his dream all through the years that he had been absent from his home that some time he would accumulate money enough to provide her with a home, where around her life every comfort would be drawn, and from her life every heart-breaking care would be driven away. But time would not wait for him, and the letter, which only in gentle words told him of his mother's death, kindled in his heart such bitter self-reproaches that for awhile the warm-hearted man's grief was inconsolable.

The Club heartily sympathized with him, but there was little said. The men who face death daily in a deep mine either come to think, after awhile, that this life hangs on too tender a thread to be grieved over so very much when that thread is broken, or, because of the nature of their occupation. which is necessarily carried on mostly in silence, they lose the faculty to say the words which in society circles are intruded upon people who are in deep sorrow.

On this evening the supper was eaten in silence, Corrigan hardly tasting anything.

As the Club took their seats Ashley found opportunity to covertly whisper to Yap Sing that Corrigan had received bad news and he must prepare something especially tempting for him to eat. · When the meal was nearly finished Yap Sing brought a mammoth dish of strawberries, a bowl of sugar and pitcher of cream, and after the noiseless manner of his race, set them in front of Corrigan's plate. No one else at the table seemed to notice the act of the Chinaman. Corrigan gave a quick glance around the table and when he saw that no one else was to be served with the berries—that it was meant as a special act of sympathy for him—his eyes filled with tears and he hastily withdrew from the room.

At his leisure during the evening Yap Sing ate the berries and the cream, remarking to himself as he did so:

"Me heap slory Meester Clorigan; me likee be heap slory ebbly day."

For an hour after supper the Club did little but smoke. At length, however, Harding, who usually spent his evenings absorbed in reading, laid aside his book and in his low and kindly voice, began to talk.

"Often when a boy I heard my father tell a story of a woman, a Sister of Charity, which, I think, may be, it will be good to tell to-night. In one of the mountain towns of Northern California a good many years ago, while yet good women, compared to the number of the men, were so disproportionately few, suddenly one day, upon the street, clad in the un-attractive garb of a Sister of Charity, appeared a woman whose marvelous loveliness the coarse garments and uncouth hood peculiar to the order could not conceal.

"There was a Sisters' Hospital in the place and this nun was one of the devoted women who had come to minister to the sick in that hospital.

"She was of medium size and height, and despite her shapeless garments it was easy to see that her form was beautiful. The hand that carried a basket was a delicate one; under her unsightly hood glimpses of a brow as white as a planet's light could be caught; the coarse shoes upon her feet were three sizes too large. When she raised her eyes from the inner depths a light like that of kindly stars shone out, and though a Sister of Charity, there was something about her lips which seemed to say that of all famines a famine of kisses was hardest to endure. There was a stately, kindly dignity in her mien, but in all her ways there was a dainty grace which, upon the hungry eyes of the miners of that mountain

11

town, seemed like enchantment. She could not have been more than twenty years of age.

"It was told that she was known as 'Sister Celeste,' that she had recently come to the Western Coast, it was believed, from France, and that was all that was known of her. When the Mother Superior at the hospital was questioned about the new sister, she simply answered: 'Sister Celeste is a sister now; she will be a glorified saint by and by.'

"The first public appearance of Sister Celeste in the town was one Sunday afternoon. She emerged from her hospital and started to carry some delicacy to a poor, sick woman, a Mrs. De Lacy, who lived on the opposite side of the town from the hospital; so to visit her the nun was obliged to walk almost the whole length of the one long, crooked street which, in the narrow cañon, included all the business portion of the town.

"When the nun started out from the hospital the town was full of miners, as was the habit in those days on Sunday afternoons, and as the Sister passed along the street hundreds of eyes were bent upon her. She seemed unconscious of the attention she was attracting; had she been walking in her sleep she could not have been more composed.

"Many were the comments made as she passed out of the hearing of different groups of men. One big, rough miner, who had just accepted an invitation to drink, caught sight of the vision, watched the Sister as she passed and then said to the companion who had asked him:

"'Excuse me, Bob, I have a feeling as though my soul had just partaken of the sacrament. No more gin for me to-day.'

" Said another: 'It is a fearful pity. That woman was born to be loved, and to love somebody better than nine hundred and ninety out of every thousand could. Her occupation is, in her case, a sin against nature. Every hour her heart must protest against the starvation which it feels: every day she must feel upon her robes the clasp of little hands which are not to be.'

" One boisterous miner, a little in his cups, watched until the Sister disappeared around a bend in the crooked street, and then cried out: ' Did you see her, boys? That is the style of a woman that a man could die for and smile while dying. Oh! Oh!' Then drawing from his belt a buckskin purse, he held it aloft and shouted: ' Here are eighty ounces of the cleanest dust ever mined in Bear Gulch; it's all I have in the world, but I will give the last grain to any bruiser in this camp who will look crooked at that Sister when she comes back this way, and let me see him do it. In just a minute and a half—but no matter, I'm better that I have seen her.'

" After that, daily, for all the following week, Sister Celeste was seen going to and returning from the sick woman's house. It suddenly grew to be a habit with everybody to uncover their heads as Sister Celeste came by.

" Sunday came around again, and it was noticed that on that morning the nun went early to visit her charge and remained longer than usual. On her return, when just about opposite the main saloon of the place, a kindly, elderly gentleman, who was universally known and respected, ventured to cross the path of the Sister, and address her as follows:

" 'I beg pardon, good Sister, but you are attending

upon a sick person. We understand that it is a woman. May I not ask if we can not in some way assist you and the woman?'

"A faint flush swept over the glorious face of Sister Celeste as she raised her eyes, but simply and frankly, and with a slight French accent, she answered:

"'The lady, kind sir, is very ill. Unless, in some way, we can manage to remove her to the hospital, where she can have an evenly warmed room and close nursing. I fear she will not live; but she is penniless and we are very poor, and, moreover, I do not see how she can be moved, for there are no carriages.'

"She spoke with perfect distinctness, notwithstanding the slight foreign accent. The accent was no impediment; rather from her lips it gave her words a rhythm like music.

"The man raised his voice: 'Boys,' he shouted, 'there is a suffering woman up the street. She is very destitute and very ill, and must be removed to the hospital. The first thing required is some money.' Then, taking off his hat with one hand, with the other he took from his pocket a twenty-dollar piece, put the money in the hat, then sprang upon a low stump that was standing by the trail and added: 'I start the subscription, those who have a trifle that they can spare will please pass around this way and drop the trifle into the hat.'

"Then Sister Celeste had a new experience. In an instant she was surrounded by a shouting, surging, struggling crowd, all eager to contribute. There was a Babel of voices, but for once a California crowd were awakened to full roar without an oath being heard. The boys could not swear in the presence of Sister Celeste.

" In a few minutes between seven and eight hundred dollars was raised. It was poured out of the hat into a buckskin purse, the purse was tied, and handed, by the man who first addressed her, to Sister Celeste, with the remark that it was for her poor and that when she needed more the boys would stand in.

"Again the nun raised her eyes and in a low voice which trembled a little, she said:

"'Please salute the gentlemen and say to them that God will keep the account.'

"The man turned around and with an awkward laugh said: 'Boys! I am authorized, by one of His angels, to say that for your contribution, God has taken down your names, and given you credit.'

"Then a wild fellow cried out from the crowd:

"'Three cheers for the Angel!'

"The cheers rang out like the braying of a thousand trumpets in accord. Then in a hoarse undertone a voice shouted 'Tiger!' and the deep-toned old-day California 'Tiger' rolled up the hillsides like an ocean roar. It would have startled an ordinary woman, but Sister Celeste was looking at the purse, and it is doubtful if she heard it at all.

"Then the first speaker called from the crowd eight men, by name, and said:

"'You were all married men in the States and for all that I know to the contrary, were decent, respectable gentlemen. As master of ceremonies I delegate you, as there are no carriages in this camp, to go to the sick woman's house, and carry her to the hospital, while the good Sister proceeds in advance and makes a place for her.'

" This was agreed to, and the Sister was told that in half an hour she might expect her patient.

"Then she hurried away, the crowd watching her and remarking that her usual stately step seemed greatly quickened.

"Long afterward, the Mother Superior related that, when Sister Celeste reached the hospital on that day, she fell sobbing into the Mother's arms, and when she could command her voice, said: ' Those shaggy men that I thought were all tigers are all angels disguised. O, Mother, I have seen them as Moses and Elias were, transfigured.'

"The eight men held a brief consultation in the street, then going to a store they bought a pair of heavy white blankets, an umbrella and four pick handles. Borrowing a packer's needle and some twine they began to sew the pick handles into the sides of the blanket, first rolling the handles around once or twice in the edges of the blanket. They then proceeded to the sick woman's house: one went in first and told the sick woman, gently, what they had come to do, and bade her have no fears, that she was to be moved so gently that if she would close her eyes she would not know anything about it. The others were called in; the blanket was laid upon the floor; the bed was lifted with its burden from the bedstead and laid on the blanket; the covers were neatly tucked under the mattress; four men seized the pickhandles at the sides, lifted the bed, woman and all from the floor, a fifth man stepped outside, raised the umbrella and held it above the woman's face, and so, as gently as ever mother rocked her babe to sleep, the sick woman was carried the whole length of the street to the hospital, where Sister Celeste and the Mother Superior received her.

"Then all hands went up town and talked the

matter over, and I am afraid that some of them drank a little, but the burden of all the talk and all the toasts, was Sister Celeste.

"After that the nun was often seen, going on her errands of mercy, and it is true that some men who had been rough and who had drank hard for months previous to the coming of the Sister, grew quiet in their lives and ceased to go to the saloons.

"One day a most laughable event transpired. Two men got quarrelling in the street which in a moment culminated in a fight. The friends of the respective men joined and soon there was a general fight in which perhaps thirty men were engaged. When it was at its height (and such a fight meant something) Sister Celeste suddenly turned the sharp bend of the street and came into full view not sixty yards from where the melee was raging in full fury.

"One of the fighters saw her and made a sound between a hiss and a low whistle, a peculiar sound of alarm and warning, so significant that all looked up.

"In an instant the men clapped their hands into their side pockets, and commenced moving away, some of them whistling low and dancing as they went, as though the whole thing was but a jovial lark. When Sister Celeste reached the spot a moment afterward, the street was entirely clear. The men washed their faces, some wag began to describe the comical scene which they made when they concluded that the street under certain circumstances was no good place for a fight; good humor was restored, the chief combatants shook hands with perfect cordiality, a drink of reconciliation was ordered all around, and when the glasses were emptied, a man cried out: 'Fill up once more, boys. I want you to drink with me the health of the only capable peace officer that we have ever had in town—Sister Celeste.' The health was drank with enthusiasm.

"The winter came on at length and there was much sickness. Sister Celeste redoubled her exertions; she was seen at all hours of the day, and was met, sometimes, as late as midnight, returning from her watch beside a sick bed.

"The town was full of rough men; some of them would cut or shoot at a word, but Sister Celeste never felt afraid. Indeed, since that Sabbath when the subscription was taken up in the street she had felt that nothing sinister could ever happen to her in that place.

"Once, however, she met a jolly miner who had been in town too long, and who had started for home a good deal the worse for liquor. She met him in a lonely place where the houses had been a few days previous burned down on both sides of the street. Emboldened by rum, the man stepped directly in front of the nun and said:

" 'My pretty Sister, I will give your hospital a thousand dollars for one kiss.'

"The Sister never wavered; she raised her calm and undaunted eyes to the face of the man, an incandescent whiteness warmed upon her cheek, giving to her striking face unwonted splendor. For a moment she held the man under the spell of her eyes, then stretching her right arm out toward the sky, slowly and with infinite sadness in her tones said:

" 'If your mother is watching from there, what will she think of her son?'

"The man fell on his knees, crying ' pardon,' and Sister Celeste, with her accustomed stately step, passed slowly on her way.

" Next day an envelope directed to Sister Celeste was received at the hospital. Within there was nothing but a certificate of deposit from a local bank for one thousand dollars, made to the credit of the hospital.

" On another occasion the nun had a still harder trial to bear. A young man was stricken with typhoid fever and sent to the hospital. He was a rich and handsome man. He had come from the East only a few weeks before he was taken down. His business in California was to settle the estate of an uncle recently deceased, who had died leaving a large property.

" When carried to the hospital Sister Celeste was appointed his nurse. The fever ran twenty-one days, and when it left him finally, he lay helpless as a child and hovering on the very threshhold of the grave for days.

" With a sick man's whim, no one could do anything for him but Sister Celeste. She had to move him on his pillows, give him his medicines and such food as he could bear. In lifting him her arms were very often around him and her bosom was so near his breast that she could feel the throbbing of his heart.

" As health slowly returned, the young man watched the nurse with steadily increasing interest.

" At length the time came when the physician said that in another week the patient would require no further attendance, but that he ought, so soon as possible, to go to the seaside, where the salt air would furnish him the tonic that he needed most.

" When the physician went away the young man said: 'Sister Celeste, sit down and let us talk.' She obeyed. 'Let me hold your hand,' he said; 'I want to tell you of my mother and my home, and with

your hand in mine it will seem as though the dear
ones there were by my side.' She gave him her hand
in silence.

"Then he told her of his beautiful home in the
East; of the love that had always been a benediction
to that home; of his mother and little sister, of their
daily life and their unbroken happiness.

"Insidiously the story flowed on until at length
he said, with returning health, his business being
nearly all arranged, he should return to those who
awaited, anxiously, his coming. And before Sister
Celeste had any time for preparation or remonstrance,
the young man added:

"'You have been my guardian angel; you have
saved my life. The world will be all dark without you.
You can serve God and humanity better as my wife
than as a lowly and poor Sister here. Some women
have higher destinies and a nobler sphere to fill on
earth than as Sisters of Charity; you were never
meant to be a nun, but a loving wife. Be mine.
If it is the poor you wish to serve, a thousand shall
bless you where one blesses you here; but come with
me, filling my mother's heart with joy and taking
your rightful place as my wife. Be my guardian
angel forever!

"The face of Sister Celeste was white as the pillow
on which her hand lay; for a moment she seemed
choking, while about her lips and eyes there was a
tremulousness as though she was about to break into a
storm of uncontrollable sobs. But she rallied under a
tremendous effort at self-control, gently disengaged
her hand from the hand that held it, rose to her feet
and said:

"'I ought not to have permitted this; ought not

to have heard what you said. However, we must bear our cross. I do not belong to the world; but do not misjudge me, I have not always been as you see me. I can only tell you this: To a woman now and then there comes a time when either her heart must break or she must give it to God. I have given mine to Him. I cannot take it back. I would not if I could.

"'If you suffer a little now, you will forget it with returning strength. I only ask that when you are strong and well and far away, you will sometimes remember that the world is full of heart aches. Comfort as many as you can. And now, God bless you, and farewell.'

"She laid her hand a moment on his brow, then drew it down upon his cheek, where it lingered for a moment like a caress, and then she was gone.

"After that the Mother Superior became the young man's nurse until he left the hospital. He tried hard, but never saw Sister Celeste again. While he remained in the place she ceased to appear on the street.

"Another year passed by and Sister Celeste grew steadily in the love of the people. With the winter months some cases of smallpox broke out. The country was new, the people careless, and no particular alarm was felt until the breaking out of ten cases in one day awakened the people to the fact that the disease prevailed generally.

"Sister Celeste labored almost without rest, night or day, until the violence of the contagion had passed; then she was stricken. She recovered, but was shockingly marked by the disease.

"She was in a darkened room, and how to break to her the news of her disfigurement was a matter of sore distress to the other nuns. But one day, to a

Sister who was watching by her bed side, she suddenly said:

"'I am almost well now, Sister. Throw back the blinds and bring me a mirror,' and, with a gentle gaiety that never forsook her when with her sister nuns, she added: 'It is time that I began to admire myself.'

"The nun opened the blinds, brought the glass, laid it upon the bed and sat down in fear and trembling.

"Sister Celeste, without glancing at the mirror, laid one hand upon it, and, shading her eyes with the other hand, for a moment was absorbed in silent prayer. Then she picked up the glass and held it before her face. The watching nun, hardly breathing and in an agony of suspense, waited. After a long, earnest look, without a shade passing over her face, Sister Celeste laid down the glass, clasped her hands and said: 'God be praised! Now all is peace. Never. never again will my face bring sorrow to my heart.'

"The waiting nun sank, sobbing, to her knees; but as she did so, she saw, on the face of the stricken woman, a smile which she declared was as sweet as the smile of God.

"With the return of health, Sister Celeste again took up her work of mercy, and for a few months more her presence was a benediction to the place. At last, however, it began to be noticed that her presence on the street was less frequent than formerly, and soon an unwelcome rumor began to circulate that she was ill. The truth of this was soon confirmed, and then, day by day, for some weeks, the report was that she was growing weaker and weaker, and finally, one morning, it was known that she was dead.

"A lady of the place who was greatly attached to Sister Celeste, because of that attachment and because of her devotion to 'Mother Church,' was permitted to watch through the last hours of the nun's life. Of the closing moments of the glorified woman's life she gave the following account:

"For an hour the dying nun had been motionless, as though hushed in a peaceful sleep. When the first rays of the dawn struck on the window, a lark lighted on the sill, and in full voice warbled its greeting to the day. Then the Sister opened her eyes, already fringed by the death frost, and in faint and broken sentences murmured:

"'A delicious vision has been sent me. *Deo gratias*, every act meant in kindness that I have ever done, in the vision had become a flower, giving out an incense ineffable. These had been woven into a diadem for me. Every word, meant in comfort or sympathy. that I have ever spoken, had been set to exquisite music, which voices and harps not of this world were singing and playing while I was being crowned. Every tear of mine shed in pity had become a precious gem. These were woven into the robes of light that they drew around me. A glass was held before me; from face and bosom the cruel scars were all gone, and to eye and brow and cheek the luster and enchantment of youth had returned, and near all radiant'—

"'The eyes, with a look of inexpressibly joyous surprise in them, grew fixed, and all was still save where on the casement the lark was repeating her song.'

"Among the effects left by Sister Celeste was found a package addressed to the same lady who had watched during the closing hours of the dead nun's life. This was brought to her by the Mother Superior. On being opened, within was found another package, tied with silver strings, sealed with wax, and the seal bore the date on which she took her vows. This in turn was opened, and a large double locket was revealed. In one side was the picture of a young man in the uniform of a French colonel. From the other side a picture had evidently been hastily removed, as though in a moment of excitement, for there were scars upon the case which had been made by a too impetuous use of some sharp instrument. On the outer edge of the case was a half-round hole, such as a bullet makes, and there were dark stains on one side of the case. Below the picture in a woman's delicate hand-writing, were the words: 'Henrie. Died at Majenta.'

"The lady called the Mother Superior aside and showed her the picture. Tears came to the faded eyes of the devoted woman.

"'Now God be praised!' said she. 'Three nights since, as I watched by the poor child. I heard her murmur that name in her fevered sleep, and I was troubled, for I feared she was dreaming of the youth she nursed back to life here in the hospital. It was not so. Her work was finished on earth, she was nearing the spheres where love never brings sorrow; her soul was already outstretching its wings to join—' the poor nun stopped, breathed short and hard a few times, and then incoherently began to tell her beads in Latin.

"While they were conversing the body of Sister Celeste lay dressed for the grave in another apartment, watched over by two Sisters. When the Mother Superior ceased speaking, the lady said to her:

"'Mother, come with me to where Sister Celeste is sleeping! When we reach the room, send the watchers away, and then do not look at me. I want to put this picture away.'

"The Mother Superior was strangely agitated, but she led the way to the room, bade the nuns there go and get some rest, then knelt by the foot of the casket, and bowed her head in prayer.

"The lady slipped the locket beneath the folds of the winding sheet, where it lay above the pulseless heart of the dead nun.

"The whole population of the place were sorrowing mourners at the obsequies of Sister Celeste, and for years afterward, every morning, in summer and winter, upon her grave, a dressing of fresh flowers could be seen.

"On the day of the funeral the miners made up a purse and gave it to Mrs. De Lacy, the consideration being that every day for a year, the grave of the Sister should be flower-crowned. The contract was renewed yearly until Mrs. De Lacy moved away. In the meantime a wild rosebush and cypress had been planted beside the grave, and they keep watch there still."

The good-night whistles had already blown when Harding finished his story. Not much was said as the Club retired, but Corrigan, understanding why the story had been told, in silence wrung Harding's hand.

CHAPTER XIV.

The Club had now been running a month. It had been most enjoyable. When Yap Sing had been installed as cook and housekeeper he was given a memorandum book. on the first page of which was written an order for such supplies as the Club might require at the stores and markets. Brewster had objected to this at first. inasmuch as the Mongolian was a stranger. and because it was not good to make bills. But he was overruled by the explanation that almost everything required, except fresh vegetables and. now and then, fresh meat, had already been provided. and that the Chinaman could not cheat very much with seven men to watch him.

But from the first day the Club fared sumptuously. Yap Sing was a thorough artist in his way. He had a trick of preparing substantials and dainties, and of arranging a table, which was wonderful. His breakfasts and suppers were masterpieces, and daily as the dinner buckets, which Yap Sing had filled, were opened at the mines, the members of the Club were the envy of all the men, underground, who were their companions. It was a change from the boarding houses, so delicious, that the members of the Club did not care to consider what the probable extra expense would be. Moreover, each had a feeling that so long as the rest were satisfied it was not worth while to interrupt the pleasant course which events were taking by intruding questions which possibly might lead to unpleasant developments.

But on pay day the bills were sent in. For provisions and crockery they amounted to more than three hundred dollars, or about one dollar and a half per day for each member of the Club. This was in addition to the stock of food purchased at the beginning.

The first thought was that Yap Sing had been robbing the Club. He was called in, confronted with the bills and questioned as to what he had to say to the amount.

He declared it to be his belief that it was "belly cheapee."

Miller took up the case for the plaintiffs and said: "But, Yap, you understand when you came here a month ago we had plenty of provisions—flour, butter, bacon, lard, tea, coffee, sugar—everything required except fresh vegetables and, now and then, fresh meat."

"Yes, me sabbe; got plentie now, allee samee," said Yap.

"But, Yap," said Miller, "you know in boarding-houses and restaurants board is only eight dollars a week. Besides what you had at the beginning, this is costing a dollar and a half a day for each one of us. What have you to say to that?"

"Me say him heap cheapee," said Yap. "Me no care for bloarding-housie; me no care for lestaulent; me heap sabbie 'em. You likie 'em, you bletter go lare eatie. You no likie loyster; you likie hashie. You no likie tlenderloin; you likie corn beefe. You no likie turkie; you likie bull beefe. You no likie plum puddie; you likie dlied apples. All litie, me cookie him; me no care. You no likie bloiled tongue, loast chickie and devil ham for dinner bucket; you likie blead and onion. All litie, me fixie him. You wantie one d——d cheapee miners' bloarding-housie. All litie, no difflence me."

12

It was hard to argue the point with the country-man of Confucius. Notwithstanding the magnificent fare, the impression was general that Yap Sing had been feeding three or four of his cousins and making a little private pocket change for himself by the transaction, but it would have been useless to try to convict him. Indeed, it would have been impossible, for when any particularly outrageous item was pointed out he would cite some special occasion when he had outdone himself in his art.

" What a time-keeper he would make for a mine!" said Carlin. " He would have his pay-roll full every day if he had to rob a graveyard of all the names on its monuments to fill it."

"What a superintendent he would make!" said Miller. " There would not be an item in the monthly accounts that he would not be prepared to explain with entire satisfaction and appalling promptness, and all the time he would have looked like a sorrow-ful statue of unappreciated innocence."

" What a mining expert he would be!" said Ashley. "With his faculty for making doubtful things look plausible, and his powers of expression, he would convince the ordinary man that he could see further into the ground than you could bore with a diamond drill."

"But his cooking is lovely; you must all admit that." said Wright.

"If there be blame anywhere, it rests on us," said Brewster, "for we could all see that we were living a little high, and yet not one of us so much as cautioned Yap to go slow."

It was finally decided that there must be a return to sound and economic principles. Yap was paid his month's salary and instructed that, in future, the fare must be reduced to plain, solid miner's food. The money to pay all the bills, together with what was due on the previous month, and also the rent, was contributed and placed in Miller's hands as treasurer and paymaster, that he might pay the accounts, and the Club settled down to its pipes and conversation.

In the meantime the honorary members had come in. As usual, the first theme was the condition of stocks. Miller believed that Silver Hill was the best buy on the lode, Corrigan had heard that day that a secret drift had been run west from the thirteen hundred level of the Con. Virginia; that up in the Andes ground an immense body of ore had been cut through, but that nothing would come of it until the Bonanza firm could gather in more of the stock. Carlin was disposed to believe that a development was about to be made in Chollar Potosi, because during the past month the superintendent had come up twice from Oakland, California, to look at the property. Strong was disposed to unload all the stocks that he had and invest in Belcher and Crown Point because the superintendent of both mines had that day assured him that they had no developments worth mentioning.

At length the conversation turned on silver. The Club had that day received a portion of their month's pay in silver, and some grumbled, thinking they should have received their full wages in gold. After a good deal had been said, the Professor, who had been quietly reading and had taken no part in the discussion, was asked for his opinion. He answered as follows:

"It is not right to pay laboring men in a depreciated currency; it is a still greater wrong that there

is a discount on silver. It is the steadiest measure of
values that mankind has ever found; it is the only
metal that three-fifths of the human race can measure their daily transactions in; its full adoption by
our Government, as a measure of values and basis of
money, would mean prosperity; its rejection during
the past five years and the denying to it its old sovereignty, have wrought incalculable loss.

" Here on the Comstock it sleeps in the same mat-
rix with gold, the proportion in bullion being about
forty-four per cent. gold to fifty-six per cent. silver.
The Nation cannot make a better adjustment than to
keep that proportion good in her securities. Five
years ago silver commanded a premium over gold.
Since then two dollars in gold to one in silver have
been taken from the earth, but silver is at a discount,
because through unwise if not dishonest legislation,
its sovereignty as a measure of values, its recognition
as money was taken away. The whole burden was
put upon gold, and the result is that the purchasing
power of gold has been enhanced, and silver is, or
seems to be, at a discount. Those who have accomplished this wrong affect to scorn the proposition that
legislation could restore to silver its old value, ignoring
the fact that the present apparent depreciation is due
entirely to unfriendly legislation, and conveniently
forgetting that with silver, everything else is at a
discount when measured by gold. That is, gold is in-
flated by the discriminations which have been made
in its favor. The chief use of silver in the world is
for a measure of values, as the chief use of wheat is
for material out of which to make bread. Were men
forbidden to make any more bread from wheaten flour
and compelled to use corn meal as a substitute, would

the present prices of wheat and corn remain respectively the same?

"Silver should be restored to its old full sovereignty, side by side with gold. Then, in this country, just as little of either metal as possible should be used in men's daily transactions. Handling gold and silver directly in trade is but continuing the barter of savage men, and is a relic of a dark age. Moreover, the loss by abrasion is very great. Both metals should be cast into ingots and their values stamped upon them. Then they should be stored in the Treasury and certificates representing their value should be issued as the money of the people. If this makes the Government a banker no matter, so long as it supplies to the people a money on which there can be no loss. The thought that this would drain our land of gold has not much force, because the trade balances are coming our way and will soon be very heavy: if the gold shall be taken away something will have to be returned in lieu of it, and after all the truth is that four-fifths of our people do not see a gold piece twice a year. Our internal commerce is very much greater than our foreign commerce, and to keep that moving without jar should be the first anxiety of American statesmen. For that purpose nothing could be better than the silver certificate.

"The Government has commenced to coin silver and has partially remonetized it. It is only partial because gold is still made the absolute measure of values and preference is reserved for it in ways which will keep silver depressed until there shall come a demand for it which cannot at once be met: then it will be discovered that it is still one of the precious metals and it will take its place in trade as it has its place here in the mines, side by side and the full brother of gold.　Were the Government to-morrow to commence to absorb and hoard all the product of our mines and keep this up for a generation, issuing certificates on the same for the full value, at the end of about thirty years there would be on deposit as security for the paper afloat more than one thousand millions of dollars.　This seems like a vast sum, but it would then amount to but ten dollars per captia for our people. You have each received two and a half times that amount to-day on account of your last month's wages, and the only serious inconvenience it has inflicted upon you is the discount which wicked legislation has given to silver.

"But long before one thousand millions in silver could be secured it would command a premium, because that would mean one-fourth of all the silver in circulation, and this old world cannot spare to one Nation that amount and still keep her commerce running and the arts supplied."

"But, Professor," said Alex, "why hoard the metals?　Why may not money be represented by paper backed by the Nation's faith?　Why pile up the metals in the Government vaults when the printing press can supply as good money as the people want?"

"That," replied the Professor. "is an argument for times of peace and prosperity only.　The failure of one crop would so lessen the faith of the people that a serious discount would fall upon the money that was only backed by faith.　And suppose Europe were to combine to fight the United States, then what would the loss be to the people?　We can only estimate the amount by thinking what the United States currency was worth in 1864.

"Such a combination is not at all impossible. There is a vast country to the south of us, the trade of which should be ours, and with the Governments of which we have notified Europe there must be no interference from beyond the Atlantic. There are channels for ships to be hewed through the Spanish American Isthmus, and their control is to become a question.

"Above all, the light and majesty of our Republic are becoming a terror to the Old World. Think of it. The immigrants that come to us annually, together with the young men and women that annually reach their majority here, are enough to supply the places of all the people of this coast were they to go away. Who can estimate the swelling strength that is sufficient to fully equip a new state annually?

"Before the spectacle thrones are toppling and kings sleep on pillows of thorns. If our soil was adjacent to Europe, the nations would combine and assail us to-morrow, in sheer self-defense. They have tremendous armies; they are accumulating mighty navies and arming them as ships were never armed before. Suppose that sometime they decide that the world's equilibrium is being disturbed by the Great Republic, even as they did when Napoleon the first became their terror, and that, as with him, they determine that our country shall be divided or crushed. What then? Of course they will maneuver to have a rebellion in our country and espouse the cause of the weaker side. This is what nearly happened in 1862; what would have surely happened had not Great Britain possessed the knowledge that if she joined with France in the proposed scheme, whatever the outcome might be, one thing was certain, for a season at least, there would be no night on the sea; the light made by British ships in flames would make perpetual day.

"Then ocean commerce was carried mostly in ships that had to trust alone to the fickle winds for headway. In twenty years more steam will be the motive power for carrying all valuable freights, and will be comparatively safe as against pursuing cruisers.

"Imagine such a crisis upon us, what then would the unsupported paper dollar be worth? But imagine that behind the Republic there was in the treasury a thousand millions of dollars in silver, the original money of the world, and another thousand millions in gold, what combination of forces could place the money of the Nation in danger of loss by depreciation?

"Gold and silver when produced are simply the measures of the labor required to produce them; they are labor made imperishable; and when either is destroyed—and demonetization is destruction— just so much labor is destroyed, and you who work have to make up the loss by working more hours for a dollar. You are supposed to receive the same wages that the miners did who worked on this lode six years ago, for a month's work. But you do not because, through the mistake of honest men or the manipulation of knaves, twenty per cent. of the twenty-five dollars paid you in silver for last month's work has been destroyed; and now those who have dealt this blow insist that money can in no wise be changed in value by legislation.

"The trouble is our law-makers do not estimate at half its worth their own country. They stand in awe of what they call the money centers of the world, and refuse to see that already the world is placed at a disadvantage by our Republic: that within thirty years all existing nations, all the nations that have existed through all the long watches of the past, will, in material wealth and strength, seem mean and poor in comparison with our own.

"Look at it! Five hundred thousand foreigners absorbed annually, and not a ripple made where they merge with the mighty current of our people! What is equal to a new State, with all its people and equipments, launched upon the Union every year—it makes me think of the Creator launching worlds—with immeasurable resources yet to be utilized; the wealth of the country already equal to that of Great Britain, with all her twelve hundred years of spoils; all our earnings our own; no five millions of people toiling to support another million that stand on guard, as is required in France and Germany and Russia and Austria and Italy; our great Southern staple commanding tribute from all the world; hungry Europe looking to our Northern States for meat and bread, and to our rivers for fish; our Western miners supplying to business the tonic which keeps its every artery throbbing with buoyant health, while over all is our flag, which symbols a sovereignty so awful in power and yet so beneficent in mercies, that while the laws command and protect, they bring no friction in their contact; rather they guarantee the perfect liberty of every child of the Republic, to seize with equal hand upon every opportunity for fortune, or for fame, which our country holds within her august grasp.

"To carry on the business of such a land an ocean of money is needed, and infinitely more will be required in future. And for this money there must be a solid basis; not merely a faith which expands with this year's prosperity and contracts with next year's calamity; not something which the death of a millionaire or a visitation of grasshoppers will throw down; but something which is the first-born child of labor, and is therefore immortal and without change. This is represented by gold and silver, and to commerce they are what 'the great twin brethren' at Lake Regillus were to Rome."

When the Professor ceased speaking. Harding said: "Professor, what you have been saying about our Republic sounds to me almost like a coincidence. Did you dream what you have been saying?"

The Professor replied that he did not, and asked what in the world prompted such a question.

Harding smiled and blushed, and then said: "Because I had a dream last night."

All wanted to hear what it was.

"You won't laugh, Carlin?" said Harding.

Carlin said he would not.

"And you will not call me a fool, Wright?" Harding asked.

Wright promised to conceal his sentiments, if necessary.

"You will not call it a mirage, Corrigan?" asked Harding.

Corrigan agreed to refrain.

"And, Colonel, you will not ask mysterious questions about who usually sits as a commission of lunacy in Virginia City?" Harding inquired.

The Colonel agreed to restrain himself.

"And, Alex, you will not expose me in the paper?" questioned Harding.

Alex promised to be merciful to the public.

In final appeal, Harding said: "And you, Professor, you will not say it is a tough, hard formation and too nearly primitive to carry any treasure?"

The Professor assured him that faults and displacements were common in the richest mineral-bearing veins.

"Well," said Harding, "I was tired and nervous last night. I could not sleep, and so determined to get up and read for an hour. I happened to pick up a volume of Roman history, and became so absorbed in it that I read for an hour or two more than I ought to. I went to bed at last and my body dropped to sleep in a moment, but my brain was still half awake, and for a while ran things on its own account in a confused sort of a way.

"I thought I was sitting here alone, when, suddenly, a stranger appeared and began to pace, slowly, up and down the room. He had an eye like a hawk, nose like an eagle's beak and an air that was altogether martial. His walk had the perfect, measured step of the trained veteran soldier. After watching him for a little space, I grew bold and demanded of him his name and business. When I spoke the sound of my own voice startled me, for he was more savage looking than a shift boss. He turned round to me—don't laugh, I pray you—and said:

"'I am that Scipio to whom Hannibal the terrible capitulated. I was proud of my Rome and my Romans. We were the "Iron Nation," truly. All that human valor and human endurance could do we accomplished. Amid the snows of the Alps and the sands of Africa we were alike invincible. We were not deficient either in brain power. We left monuments enough to abundantly establish that fact. To us the whole civilized world yielded fealty, but we were barbarians after all.   Listen!'

"Just then there floated in through the open window what seemed a full diapason of far-off but exquisite music.

"'Do you know what that is?' he asked. 'It is the echo of the melody which the children of this Republic awaken, singing in their free schools.   It smites upon and charms the ear of the sentinel angel, whose station is in the sun, through one-eighth of his daily round: those echoes that with an enchantment all their own ride on the swift pinions of the hours over all the three thousand miles between the seas.

"'My Rome had nothing like that.   We trusted alone to the law of might, and though we tried to be just. the slave was chained daily at our gates: we sold into slavery our captives taken in war; we fought gladiators and wild beasts for the amusement of our daughters and wives: we never learned to temper justice with mercy; only the first leaves of the book of knowledge were opened to us: our brains and our bodies were disciplined, but our hearts were darkened and we perished because we were no longer fit to rule.

"'Whether by evolution the world has advanced, or whether, indeed. the lessons of that Nazarene, whom our soldiers crucified, are bearing celestial fruit, who knows! But surely our Rome, with all its power, all its splendor, all its heroic men and stately women; its victories in the field, its pageants in the Imperial City on the days when, returning from a conquest, our chieftians were laurel-crowned: our art, our eloquence —all, were nothing compared with this song of songs. It started at first where the sullen waves wash against Plymouth Rock; it swelled in volume while the deep woods gave place to smiling fields; over mountain and desert it rolled in full tones and only ceases, at last, where the roar of the deep sea, breaking outside the Golden Gate, or meeting in everlasting anger the Oregon upon her stormy bar, gives notice that the pioneer must halt at last in his westward march.'

"As he ceased to speak the melody was heard again, sweeter, clearer and fuller than before. My guest faded away before me and I awoke. In all the air there was no sound save the deep respirations of the hoisting engine in the Norcross works, and the murmur of the winds, as on slow beating wings they floated up over the Divide and swept on, out over the desert."

The verdict of the Club was that if old Scipio talked in that strain he had softened down immensely since the days when he was setting his legions in array against the swarthy hosts of the mighty Carthagenian.

After a while Corrigan spoke: "You native Americans," he said, "at least the majority of yees, do not half appreciate your country. I was but a lad whin, after a winter of half starvation, in the care of an uncle, I lift Ireland in an English imigrant ship. One mornin' as me uncle and meself were watchin' from the deck a sail rose out of the say directly in our path. It grew larger and larger, in a little while the hull appeared, and soon after we could discern that it was a frigate. The wind was off her beam, blowing fresh; every sail was crowded on, and as her black beak rose and fell with the says, I thought her more beautiful than the smile of the sunlight on the hills of Kildare. Half careened as she was under the pressure on her sails, but still resolutely rushing on, she made a pictur' of courage which has shone before

me eyes a thousand times since, when me heart has
been heavy. She drew quite near, and as she swung
upon her tack her flag was dipped in salute. Then
me uncle bent and said: 'Barney, lad, mark will that
flag! That is an Amirican ship of war.'

"Great God! Child that I was, I think in that moment I knew how the young mother feels, when in the
curtained dimness of her room, she half fainting,
hears the blissful whisper that unto her is born a son.

"There was the ensign of the land which held all
joy in thought for us: which to us opened the gates of
hope: that wondrous land in the air of which the
pallid cheek of Want grows rosy red and Irish hearts
cast off hereditary dispair.

"I rushed forward, where thray hundred imigrants
were listlessly lounging about the deck, and, in mad
excitement, shouted: 'See! See! It is the Amirican
flag!' Just then the sunlight caught in its folds and
turned it to gold.

"O, but thin there was a transformation sane.
Ivery person on that deck sprang up and shouted.
Men waved their hats and women embraced each
other, and with a mighty 'All Hail' those Irish imigrants—Irish no longer, but henceforth forever to be
Amiricans—greeted that flag. In response the ma-
rines manned the yards, and off to us across the
wathers came the first ringing Amirican chare that we
had iver heard. We answered back with a yell like
that which might have been awakened at Babel. It
was not a disciplined chare, but simply a wild cry of
joy, and it was none the less hearty that over us
swung haughtily the red cross of St. George.

"You native Amiricans are like spiled children,
that niver having known an unsatisfied want, surfeit
on dainties."

Corrigan relapsed into silence, but his eyes were glistening and there was a tremble about his lips. His mind was still in the burial place, where "memory was calling up its dead."

While the spell of Barney's words was still upon the Club, Yap Sing softly opened the door and announced that the evening luncheon was ready. The heathen had inaugurated these luncheons on the first day of his coming. They were at once accepted and had become a regular thing. Seeing that they were received approvingly, Yap had exhausted every device to make them a marked feature of the Club.

On this occasion the table was fully set, but there was no food on the table. Beside each plate stood a glass of water and a dish of salt. When the company was seated, Yap went to the cooking range, took out and set upon the table an immense platter which was piled high with huge baked potatoes, after which, with a face utterly destitute of expression, he went to his bench in the corner of the room and sat down.

Wright, who was nearest him, said: "What is the matter, Yap? Are you sick?"

"Nothing matter; me no sickie," said Yap.

"But why do you not bring on the supper?" asked Wright.

"No catchie any more," was the answer.

"What! Just potatoes straight, Yap?" What is the matter?" said Wright.

"I no sabbie what's the matter," said the sullen Oriental. "You livie belly cheapie now. Potato belly good. Blenty potato, blenty saltie, blenty cold water; no makie you sickie; I dink belly good."

The Club took in the situation with great hilarity;

the cause of Yap Sing's frugality was briefly explained to the guests: each seized a potato and commenced their meal.

At length Carlin asked Yap Sing if he could not furnish a little butter with the salt. Yap shook his head resolutely, and said:

"No catchie. Blutter five bittie [sixty-two and a half cents] one pound. No buy blutter for five bittie to putee on potato: too muchie money allee time pay out for hashie."

Then Ashley asked for a pickle, but Yap Sing was firm. Said he: "Pickle slix bittie one bottle; no can standee."

A great many other things were banteringly asked for, from cold tongue and horse-radish to blackberry jam; but the imperturbable face of the Mongolian never relaxed and his ears remained deaf to all entreaties.

The potatoes were eaten with a decided relish, though there was no seasoning except salt, and when the repast was over the Club still sat at the table while the Colonel delivered a dissertation upon the virtues of the potato in general and upon the Nevada potato in particular. He insisted that the potato was the great modern mind food, and instanced the effect of potato diet upon the people of Ireland, pointing out that the failure of a crop there meant mental prostration and despair, while the news of a bountiful crop was a certain sign of a lively revolution within the year. From a scientific standpoint he demonstrated that no where else on the continent were the conditions absolutely perfect for producing potatoes that were potatoes, except upon the high, dry, slightly alkaline table lands between the Sierras and the Wasatch Range, and, giving his lively imagination full play, he pictured that region as it would be fifty years hence; when transportation shall be reduced; when artesian wells shall be plenty; when the rich men of the earth will not be able to give entertainments without presenting their guests with Nevada or Utah potatoes, and when to say that a man has a potato estate in the desert will be as it now is to say that a man has a wheat farm in Dakota, an orange orchard in Los Angeles, or a cotton plantation in Texas.

While talking, the Colonel managed, between sentences, to dispose of a second potato.

When the pipes were resumed, the joke of Yap Sing was fully discussed, and finally the Chinese question came up for consideration.

Strong took up this latter theme and said:

"The men of the Eastern States think that we of the West are a cruel, half-barbarous race, because we look with distrust upon the swelling hosts of Mongolians that are swarming like locusts upon this coast. They say: 'Our land has ever been open to the oppressed, no matter in what guise they come. The men of the West are the first to stretch bars across the Golden Gate to keep out a people. And this people are peaceable and industrious; all they petition for is to come in and work. Still, there is a cry which swells into passionate invective against them. It must be the cry of barbarism and ignorance. It surely fairly reeks with injustice and cruelty and sets aside a fundamental principle of our Government which dedicates our land to freedom and opens all its gates to honest endeavor.'

"Those people will not stop to think that we
13

came here from among themselves. We were no more ignorant, we were no worse than they when we came away. We have had better wages and better food since our coming than the ordinary men of the East obtain. Almost all of us have dreamed of homes, of wives and children that are men's right to possess, but which are not for us; and though they of the East do not know it, this experience has softened, not hardened our hearts, toward the weak and the oppressed. If they of the East would reflect they would have to conclude that it is not avarice that moves us; that there must be a less ungenerous and deeper reason.

"Our only comfort is, that, by and by, maybe while some of us still live, those men and women who now upbraid us, will, with their souls on their knees, ask pardon for so misjudging us.

"We quarantine ships when a contagion is raging among her crew; we frame protective laws to hold the price of labor up to living American rates; New England approves these precautions, but when we ask to have the same rules, in another form, enforced upon our coast, her people and her statesmen, in scorn and wrath, declare that we are monsters.

"There is Yap Sing in the kitchen. You have just paid him forty dollars for a month's work. All the clothes that he wears were made in China. If he boarded himself, as nearly as possible, he would eat only the food sent here from China. Of his forty dollars just received, thirty at least will be returned to China and be absorbed there. There are one hundred thousand of his people in this State and California. We will suppose that they save only thirty cents each per day. That means, for all, nine hundred thousand dollars per month, or more than ten million dollars per annum that they send away. This is the drain which two States with less than one million inhabitants are annually subjected to. How long would Massachusetts bear a similar drain, before through all her length and breadth, her cities would blaze with riots, all her air grow black with murder? Ireland, with six times as many people, and with the richest of soils, on half that tax, has become so poor that around her is drawn the pity of the world.

"'But,' say the Eastern people, 'you must receive them, Christianize them, and after awhile they will assimilate with you.'

"Waiving the degradation to us, which that implies, they propose an impossibility. They might just as well go down to where the Atlantic beats against the shore, and shout across the waste to the Gulf stream, commanding it to assimilate with the 'common waters' of the sea. Not more mysterious is the law that holds that river of the deep within its liquid banks, than is the instinct which prevents the Chinaman from shaking off his second nature and becoming an American. He looks back through the halo of four thousand years, sees that without change, the nation of his forefathers has existed, and with him all other existing nations except Japan and India and Persia, are parvenues.

"For thousands of years, he and his fathers before him, have been waging a hand-to-hand conflict with Want. He has stripped and disciplined himself until he is superior to all hardships except famine, and that he holds at bay longer than any other living creature could.

"Through this training process from their forms

everything has disappeared except a capacity to work; in their brains every attribute has died except the selfish ones; in their hearts nearly all generous emotions have been starved to death. The faces of the men have given up their beards, the women have surrendered their breasts and the ability to blush has faded from their faces.

"Like all animals of fixed colors they change neither in habits nor disposition. In four thousand years they have changed no more than have the wolves that make their lairs in the foothills of the Ural mountains, except that they have learned to economize until they can even live upon half the air which the white man requires to exist in. They have trained their stomachs until they are no longer the stomachs of men; but such as are possessed by beasts of prey; they thrive on food from which the Caucasian turns with loathing, and on this dreadful fare work for sixteen hours out of the twenty-four.

"The moral sentiments starved to death in their souls centuries ago. They hold woman as but an article of merchandise and delight to profit by her shame.

"Other foreigners come to America to share the fortunes of Americans. Even the poor Italian, with organ and monkey, dreams while turning his organ's crank, that this year or next, or sometime, he will be able to procure a little home, have a garden of his own, and that his children will grow up—sanctified by citizenship—defenders of our flag.

"But the Chinaman comes with no purpose except for plunder; the sole intention is to get from the land all that is possible, with the design of carrying it or sending it back to native land. The robbery is none the less direct and effective for being carried on with a non-combatant smile instead of by force.

"It is such a race as this that we are asked to welcome and compete with, and when we explain that the food we each require—we, without wife or child to share with—costs more in the market daily than these creatures are willing to work for and board themselves; the question, with a lofty disdain, is asked: 'Are you afraid to compete with a Chinaman?'

"It is an unworthy question, born of ignorance and a false sentimentality; for no mortal can overcome the impossible.

"In the cities these creatures fill the places of domestics and absorb all the simpler trades. The natural results follow. Girls and boys grow up without ever being disciplined to labor. But girls and boys must have food and clothes. If their parents can not clothe and feed them other people must; If poor girls with heads and hands untrained have nothing but youth and beauty to offer for food, when hungry enough they will barter both for bread.

"The vices and diseases which the Chinese have already scattered broadcast over the west, are maturing in a harvest of measureless and indescribable suffering.

"The Chinese add no defense to the State. They have no patriotism except for native land; they are all children of degraded mothers, and as soldiers are worthless.

"Moreover it is not a question of sharing our country with them; it is simply a question of whether we should surrender it to them or not. When the western nations thoroughly understand the Chinese they will realize that with their numbers, their imitative faculties, their capacity to live and to work on food which no white man can eat, with their appalling thrift and absence of moral faculties, they are, to-day. the terror of the earth.

"The nations forced China to open her gates to them. It was one of the saddest mistakes of civilization.

"To ask that their further coming be stopped, is simply making a plea for the future generations of Americans. a prayer for the preservation of our Republic. It springs from man's primal right of self-preservation, and when we are told that we should share our country and its blessings with the Chinese, the first answer is that they possess already one-tenth of the habitable globe; their empire has everything within it to support a nation: they have, besides. the hoarded wealth of a hundred generations, and if these were not enough, there are still left illimitable acres of savage lands. Let them go occupy and subdue them.

"The civilization of China had been as perfect as it now is for two thousand years when our forefathers were still barbarians. While our race has been subduing itself and at the same time learning the lessons which lead up to submission to order and to law; while, moreover, it has been bringing under the ægis of freedom a savage continent, the Mongolian has remained stationary. To assert that we should now turn over this inheritance (of which we are but the trustees for the future), or any part of it, to 'the little brown men,' is to forget that a nation's first duty is like a father's, who, by instinct, watches over his own child with more solicitude than over the child of a stranger, and who, above all things, will not place his child under the influence of anything that will at once contaminate and despoil him.

"Finally, by excluding these people no principle of our Government is set aside, and no vital practice which has grown up under our form of government. Ours is a land of perfect freedom, but we arrest robbers and close our doors to lewd women. While these precautions are right and necessary it is necessary and right to turn back from our shores the sinister hosts of the Orient."

With this the whole Club except Brewster heartily agreed. Brewster merely said: "Maybe you are right. but your argument ignores the saving grace of Christianity, and maybe conflicts with God's plans."

Then the good-nights were said.

CHAPTER XV.

The next evening when supper was prepared, Harding was not present. He had bruised one hand so badly in the mine the previous day, that he was forced to have it bound up and treated with liniments and had not worked that day. Thinking he would be home soon the rest ate their suppers, but it was an hour before he came. When he arrived he had a troubled look. and being pressed to tell what had gone wrong, he stated that he had met a group of five miners from the Sierra Nevada day shift, men whom they all knew, who, without provocation. had commenced abusing him; jeering him about joining with six or seven more miners, hiring a house and a cook, and putting on airs; that finally they dared him to fight, and when he offered to fight any one of them, they said it was a mere "bluff." that he would not fight a woman unless she were sick, and further declared their purpose at some future time to go up and "clean out" the whole outfit.

Harding was the younger member of the Club; the rest knew about his former life; how his father, joining the reckless throng of the early days. lived fast. and suddenly died, just as the boy came from school: how the young man had put aside his hopes. learned mining, and with a brave purpose was working hard and dreaming of the time when he would wipe away every reproach which rested on his father's memory.

To have him set upon by roughs, causelessly. was like a blow in the face to every other member of the Club. When Harding had told his story. Miller said: "Who did you say these men were, Harding?"

Harding told their names.

"Why, they are not miners at all," said Carlin. "They are a lot of outside bruisers who have come here because there is going to be an election this year, and they have got their names on a pay roll to keep from being arrested as vagrants. You did just right, Harding, to get away from them with your crippled hand without serious trouble."

"Indeed you did. Harding," said Brewster. "One street fight at your age might ruin you for life."

"That is quite true," said Miller; "I am glad you had no fight."

Said Corrigan: "You offered to fight any one of the blackguards, and whin they refused, you came away? It was the proper thing to do."

"Did you have any weapons with you, Harding?" asked Ashley.

"Not a thing in the world," was the reply.

"I am glad of that," said Ashley. "The temptation to wing one or two of the brutes, would have been very great had you been 'fixed.'"

"I am glad it was no worse." said Wright. "You said it was down by the California Bank corner?"

"No," replied Harding; "it was by the Fredericksburg Brewery corner, on Union Street, just below C."

"You managed the matter first-rate, Harding," said Wright. "Do not think any more about it."

Harding, thus reassured by his friends, felt better, but said if three of the Club would go with him he would undertake to do his part to bring hostilities to a successful close with the bullies.

Ashley and Corrigan at once volunteered, but Wright and Carlin interfered and said it must not be, and Brewster expostulated against any such thing.

Corrigan and Ashley caught a look and gesture from Wright which caused them to subside, and Harding at length went out to supper.

When Harding came in from up town, Miller was making arrangements to go out, as he said, to meet a broker as per agreement. As Harding went to supper, Miller went out and Brewster resumed the reading of a book in which he was engaged. The Professor, Colonel and Alex had not yet come in.

Significant glances passed between the others, and soon Wright arose and said: "Boys! the Emmetts drill to-night; suppose we go down to the armory and look on for half an hour."

The rest all agreed that it would be good exercise,

and quietly the four men went out, Wright saying as he started: "Brewster, if the others come, tell them we have just gone down to the Emmetts armory, and will be back in half an hour or so."

The Professor and Alex shortly after came in, a little later the Colonel and Miller. It was nearly an hour before the others returned. When they did they were in the best possible humor; spoke of the perfectness of the Emmetts' drill; told of something they had heard down town which was droll, while Barney in particular was full of merriment over a speech that had that day been made by a countryman of his, Mr. Snow, in a Democratic convention, and insisted upon telling Brewster about it.

Brewster laid down his book and assumed the attitude of a listener.

"It was this way," said Barney. "The convintion had made all its nominations, when it was proposed that on Friday nixt a grand mass-ratification matin' should be hild at Carson City, the matin' to be intinded for the inauguratin' of the campaign, where all the faithful from surroundin' counties might mate and glorify, and thus intimidate the inemy from the viry commincement.

"The proposition was carried by acclamation, and jist thin a mimber sprang up and moved that the matin' should be a barbecue. This motion likewise carried by an overwhilmin' vote. Whin the noise died away a bit, my ould friend Snow, he of the boardin' house, arose and made a motion. It was beautiful. Listen!

"'Mr. Spaker! Bain that the lift of the Dimocratic party do not ate *mate* of a Friday, I move yees, sir, that we make it a *fish* barbecue.'"

A great laugh followed Barney's account of the motion, and then the usual comparison of notes on stocks took place. Miller was sure that Silver Hill was the best buy on the lode; Corrigan had been told by a Gold Hill miner that Justice was looking mighty encouraging; the Colonel had heard the superintendent of the Curry tell the superintendent of the Belcher that he was in wonderfully kindly ground on the two thousand foot level; the Professor had that day heard the superintendent of the Savage declare that the water was lowering four feet an hour, while all were wondering when the Sierra Nevada would break, as it was too high for the development. By all is meant all but Brewster and Harding; they never joined in any conversations about stocks.

At length the stock talk slackened, when Corrigan again referred to the fish barbecue resolution. Naturally enough, the conversation drifted into a discussion of the humor of the coast, when the Colonel said:

"There is not much pure humor on this coast. There is plenty of that material called humor, which has a bitter sting to it, but that is not the genuine article. The men here who think as Hood wrote, are not plenty. I suspect the bitter twang to all the humor here comes from the isolation of men from the society of women, from broken hopes, and it seems to me is generally an attempt to hurl contempt, not upon the individual at whom it is fired, but at the outrageous fortunes which hedge men around. The coast has been running over with that sort of thing, I guess since 'forty-nine.'

"A man here, fond of his wife and children, said to a friend a day or two after they went away for a visit to California: 'Did you ever see a motherless colt?'

"'Oh, yes,' was the reply.

"'Then,' said the man, 'you know just how I feel.'

"'Yes,' said the friend. 'I suppose you feel as though you are not worth a dam.'

"I know a brother lawyer who is somewhat famous for getting the clients whom he defends convicted. One morning he met a brother attorney, a wary old lawyer, and said to him: 'I heard some men denouncing you this morning and I took up your defense.'

"'What did you say?' the other asked.

"'Those men were slandering you and I took it upon myself to defend you,' said the first lawyer.

"The old lawyer took the other by the arm, led him aside, then putting his lips close to the ear of his friend, in a hoarse whisper said: 'Don't do it any more.'

"'I am going to lecture to-night at ('——,' said a pompous man.

"'I am glad of it,' was the quick answer. 'I have hated the people there for years. No punishment is too severe for them.'

"'I am particular who I drink with,' said a man curtly to another.

"'Yes?' was the answer. 'I outgrew that foolish pride long ago. I would as soon you would drink with me as not.'

"'I do not require lecturing from you,' said a man. 'I am no reformed drunkard.'

"'Then why do you not reform?' was the response.

"This coast is full of the echoes of such things."

The Professor spoke next. "I think," said he,

"that there is more extravagance in figures of speech on this coast than in any other country. Marcus Shults had a difficulty in Eureka the other day, when I was there. He told me about it. Said he: 'I told him to keep away; that I was afraid of him. I wanted some good man to hear me say that. but I had my eye on him every minute, and had he come a step nearer, why—when the doctors would have been called in to dissect him they would have thought they had struck a new lead mine.'"

Here Wright interrupted the Professor. "Marcus was from my State, Professor. Did you ever hear him explain why he did not become a fighter?"

The Professor answered that he never had, when Wright continued:

"Marcus never took kindly to hard work. Indeed, he seems to have constitutional objections to it. As he tells the story, while crossing the plains he made up his mind that, upon reaching California, he would declare himself and speedily develop into a fighter. His words, when he told me the story, were: 'They knew me back in Missouri, and I was a good deal too smart to attempt to practice any such profession there, but my idea was that California was filled with Yankees, and in that kind of a community I would have an easy going thing. Well, I crossed the Sierras and landed at Diamond Springs, outside of Placerville a few miles, and when I had been there a short time I changed my mind.'

"Of course at this point some one asks him why he changed his mind, whereupon he answeres solemnly:

"'The first day I was there a State of Maine man cut the stomach out of a Texan.'

" Marcus was with the boys during that first tough winter in Eureka. One fearfully cold day a man was telling about the cold he had experienced in Idaho. When the story was finished Marcus cast a look of sovereign contempt upon the man and said:

" ' You know nothing about cold weather, sir; you never saw any. You should go to Montana. In Montana I have seen plenty of mornings when were a man to have gone out of a warm room. crossed a street sixty feet wide and shaken his head, his ears would have snapped off like icicles.'

" The stranger, overawed, retired."

Alex spoke next: " The other day Dan Dennison asked me to go and look at a famous trotting horse that he has here. We went to the stable, and when the stepper was pointed out I started to go into the stall beside him, whereupon Dan caught me by the arm, drew me back, and said:

" ' Be careful! Sometimes he deals from the bottom.'

" He stripped the covers from the horse and backed him out where I could look at him. The horse was not a beauty by any means and I intimated my belief of that fact to Dan.

" ' No,' said Dennison. ' The truth is—' He hesitated a moment and then the words came in a volley:

" ' He's deformed with speed.'

" There is a lawyer down town. you all know him. He has a head as big as the old croppings of the Gould and Curry, but like some other lawyers that practice at the Virginia City bar (here he glanced significantly at the Colonel), he is not an exceedingly bright or profound man. He was passing a downtown office yesterday when a man, who chanced to be standing in the office, said to the bookkeeper of the establishment:

"'Look at Judge ———. His head is bigger than Mount Davidson, but I am told that where his brains ought to be there is a howling wilderness.'

"The bookkeeper stopped his writing, carefully wiped his pen, laid it down, came out from behind his desk, came close up to the man who had spoken to him, and said:

"'Howling wilderness? I tell you, sir, that man's head is an unexplored mental Death Valley.'"

"Yes," said the Colonel, "his is a queer family. He has a brother who is a journalist; he has made a fortune in the business. His great theme is sketching the lives and characters of people."

"But has he made a fortune publishing sketches of that description?" asked Miller.

"Oh, no," replied the Colonel; "he has made his money by refraining from publishing them. People have paid him to suppress them."

"Colonel," asked Strong, "did it never occur to you that other fortunes might be made the same way by people just exactly adapted to that style of writing?"

"If it had," was the reply. "I should have considered that the field here was fully occupied."

"You might write a sketch of your own career," suggested the Professor.

"Don't do it, Colonel," said Alex.

"Why not?" asked Ashley.

"There is a law which sadly interferes with the circulation of a certain character of literature," said Alex.

"Alex," said the Colonel, "what a painstaking and delicate task it will be, under that law, to write your obituary."

"There will be great risk in writing yours, Colonel," said Alex; "but it will be a labor of love, nevertheless; a labor of love. Colonel."

"If you have it to do. Alex, don't forget my strongest characteristic," said the Colonel; "that lofty generosity, blended with a self-contained dignity, which made me indifferent always to the slanders of bad men."

It was always a delight to the Club to get these two to bantering each other.

Ashley here interposed and said: "You all know Professor ———. One night in Elko, last summer. he was conversing with Judge F — of Elko. Both had been indulging a little too much; the Professor was growing talkative and the Judge morose.

"The Professor was telling about the battle of Buena Vista, in which he. a boy at the time, participated. In the midst of the description the Judge interrupted him with some remark which the Professor construed into an impeachment of his bravery.

"He leaned back in his chair and sat looking at the Judge for a full minute, as if in an astonished study, and then in a tone most dangerous, said:

"'I do not know how to classify you, sir. I do not know, sir, whether you are a wholly irresponsible idiot, or an unmitigated and infamous scoundrel, sir.'

"He was conscientious and methodical even in his wrath. He would not pass upon the specimen of natural history before him until certain to what species it belonged."

Said Miller: "Did you ever hear how Judge T—— of this city met a man who had been saying disrespectful things about him, but who came up to the Judge in a crowd and, with a smile, extended his

hand? The Judge drew back quickly, thrust both hands in his side pockets and said:

"'Excuse me, sir; I have just washed my hands.'"

"I heard something yesterday of a rough man whom you all know, Zince Barnes," said the Professor, "which seemed to me as full of bitter humor as anything I have heard on this mountain side. You know that politics are running pretty high.

"Well, an impecunious man—so the story goes—called upon a certain gentleman who is reported to be rich and to have political aspirations, and tried to convince him that the expenditure of a certain sum of money in a certain way would redound amazingly to the credit, political, of the millionaire. The man of dollars could not see the proposition through the poor man's magnifying glasses, and the patriot retired baffled.

"A few minutes later, and while yet warm in his disappointment, he met Zince Barnes, told him of the interview and closed by expressing the belief that the millionaire was a tough, hard formation.

"'Hard!' said Zince. 'I should think so. The tears of widows and orphans are water on his wheel.'"

At this Corrigan 'roused up and said: "Speakin' of figures of spache, I heard some from a countrywoman of mine one bitter cowld mornin' last March. It was early; hardly light. John Mackay was comin' down from the Curry office on his way to the Con. Virginia office, and whin just opposite the Curry works, he met ould mother McGarrigle, who lives down by the freight depot. I was in the machane shop of the Curry works; they were just outside, and there being only an inch boord and about ten feet of

14

space between us, I could hear ivery word plain, or rather I could not help but hear. The conversation ran about after this style:

"'Mornin', Meester Mackay, and may the Lord love yees.'

"'Good morning, madam.'

"'How's the beautiful wife and the charmin' childers over the big wathers, Mr. Mackay?'

"'They are all right.'

"'God be thanked intirely. Does yees know, Mr. Mackay, that in the hull course of me life I niver laid eyes upon childer so beautiful loike yees. Often and often I've tould the ould man that same. And they're will, are they?'

"'Yes, they are first-rate. I had a cable from them yesterday.'

"'A tilligram, was it? Oh, but is not that wonderful, though! A missige under the say and over the land to this barbarous place. It must have come like the smile of the Good God to yees.'

"'Oh, I get them every day.'

"'Ivery day! And phat do they cost?'

"'Oh, seven or eight dollars; sometimes more. It depends upon their length.'

"'Sivin or eight dollars! Oh, murther! But yees desarve it, Mr. Mackay. What would the poor do without yees in this town, Mr. Mackay? Only yisterday I was sayin' to the ould man, says I: "Mike, it shows the mercy of God whin money is given to a mon like Mr. John Mackay. It's a Providence he is to the city. God bless him." I did, indade.'

" By this time Mackay began to grow very ristless.

"'What can I do for you this morning, Mrs. McGarrigle?'

"'It's the ould mon, Lord love yees, Mr. Mackay. It's no work he's had for five wakes, and it's mighty little we have aither to ait or to wear. It's work I want for him.'

"'I am sorry, but our mines are full. Indeed, we are employing more men than we are justified in doing.'

"'But Mr. Mackay, it's so poor we are, and so hard it is getting along at all; put him on for a month and may all the saints bless yees.'

"'The city is full of poor people, madam. To determine what to do to mitigate the distress here occupies half our time.'

"'Yis, but ours is a particular hard case intirely. I am dilicate meself. I know I don't look so. but I am; and yees ought ter interpose to help a poor countryman of yees own in trouble.'

"By this time Mackay was half frozen and thoroughly out of patience. In his quick, sharp way he said: 'Madam, we cannot give all the men in the country employment.'

"The mask of the woman was off in an instant. With a scorn and hate unutterable she burst forth in almost a scrame.

"'Oh, yees can't. Oh, no! Yees forgits fen yees was poor your ownsilf, ye blackguard. Refusin' a poor man work, and shakin the mountains and churnin' the ocean avery day wid your siven and eight dollar missages. Yees can't employ all the min in the counthry. Don't yees own the whole counthry? And do yees think we'd apply to yees at all if we could find a dacant mon in the worreld? May the divil fly away wid yees, and whin he does yees may tell him for me if he gives a short bit for yer soul he'll chate himself worse nor he's been chated since he bargained with Judas Iscariot. Thake that, sur, wid me compliments, yees purse-proud parvenu.'

" When the woman began to rave. Mackay walked rapidly away, but she niver relaxed the scrame of her tirade until Mackay disappeared from sight. Thin she paused for a moment, thin to herself she muttered, ' But I got aven wid him oneway.' She thin turned and walked away toward her cabin.

" It was a case where money was no assistance to a man."

" There is a good deal of humor displayed in courts of justice at times, is there not. Colonel?" asked Wright.

" Oh, yes," was the reply. " Anyone would think so who ever heard old Frank Dunn explain to a court that the reason of his being late was because he had no watch, and deploring meanwhile his inability to purchase a watch because of the multitude of unaccountable fines which His Honor had seen proper, from time to time, to impose upon him."

" In that first winter in Eureka," said Wright. " I strolled into court one day when a trial was in progress.

" Judge D—— was managing one side and a volunteer lawyer the other. The volunteer lawyer had the best side, and to confuse the court, Judge D——, in his argument, misquoted the testimony somewhat. His opponent interrupted and repeated exactly what the witness had testified to.

" Turning to his opponent, Judge D——, with a sneer, said:

" ' I see, sir, you are very much interested in the result of this case.'

"'Oh, no,' was the response. 'I am doing this for pure love. I do not make a cent in this case.'

"Then Judge D——, with still more bitterness, said:

"'That is like you. You try cases for nothing and cheat *good* lawyers out of their fees.'

"With a look of unfeigned astonishment the other lawyer said:

"'Well, what are *you* angry about? How does that interfere with *you?*'"

Here Brewster, who had been reading, laid down his book and said:

"I heard of a case as I came through Salt Lake City some years ago, which, if not particularly humorous, revealed wonderful presence of mind on the part of the presiding judge. It may be the story is not true, but it was told in Salt Lake City as one very liable to be true.

"A miner, who had been working a placer claim in the hills all summer—so the story ran—and who had been his own cook, barber, chambermaid and tailor, came down to Salt Lake City to see the sights and purchase supplies. He had dough in his whiskers, grease upon his overalls, pine twigs in his hair, and altogether did not present the appearance of a dancing master or a millionaire. Hardly had he reached the city when he thought it necessary to take something in order to 'brace up.' One drink gave him courage to take another, and in forty minutes he was dead drunk on the sidewalk.

"The police picked him up and tossed him into a cell in the jail, disdaining to search him, so abject seemed his condition.

"Next morning he was brought before the Police

Judge and the charge of D. D. was preferred against
him.

"'You are fined ten dollars, sir,' was the brief sentence of the Court. The man unbuttoned two pairs
of overalls and from some inner recess of his
garments produced a roll of greenbacks as big as a
man's fist. It was a trying moment for the Judge,
but his presence of mind did not fail him. He raised
up from his seat, leaned one elbow on his desk and, as
if in continuation of what he had already said, thun-
dered out: 'And one hundred dollars for contempt
of court.'

"The man paid the one hundred and ten dollars
and hastily left the court and the city."

Miller was the next to speak. Said he: "Once in
Idaho I heard a specimen of grim humor which
entertained me immensely. There was a man up
there who owned a train of pack mules and made a
living by packing in goods to the traders and packing out ore to be sent away to the reduction works.
He was caught in a storm midway between Challis
and Powder Flat. It was mid-winter; the thermometer at Challis marked thirty-four degrees below
zero. He was out in the storm and cold two days
and one night, and his sufferings must have been indescribable. When safely housed and ministered to
at last a friend said to him: 'George, that was a
tough experience, was it not?'

"'Oh, regular business should never be called
tough,' said he, 'but since I began to get warm I have
been thinking that, if I make money enough, may be
in three or four years I will get married, if I can de-
ceive some woman into making the arrangement.
If I should succeed, and if after a reasonable time a

boy should be born to us, and if the youngster should "stand off" the colic, teething, measles, whooping cough, scarlet fever and falling down stairs, and grow to be ten or twelve years old, and have some sense, if I ever tell him the story of the past two days of my life and he don't cry his eyes out, I will beat him to death, sure.'"

The Professor was reminded by the anecdote of something which transpired in Belmont, Nevada, the previous winter. Said he: "I went to Belmont to examine a property last winter and while there Judge —— came in from a prospecting trip down into the upper edge of Death Valley. I saw him as he drove into town, and went to meet him. He was in no very good spirits. On the way to his office he said: 'I was persuaded against my better judgment to go on that trip. The thief who coaxed me away told a wonderful story. He had been there; he had seen the mine, but had been driven away by the Shoshones; he knew every spring and camping place. It would be just a pleasure trip. So, like an idiot, I went with him. It was twice as far as he said, and we got out of food; he could not find one particular spring, and we were forty hours without water. We had to camp in the snow, and the only pleasure I had in the whole journey was in seeing my companion slip and sit down squarely on a Spanish bayonet plant. It was a double pleasure, indeed; one pleasure to see him sit down and another pleasure to see him get right up again without resting at all, and with a look on his face as though a serious mistake had been made somewhere.'

"By this time we had reached the Judge's office. On the desk lay a score of letters which had been accumulating during his absence. Begging me to excuse him for five minutes, he sat down and commenced to run through his mail.

"Suddenly he stopped, seized a pen and wrote rapidly for two or three minutes. Then he threw down the pen and begged my attention. First he read a letter which was dated somewhere in Iowa. The writer stated that he had a few thousand dollars, but had determined to leave Iowa and seek some new field, and asked the Judge's advice about removing to Nevada. I asked the Judge if he knew the man.

"'Of course not,' said he. 'He has found my name in some directory, and so has written at random. He has probably written similar letters to twenty other men. Possibly he is writing a book descriptive of the Far West by an actual observer,' continued the Judge.

"'How are you going to reply?' I asked.

"'That is just the point,' he answered. 'I have written and I want you to tell me if I have done about the right thing. Listen.'

"At this he read his letter. It was in these identical words:

My Dear Sir:—Your esteemed favor is at hand and after careful deliberation I have determined to write to you to come to Nevada. I cannot, in the brief space to which a letter must necessarily be confined, enter into details; but I can assure you that if you will come here, settle and invest your means, the final result will be most happy to you. A few brief years of existence here will prepare you to enjoy all the rest and all the beatitudes which the paradise of the blessed can bestow, and if, perchance, your soul should take the other track, hell itself can bring you no surprises. Respectfully, etc.

"He mailed the letter, but at last accounts the gentleman had not come West."

"That," said Alex, "reminds me of Charley

O——'s mining experience. An Eastern company purchased a series of mines at Austin and made Charley superintendent of the company at a handsome salary. Charley proceeded to his post of duty, built a fine office and drew his salary for a year. He did his best, too, to make something of the property, but it is a most difficult thing to make a mine yield when there is no ore in it. The result was nothing but 'Irish dividends' for the stockholders. It was in the old days, before the railway came along.

"One morning, when the overland coach drove into Austin, a gentleman dismounted, asked where the office of the Lucknow Gold and Silver Consolidated Mining and Milling Company was, and being directed, went to the office and without knocking, opened the door and walked in. Charley was sitting with his feet on the desk, smoking a cigar and reading the morning paper.

"'Is Mr. O—— in?' politely inquired the stranger.

"'I am Mr. O——,' responded Charley. The stranger unbuttoned his coat, dived into a side pocket and drawing out a formidable envelope, presented it to O——.

"Charley tore open the envelope and found that the letter within was a formal notice from the secretary of the company that the bearer had been appointed superintendent and resident manager of the L. G. and S. C. M. & M. Co., and requesting O—— to surrender to him the books and all other property of the company. After reading the letter Charley looked up and said to the stranger:

"'And so you have come to take my place?'

"'It seems so,' was the reply.

"'On your account I am awfully sorry,' said Charley.

"The stranger did not believe that he was in any particular need of sympathy.

"'But you will not live six months here,' said Charley.

"The stranger was disposed to take his chances.

"This happened in August. Charley took the first stage and came in to Virginia City. In the following December the morning papers here contained a dispatch announcing that Mr. ——, superintendent of the Lucknow Gold and Silver Consolidated Mining and Milling Company, was dangerously ill of pneumonia. On the succeeding morning there was another dispatch from Austin saying that Mr. ——, late superintendent of the Lucknow Gold and Silver Consolidated Mining and Milling Company, died the previous evening and that the body would be sent overland to San Francisco. to be shipped from there to the East. Two days after that, about the time the overland coaches were due, Charley was seen wading through the mud down to the Overland barn. He went in and saw two coaches with fresh mud upon them. The curtains of the first were rolled up. The curtains of the second were buckled down close. O—— went to the second coach, loosened one of the curtains and threw it back; then reaching in and tapping the coffin with his knuckles, said: 'Didn't I tell you? Didn't I tell you? You thought you could stop my salary and still live. See what a fix it has brought you to!' And then he went away. No one would ever have known that he had been there had not an 'ostler overheard him.

"Speaking of Austin, I think the remark made by Lawyer J. B. Felton of Oakland, California, regarding the mines of Austin, was as cute as anything I ever heard. When the mines were first discovered Felton was induced to invest a good deal of money in them.

"The mines were three hundred and fifty miles from civilization, there being no reduction works of any kind, and pure silver would hardly have paid. So Felton did not realize readily from his investment. After some months had gone by Felton was standing on Montgomery street, San Francisco, one day when a long procession, celebrating St. Patrick's day, filed past. Of course Erin's flag was 'full high advanced' in the procession. Turning to a friend, Felton said: 'Can you tell why that flag is like a Reese River mine?'

"The friend could not.

"Said Felton: 'It's composed mostly of sham rock and a blasted lyre!'"

Ashley was next to speak.

"After all," said he, "the funniest things are sometimes those which are not meant to be funny at all. Steve Gillis, in a newspaper office down town, perpetrated one the other day. An Eastern editor was here, and when he found out how some of the men in the office were working he was paralyzed, and said to Gillis:

"'There's ——, you will go into his room some day and find him dead. He will go like a flash some time. No man can do what he is doing and stand it.'

"'Do you think so?' asked Gillis.

"'Indeed I do; I know it,' said the man.

"'Then,' said Gillis, 'you ought to be here. You would see the most magnificent funeral ever had in Virginia City.'"

By this time it was very late and the Club dispersed for the night.

Next morning Harding who was reading the morning paper, came upon this item:

A LIVELY SCRIMMAGE.

Last evening, about seven-thirty o'clock, there was a terrific fight on Union Street, near the depot; four men against five. It lasted but a few minutes, but the five men were dreadfully beaten. No one seemed to know the origin of the fight. A boy who was standing across the street says the men met, a few low words passed between them, and then the fight ensued. The four men, who seem to have been the assailants, hardly suffered any damage, but the five others were so badly beaten that two of them had to be carried home, while the other three had fearful mansard roofs put upon them.

There were no arrests; indeed little sympathy was felt for the injured men, for though at present at work in the mines, they are known as bullies and roughs by trade.

No one seems to know who the victors were, except that they were miners. One man told our reporter that he knew one of the men by sight; that he was, he thought, a Gold Hill miner. No weapons were drawn on either side, and no loud words were spoken, but it was as fierce an encounter as has been seen here since the old fighting days.

Harding looked up from the paper and said:

"Wright, what was it you said about the drill of the Emmett Guards, last night?"

"They are splendid, those Emmetts," was the reply, with an imperturbable face.

CHAPTER XVI.

Pay day was on the fifth of the month. On the night of the thirteenth, when the Club met at the usual hour for supper, Miller was not present. He was never as regular as the others, so the rest did not wait supper for him. After supper the Club settled down to their pipes, the Professor, the Colonel and

Alex came in, and the usual discussion about stocks was indulged in for some minutes. the chief matter dwelt upon being the steady and unaccountable rise in Sierra Nevada. At length it was noticed that Carlin did not join as usual in the conversation. and Ashley asked him what he seemed so cast down about.

At this Carlin shook himself together and said: "I will be glad if you will all give me your attention for a moment." He took a letter from his pocket and read as follows:

CARLIN: When you receive this I shall be on my way, by horseback (overland), to Eastern Nevada. I am going to Austin, and if I do not obtain employment there, shall continue on to Eureka. You can find me in one place or the other by Sunday.

The evening of pay day, with the money which the Club had placed in my hands to pay the bills, I went down town to carry out the wishes of the Club, when I met a friend, who is in the close confidence of the "big ring" of operators. He called me aside and told me that he had inside information that within three days Silver Hill would commence to jump, that within a week the present value would be multiplied by five or six and more likely by ten. That there would be an immediate and great advance he assured me was absolutely certain. He told me how he had received his information, and it seemed to me to be conclusive.

I found a broker, unloaded my pockets, and bade him buy Silver Hill; to buy on a margin all he could afford to. The stock has fallen thirty per cent., and the indications are that it will go still lower. Yesterday I suppose it was sold out, for on the previous day I received a notice from the broker to please call at his office at once. My courage, that never failed me before, broke down. I could not go. The amount of money belonging to the Club which I had was altogether $575.00. Of course it is lost. It is a clear case of breach of trust, if not of embezzlement. You can make me smart for it, if you feel disposed to, or if you can give me the time, I can pay the money in about eight months after I get to work. That is, I can send you about eighty dollars per month. If wanted I will be in Austin or Eureka.

I might make this letter much longer, but I suspect by the time you will have read this much, you will think it long enough. Believe me none of you can think meaner of me than I do of myself.

JOE MILLER.

After the reading of the letter, Wright was the first to find his voice. Said he: "It is too bad. I knew Miller was reckless, but I believed his recklessness never could go beyond his own affairs. I had implicit faith in him."

"Had he only told us," said Ashley, "that he wanted to use the money, he could have had five times the sum."

"What I hate about it, is the want of courage and the lack of faith in the rist of us," said Corrigan. "Why did he not come loike a mon and say, 'Boys, I have lost a trifle of your money in the malstroom of stocks; be patient and I will work out?'"

"It is a pitiable business," said Carlin. "The money—that is the loss of it—does not hurt at all. But it was Miller who proposed the forming of this Club, and he is the one who first betrays us, and then lacks the sand to tell us about it frankly. But no matter. Jesus Christ failed to secure twelve men who were all true. What do you think of it, Brewster?"

"What Miller has done," said Brewster, "is but a natural result when a working man goes down into the pit of stock gambling. The hope in that business is to obtain money without earning it. It is a kind of lunacy. In a few months, men so engaged lose everything like a steady poise to their minds. They take on all the attributes which distinguish the gambler. Their ideas are either up in the clouds or down in the depths Worst of all, they forget that a dollar means so many blows, so many drops of sweat, that a dollar, when we see it, means that sometime, somewhere, to produce that dollar, an honest dollar's worth of work was performed, that when that dollar is transferred to another, another dollar's worth of work in some form must be given in return, or the eternal balance of Justice will be disarranged. Miller reached the point where he did not prize his own dollars at their true value. It ought not to be expected that he would be more careful of ours."

"Colonel, what is your judgment about the business?" Carlin asked.

"It seems to me," was the reply, "that when he went away Miller insulted all of you—all of us, for that matter. His conduct assumes that we are all pawnbrokers who would go into mourning over a few dollars lost."

"Oh, no, I think not," said Strong. "Miller is a sensitive, high-strung man. He has been in all sorts of dangers and difficulties and has never faltered. At last he found himself in a place where, for the first time, he felt his honor wounded, and his courage failed him. He is not running away from us, he is trying to run away from himself."

"What is your judgment, Professor?" asked Carlin.

"As they say out here, Miller got off wrong," said the Professor; "and he seems blinded by the mistake so much that he cannot see his best way back."

"Harding, why are you so still?" asked Carlin.

"I am sorry for Miller," said Harding. "He is the best-hearted man in the world."

"It is a most unpleasant business. What shall we do about it?" asked Carlin. "I wish all would express an opinion."

"What ought to be done, Carlin?" asked Wright.

Carlin answered: "The business way would be to formally expel him from the Club, and to write him that, without waiving any legal rights, we will give him the time he requires in which to settle."

"That would no doubt be just." said Wright.

"There would be no injustice in it, from a business standpoint," said Ashley.

"He certainly," said Brewster, "would have no right to complain of such treatment."

Said Corrigan: "The verdict of the worreld would be that we had acted fairly."

"No one," said the Colonel, "could blame you for firing him out. He has not only wronged you directly, but at the same moment has attacked your credit in the city where you are owing bills."

"That is true," said the Professor.

"It is only a matter of discretion what to do," said Alex. "All the direct equities are against Miller."

"There is no decision so fair as by a secret ballot," said Harding. "Let us take a vote on the proposition of Miller's expulsion, and all must take part."

This was agreed to. Nine slips of paper were prepared, all of one size and length, one was given to each man to write "expulsion, yes," or "expulsion, no," as he pleased. A hat was placed on the table for a ballot-box: each in turn deposited his ballot and resumed his seat.

The silence was growing painful when Brewster said: "Carlin, Miller wrote back to you; you will have to write to him. Suppose you be the returning board to count the votes and make up the returns."

Carlin arose and went to the table. There he paused, and his face wore a look of extreme trouble; but he shook off the influence, whatever it was, stretched out his hand in an absent-minded way, picked up a ballot and slowly brought it before his

eyes. He looked at it, turned it over and looked on the other side, then with a foolish laugh he said: "Why, the ballot is blank."

He transferred it to his left hand, picked up another ballot with his right hand; looked at it; it, too, was blank.

So in turn he took up one after another. They all were blank.

As he called the last one and started to resume his seat. Harding, in a low voice, as to himself, said: "Thank God!"

All looked a little foolish for a moment, and then the Colonel said: "Why, Carlin, you are not much of a returning board, after all."

Said Corrigan: "It sames the convintion moved to make it unanimous."

Said Carlin: "I could not vote to expel Miller. He has long been my friend. I know how sensitive he is. He wronged us a little, but I just could not do it."

Said Brewster: "I could not do it, because that would be the quickest way to cause a man, when on the down grade, to keep on. To make him feel that those who have been most intimate with him, despise him, may be exact justice, but it seldom brings reformation."

Said the Colonel: "I could not do it in his absence. It would have had a look of assassination from behind."

"I could not do it," said the Professor. "The news would have got out and the Club would have been disgraced."

"It was not much more than an error of judgment on Miller's part," said Wright. "He never intended

15

to wrong us out of a penny. Crime is measured only by the intention."

"That is the true inwardness of the whole business, Wright, and that thought kept my ballot blank," was Alex's suggestion.

"I could not do it," said Ashley. "His expulsion would have looked as though we measured friendship by dollars. If a man ever needs friends, it is when he is in trouble."

"I could not do it," chimed in Corrigan. "Suppose all our mistakes shall be remimbered against us, how will we iver git admitted to the great Club above?"

"I could not do it, because I love him," said Harding.

"I feared," said Brewster, "that things were going wrong with Miller a week ago, when I noticed that in lieu of the costly chair which he first brought to the Club, he was using that old, second-hand cheap affair."

"I think," said Harding, "that I have a right to tell now what has been a secret. You know Miller and myself worked together. We were coming up from the mine one evening, ten days ago, when we chanced to pass old man Arnold's cabin —Arnold, who was crippled by a fall in the Curry some months ago. The old man was sitting outside his cabin and resting his crippled limb on a crutch. Miller stopped and asked him how he was getting on, and talked pleasantly with him for a few minutes, when an express wagon came by. Miller left the old man with a pleasant word, asked me if I would not wait there a few minutes, hailed the expressman, jumped upon his wagon, said something to the man which I did not understand, and the wagon was driven rapidly away.

"In a few minutes it returned; Miller sprang down: the expressman handed him the great easy chair; he carried it into the door of the cabin, setting it just inside; then lifted the old man in his arms from his hard chair, placed him in the soft cushions of the other, moved it gently until it was in just the position where the old man could best enjoy looking at the descending night: then, picking up the old battered chair, he said, cheerily: 'Arnold, I want to trade chairs with you,' and walked so rapidly away that the old man could not recover from his surprise enough to thank him. This old chair is the one he brought away.

"Coming home he said to me: 'Harding, don't give me away on this business, please. We are all liable to be crippled some time, and to need comforts which we do not half appreciate now. I would have given the old man the chair two weeks ago, but I did not have it quite paid for at that time.'

"'I tell you the story now because I do not think there is any obligation to keep it a secret any longer."

When Harding had finished there was not one man present who was not glad that the vote had resulted unanimously against the generous man's expulsion.

The next question was as to the form of the letter that should be sent Miller. This awakened a good deal of discussion. It was finally decided that each should write a letter, and that the one which should strike the Club most favorably should be sent, or that from the whole a new letter should be prepared. Writing materials were brought out and all went to work on their letters. For several minutes nothing but the scratching of pens broke the silence.

When the letters were all completed, Carlin was called upon to read first.   He proceeded as follows:

VIRGINIA CITY, August 13th, 1878.

FRIEND MILLER:—The Club has talked everything over.   All think you made a great mistake in going away, and that it would be better for you to return to your work.   Your old place in the Club will be kept open for you.   Sincerely yours,

TOM CARLIN.

Wright read next as follows:

VIRGINIA CITY, August 13th, 1878.

JOE:—I make a poor hand at writing.   I have been banging hammers too many years.   But what I want to say is, you had better, so soon as your visit is over, come along back.   There wasn't a bit of sense in your going away.   Your absence breaks up the equilibrium of the Club amazingly.   The whole outfit is becoming demoralized, and the members are growing more garrulous than so many magpies.   We shall look for you within a week.   We all want to see you.

Your sincere friend,

ADRIAN WRIGHT.

The Colonel responded next.

VIRGINIA CITY, August 13th, 1878.

MILLER:—You made a precious old fool of yourself, rushing off as you did.   Are you the first man who has ever been deceived by Comstock "dead points?"   If you think you are, try and explain how it is that while some thousands of bright fellows have devotedly pursued the business during the past fifteen years, you can, in five minutes, count on your fingers all that have saved a quarter of a dollar at the business.

The whole Club join me in saying that you ought to return without delay.   Yours truly,

SAVAGE.

The Professor's letter, which was next read, was as follows:

VIRGINIA CITY, August 13th, 1878.

DEAR MILLER:—We do not like your going away.   The act was deficient in candor, and seems to have a look as though you estimated yourself or the Club at too low a figure.   Suppose you did get a little off; the true business would have been to have told us all about it. We would have "put up the mud" and carried the thing along until it came your way. But what is done is done. The thing to decide now is what it is best for you to do. Austin is no place for you. The mines there are rich, but the veins are small and the district restricted In that camp the formation makes impossible the creation of a big body of ore; the fissures are necessarily small. You would die of asphyxia within a month or go blind searching for a place where an ore body "could make." Eureka is open to other objections. It would require six months for you to become acclimated there, and the chances are that within that time you would be tied up in a knot with lead colic. The proper course to pursue is to come back. The Club are all agreed on that proposition. Yours truly,

STONEMAN.

Ashley's letter, in these words, followed:

VIRGINIA CITY, August 13th, 1878.

DEAR FRIEND JOE: Your going away has caused us ever so much trouble. It was foolish and cruel of you to imagine--even when you were in trouble that any of the Club weighed friendship on old-fashioned placer diggings gold scales. We are sorry for your misfortune, but it is on *your* account that we are sorry. It is not so serious that it canno: be made up in a little while, if you do not persist in remaining in some place where there are no opportunities to do any good for yourself. It may be a long time, among strangers, before you can obtain employment. Because you have made one mistake, do not make an ther, but without delay come back. This is Tuesday. It will take you until about Saturday next to get to Austin. You will be pretty badly used up and will have to rest a day. But on Sunday evening you ought to start back by stage and rail. That will bring you home a week from to-day. A week from to-night then, we shall expect your account of how big the mosquitoes are at the sink of the Carson, and what your opinion is of Churchill County as a location for a country residence. Yours fraternally,

HERBERT ASHLEY.

Alex's letter was very brief, as follows:

VIRGINIA CITY, August 13th, 1878.

Come back, Joe. Were your precedent to be strictly followed, we should suddenly lose a majority of our most respected citizens. In the interest of society and of the Club come. ALEX.

To MR. JOE MILLER, Austin.

Corrigan did not like to read his letter, but the Club insisted, and after declaring that the Club would get "a dale the worst of it," he proceeded as follows:

Virginia City, Nevada, August 13th, 1878.

Dear Auld Jo:—It's murthered yees ought to be for doing onything phat compills me to write you a lether. Whin I commince to write I fale as though all the air pipes were shut off intirely. I would sooner pick up a thousand dollars in the strate, ony day, than to have to hould a pin in me hand and make sinse in my head at the same moment. You know that same, too, and hince phy did yees go away and force all this work upon me? Is it in love wid horse-back exercise that ye are? We have been talkin' your case over, quiet loike, in the Club, and we have unanimously rached the irresistible conclusion that it was an unpatriotic thing for yees to do –to propose this Club business and thin dezart it just whin our habits had become fixed, so to spake; and it would become a mather of sarious inconvanience for us to change. In this wurreld a man can shirk onything excipt his duty, and it is a plain proposition that it is your duty immejitely to come back. My poor fingers are cramped to near brakin' by this writin', and it is your falt, the whole of it, ond I pray yees don't let it happen ony more.

Faithfully,

B. Corrigan.

P. S.—Should you nade a bit of coin to return comfortably draw on me through W. F. & Co.　　　　　　Barney.

Harding read next.

Virginia, August 13th, 1878.

Dear Friend Miller:—Enclosed I send certificate of deposit for $100. The Club desire, unanimously, that you return without a moment's unnecessary delay. All agree that this is the best field for you. I will see the foreman in the morning, tell him you have been called away for a week and get him to hold your place for you. It was very wicked of you to go away. You can only get forgiveness by hurrying back.　　　　　　Lovingly,

Harding.

Brewster's was the final letter, and was in these words:

Virginia City, Nevada,
8th month, 13th day, A. D. 1878.

Mr. Joseph Miller:

Dear Sir and Friend:—I have this evening, with great pain, learned that you have left this place, and, moreover, have heard explained the reasons which prompted that course on your part. It would be a lack of candor on my part not to inform you that I sincerely deplore the wrong which you have done yourself and us. At the same time I believe that the real date of the wrong was when you permitted yourself first to engage in stock gambling. This world is framed on a foundation of perfect justice. The books of the Infinite always exactly balance. In the beginning it was decreed that man should have nothing except what he earned. It was meant that the world's accumulations of treasures— in money, in brain, in love, or in any other material that man holds dear— should, from day to day, and from year to year, represent simply the honest effort put forth to produce the treasure.

Men have changed this in form. Some men get what they have not earned; but the rule is inexorable and cannot be changed. The books must balance.

So when one man gets more than his share, the amount has to be made up by the toil of some other man or men. This last is what you have been called upon to do, and, naturally, you suffer.

But I acquit you of any sinister intention toward us. So do we all. Your fault was when you first attempted to set aside God's law. You may recall what was said a few nights ago. "The decree which was read at Eden's gate is still in full force, and behind it, just as of old, flashes the flaming sword."

We have thoughtfully considered your case. The unanimous conclusion is that you should at once return; that here among friends and acquaintances, with the heavy work which is going on, you have a far better opportunity to recover your lost ground than you possibly could among strangers.

Moreover, you are familiar with this lode and the manner of working these mines. You are likewise accustomed to this climate, hence I conclude that your chances against accident or disease would be from fifteen to twenty per cent. in favor of your returning.

In conclusion, I beg, without meaning any offense, but on the other hand, with a sincere desire to serve you, to say that I have a few hundred dollars on hand, enough perhaps to cover all your indebtedness here. If you would care to use it, it shall be yours, *in hearty welcome*, until such time as you can conveniently return it.

I beg, sir, to subscribe myself your friend and servant,

JAMES BREWSTER.

"God bless you, Brewster," said Harding impetuously.

"That is a boss lether." said Corrigan.

"I could not do better than that myself," was Ashley's comment.

"It is a diamond drill. and strikes a bonanza on the lower level," said Carlin.

"The formation is good. the pay chute large, the trend of the lode most regular, the grade of the ore splendid," said the Professor.

Wright said: " It is a good letter, sure."

"It reads as I fancy the photographs of the Angels of Mercy and Justice look when taken together," suggested Alex.

The Colonel remarked that the letter established the fact that Brewster was not so bad a man as he looked to be.

What should be sent to Miller was next discussed again. It was finally determined that all the letters should be sent except Harding's: that he should re-write his. and instead of sending the certificate of deposit. should, like Corrigan. instruct Miller to draw on him if he needed money. and that any such drafts should be shared by the whole Club.

Then the money to pay the bills was raised among the old members of the Club. and placed in Carlin's hands to be paid out next day.

When all was finished a sort of heaviness came upon the company. There was an impression of sorrow upon them. They had been happy in their innocent enjoyment. but suddenly one who was a favorite, who was at heart the most generous one of the company. had failed them. and they brooded over the change.

At length Harding roused himself and said: " Miller must be sleeping somewhere down in the desert to-night. I wish I could call to him by telephone and bring him back.

"That reminds me." said Alex. "of something that I heard of yesterday. Down at the Sisters' Academy there is a telephone. There is a little miss attending that school, and every morning at a certain hour there is a ring at a certain house down town. The response goes back, 'Who is it?' and then the conversation goes on as follows: 'Is that you, papa?' 'Yes!' 'Good morning, papa!' 'Good morning, little one.' 'Is mamma there?' 'Yes.' 'Say good morning and give my love to mamma.' 'Yes.' 'Good bye.' 'Good bye.'

"In the evening the same call is made; the same answer; and then from the still convent on noiseless pinions these words go out through the night, and pulsate on the father's ear: 'Good night, papa! Good night, mamma! a kiss for each of you!' and then the weird instrument materializes two kisses for the father's ear.

"He is a rough fellow, but he declares that since he commenced to receive those kisses, he knows that an answer to prayer is not impossible; that if that child's voice can come to him, stealing past the night patrol unheard, stealing in clear and distinct and like a benediction, while the winds and the city are roaring outside, there is nothing wonderful in believing that on the invisible wire of faith the same voice could send its music to the furthest star, and that the Great Father would bend His ear to listen."

"It is a pretty story," said Brewster. "The telephone is the most poetical of inventions. There is a metallic sound to the click of the telegraph, as though its chief use was to further the work and the worry of mankind. There is something like a sob to the perfecting press, as though saddened by the very thought of the abuses it must reform. There is a something about a steam engine which reminds one of the heavy respirations of the slave, toiling on his chain, but the telephone has a voice for but one ear at a time, and when it is a voice that we love its messages come like caresses.

"Not the least of its triumphs is that it has broken the silence of the convent.

"At last voices from the outer world thrill through the thick walls, and the patient women who are immured there hear the good nights and the kisses which by loving lips are sent away to loving homes. How their starved hearts must be thrilled by those messages! Sometimes, too, they must realize that the course of Nature cannot be changed: that the beginning of heaven is in the love which canopies true homes on earth. But with that thought there comes another, that from the Infinite, to palace, convent and humble homes alike, celestial wires, too fine for mortal eyes to discern, stretch down, and all alike are held in one sheltering hand. Sometime all these wires will work in accord, and the 'good-nights and the kisses in the souls of men will materialize into harmony and fill the world with music."

"That is, Brewster," said Corrigan, "supposin' the wires do not get crossed and the girls do not kiss the wrong papas."

"Suppose, Brewster," said the Colonel, "that at the final concert it shall be discovered that certain gentlemen have not settled their monthly rents for a long time, and their connection has been cut off?"

"There is no music where there are no ears to hear," said Wright. "What if some souls are born deaf and dumb?"

"Suppose," said the Professor, "that there are souls which have no ear for music?"

"I do not know," said Brewster, "but I fancy that

the fairest final prizes may not be to the best
musicians, but to those who made the sorest sacrifices in order to get a ticket to the concert."

With this the good nights were repeated.

CHAPTER XVII.

At length there came a day when there was real
trouble in the Club. The foreman of the mine in
which Wright was at work ordered Wright and a fellow miner to go to the surface to assist in handling
some machinery which was to be sent down into the
mine.

The two men stepped upon the cage and three
bells were sounded—the signal to the engineer at the
surface that men were to be hoisted and all care used.

The cage started from the 2,400-foot level. Nothing
unusual happened until, as they neared the surface,
Wright said to his comrade: "By the way we are
passing the levels, it seems to me they must be in a
hurry on top."

The other miner answered: "I guess it is all right;"
but hardly were the words spoken, when they shot up
into the light; in an instant the cage went crashing
into the sheaves and was crushed, the men being
thrown violently out.

Wright's companion, as he fell, struck partly on
the curbing of the shaft, rolled in and was of course
dashed to pieces.

Wright was thrown outside the shaft, and though
not killed outright, two or three ribs were broken, one

lung was badly injured, besides he was otherwise terribly bruised.

People unfamiliar with mining may not understand the above. On the Comstock the hoisting engines are set from forty to eighty feet from the mouths of the shafts. Directly over the shafts are frames from thirty to fifty feet in height, on which pulleys (rimmed iron wheels) are fastened. The cages are lowered and raised by flat, plaited, steel wire cables, which are generally four or five inches wide and about three-eighths of an inch in thickness.

This cable is first coiled on the reel of the engine, then the loose end is drawn over the pulley, then down to the cage, to which it is made fast. The wheel of a pulley is called a sheave, and by habit it has grown to be a common expression to call the block and wheel in hoisting works " the sheaves." At intervals of one or two hundred feet on the cables they are wound with white cloth, as a guide to the engineer, as the cable is uncoiled in lowering or coiled in hoisting. Also, on the outer rim of the reel, is a dial with figures or marks at regular intervals, and a hand (like the hand of a clock) which perpetually indicates to the engineer about where the cage is in all stages of lowering or hoisting.

These engineers work eight hour shifts, and sometimes twelve. Of the nature of their work an idea can be formed by the statement that during the two or three years when the great Bonanza in the California and Con. Virginia mines was giving up its treasure, through two double-compartment shafts, all the work of those two mines was carried on. The main ore body was between the 1,300-foot and 1,700-foot levels. Every day from six hundred to eight hundred men were lowered into and hoisted out of the mine. One hundred thousand feet (square measure) of timbers were lowered daily (three million feet per month); nearly or quite one thousand tons of ore was hoisted daily; the picks, drills and gads were sent up to be sharpened and returned; the powder used and five tons of ice daily were lowered, and besides this work, there was machinery to lower and hoist; the waste rock to be handled and visitors and officers of the mine to be lowered and hoisted. The cages are about four feet six inches in length and three feet in width, and are simply iron frames with a wooden floor and iron bonnet over the top and made to exactly fit the size of the shaft. Three of these compartments had double cages—one above the other, and one had three cages. A three-decker carries three tons of ore or twenty-seven men at a time.

Of course when such work is being driven, the eyes of an engineer have to be every moment on their work. Men follow the occupation for months and years without an accident or mistake, but now and then, through the ceaseless strain, their nerves break down; something like an aberration of the mind comes over them and they watch, dazed like sleep-walkers, as the cage shoots out of the shaft and mounts up into the sheaves and cannot command themselves enough to move the lever of the engine which is in their hand.

Such an accident as this overtook Wright and his companion. Poor Wright was carried home by brother miners. The accident happened only about an hour before the time for changing shifts and hardly was Wright laid in his bed before the other members of the Club met at their home.

The best surgical talent of the city was called; the

members of the Club took turns in watching; there was not a moment that one or the other was not bending over their friend.

At first, when he rallied from the shock of the injury, Wright told all about the accident. He further told his friends that he had no near relatives, instructed the Club, in the event of his death, to open his trunk, burn the papers and divide the little money there among themselves, designated little presents for each one and said: "Miller will be grieved if I die, and may think my heart was not altogether warm toward him, so give him my watch; it is the most valuable trinket that I have."

When the first reaction from the shock came, his friends were encouraged to believe he would recover; but it was a vain hope. He soon went into a half unconscious, half delirious state, from which it was hard to 'rouse him for even a few minutes at a time.

He lay that way for two days and nights and then died.

On the afternoon of the second day it was clear that he was almost gone—the spray began to splash upon his brow from the dark river—and all the Club grouped around him.

Out of the shadow of death his mind cleared for a moment. In almost his old natural tones, but weak, like the voices heard through a telephone, he said:

"I have seen another mirage, boys. It was the old home under the Osage shadows. It was all plain; the old house, the orchard, the maples were red in the autumn sun, and my mother, who died long ago, seemed to be there, smiling and holding out her arms to me.

"It was all real, but you don't know how tired I

am. Carlin, old friend, turn me a little on my side and let me sleep."

Gently as mothers move their helpless babes, the strong miner turned his friend upon his pillows.

He breathed shorter and shorter for a few minutes, then one long sigh came from his mangled breast, and all was still.

There was perfect silence in the room for perhaps five minutes. Then Brewster, with a voice full of tears, said: "God grant that the mirage is now to him a delicious reality," and all the rest responded, "Amen."

The undertaker came, the body was dressed for the grave and placed in a casket, and the Club took up their watch around it.

Now and then a subdued word was spoken, but they were very few. The hearts of the watchers were all full, and conversation seemed out of place. Wright was one of the most manly of men, and the hearts of the friends were very sore. The evening wore on until ten o'clock came, when there fell a gentle knock on the outer door. The door was opened and by the moonlight four men could be seen outside. One of them spoke:

"We 'eard as 'ow Hadrian wur gone, and thot to sing a wee bit to he as 'ow the lad might be glad."

They were the famous quartette of Cornish miners and were at once invited in.

They filed softly into the room—the Club rising as they entered—and circled around the casket. After a long look upon the face of the sleeper they stood up and sang a Cornish lament. Their voices were simply glorious. The words, simple but most pathetic, were set to a plaintive air, the refrain of each stanza ending in some minor notes, which gave the impression that tears of pity, as they were falling, had been caught and converted into music.

The effect was profound. The stoicism of the Club was completely broken down by it. When the lament ceased all were weeping, while warm-hearted and impetuous Corrigan was sobbing like a grieved child.

The quartette waited a moment and then sang a Cornish farewell, the music of which, though mostly very sad, had, here and there, a bar or two such as might be sung around the cradle of Hope, leaving a thought that there might be a victory even over death, and which made the hymn ring half like the *Miserere* and half like a benediction.

When this was finished and the quartette had waited a moment more, with their magnificent voices at full volume, they sang again—a requiem, which was almost a triumph song, beginning:

> Whatever burdens may be sent
> For mortals here to bear,
> It matters not while faith survives
> And God still answers prayer.
> I will not falter, though my path
> Leads down unto the grave;
> The brave man will accept his fate,
> And God accepts the brave.

Then with a gentle "Good noight, lads," they were gone.

It was still in the room again until Corrigan said: "I hope Wright heard that singin'; the last song in particular."

"Who knows?" said Ashley. "It was all silence here; those men came and filled the place with music. Who knows that it will not, in swelling waves, roll on until it breaks upon the upper shore?"

"Who knows," said Harding, "that he did not hear it sung first and have it sent this way to comfort us? I thought of that when the music was around us, and I fancied that some of the tones were like those that fell from Wright's lips, when, in extenuation of Miller's fault, he was reminding us that it was the intent that measured the wrong, and that Miller never intended any wrong. Music is born above and comes down; its native place is not here."

"He does not care for music," said the Colonel. "See how softly he sleeps. All the weariness that so oppressed him has passed away. The hush of eternity is upon him, and after his hard life that is sweeter than all else could be."

"Oh, cease, Colonel," said Brewster. "Out of this darkened chamber how can we speak as by authority of what is beyond. As well might the mole in his hole attempt to tell of the eagle's flight.

"We only know that God rules. We watched while the great transition came to our friend. One moment in the old voice he was conversing with us; the next that voice was gone, but we do not believe that it is lost. As we were saying of the telephone, when we speak those only a few feet away hear nothing. The words die upon the air, and we explain to ourselves that they are no more. But thirty miles away, up on the side of the Sierras, an ear is listening, and every tone and syllable is distinct to that ear. Who knows what connections can be made with those other heights where Peace rules with Love?

"Our friend whose dust lies here was not called from nothing simply to buffet through some years of

toil and then to return to nothing through the pitiless gates of Death. To believe such a thing would
be to impeach the love, the mercy and the wisdom of
God. Wright is safe somewhere and happier than he
was with us. I should not wonder if Harding's
theory were true, and that it was to comfort us that
he impelled those singers to come here."

"Brewster," said Alex, "your balance is disturbed
to-night. You say 'from out our darkened chamber
we cannot see the light,' and then go on to assert that
Wright is happier than when here. You do not
know: you hope so, that is all. So do I, and by the
calm that has pressed its signet on his lips, I am willing to believe that all that was of him is as much at
rest as is his throbless heart, and that the mystery
which so perplexes us—this something which one
moment greets us with smiles and loving words, but
which a moment later is frozen into everlasting
silence—is all clear to him now. I hope so, else the
worlds were made in vain, and the sun in heaven, and
all the stars whose white fires fill the night, are
worthy of as little reverence as a sage brush flame;
and it was but a cruel plan which permitted men to
have life, to kindle in their brains glorious longings
and in their hearts to awaken affections more dear
than life itself."

Then Harding, as if to himself repeated: "It matters not while Faith survives, and God still answers
prayer."

Half an hour more passed, then the Colonel arose,
looked long on the face in the casket and said:

"How peaceful is his sleep. The mystery of the
unseen brings no look of surprise to his face. Around
him is the calm of the dreamless bivouac: the brood-

ing wings of eternal rest have spread their hush above him. To-morrow the merciful earth will open her robes of serge to receive him; in her ample bosom will fold his weary limbs, and while he sleeps will shade his eyes from the light. In a brief time, save to the few of us who love him, he will be forgotten among men. Days will dawn and set; the seasons will advance and recede; the years will ebb and flow; the tempest and the sunshine will alternately beat upon his lonely couch, until ere long it will be leveled with the surrounding earth; his body will dissolve into its original elements and it will be as though he had never lived. The great ocean of life will heave and swell, and there will be no one to remember this drop that fell upon the earth in spray and was lost.

" This is as it seems to us, straining our dull eyes out upon the profound beyond our petty horizon. But who knows? We can trace the thread of this life as it was until it passed beyond the range of our visions, but who of us knows whether it was all unwound or whether in the 'beyond' it became a golden chain so strong that even Death can not break it, and thrilled with harmonies which could never vibrate on this frail thread that broke to-day?"

Then the Colonel sat down and the Professor stood up, and with his left hand resting on the casket, said:

" Three days ago this piece of crumbling dust was a brave soldier of peace. I mean the words in their fullest sense. Just now our brothers in the East are fearful lest so much silver will be produced that it will become, because of its plentifulness, unfit to be a measure of values. They do not realize what it costs or they would change their minds. They do not know how the gnomes guard their treasures, or what defense

Nature uprears around her jewels. They revile the stamp which the Government has placed upon the white dollar. Could they see deeper they would perceive other stamps still. There would be blood blotches and seams made by the trickling of the tears of widows and orphans, for before the dollar issues bright from the mint, it has to be sought for through perils which make unconscious heroes of those who prosecute the search. For nearly twenty years now, on this lode, tragedies like this have been going on. We hear it said: 'A man was killed to-day in the Ophir,' or 'a man was dashed to pieces last night in the Justice,' and we listen to it as merely the rehearsal of not unexpected news. Could a list of the men who have been killed in this lode be published. it would be an appalling showing. It would outnumber the slain of some great battle.

"Besides the deaths by violence. hundreds more, worn out by the heat and by the sudden changes of temperature between the deep mines and the outer air, have drooped and died.

"The effect is apparent upon our miners. Their bearing perplexes strangers who come here. They do not know that in the conquests of labor there are fields to be fought over which turn volunteers into veteran soldiers quite as rapidly as real battle fields. They know nothing about storming the depths; of breaking down the defences of the deep hills. They can not comprehend that the quiet men whom they meet here on the streets are in the habit of shaking hands with Death daily until they have learned to follow without emotion the path of duty, let it lead where it may, and to accept whatever may come as a matter of course.

"Such an one was this our friend, who fell at his post; fell in the strength of his manhood, and when his great heart was throbbing only in kindness to all the world.

"One moment he exulted in his splendid life, the next he was mangled and crushed beyond recovery.

"Still there was no repining, no spoken regrets. For years the possibility of such a fate as this had been before his eyes steadily; it brought much anguish to him, but no surprise.

"He had lived a blameless life. As it drew near its close the vision of his mother was mercifully sent to him, and so in his second birth the same arms received him that cradled him when before he was as helpless as he is now.

"By the peace that is upon him, I believe those arms are around his soul to-night; I believe he would not be back among us if he could.

"We have a right on our own account to grieve that he is gone, but not on his. He filled on earth the full measure of an honest, honorable, brave and true life. That record went before him to Summer Land. I believe it is enough and that he needs neither tears nor regrets."

The Professor sat down and Corrigan then arose and went and looked long and fondly upon the upturned face. At last in a low voice he said:

"Auld frind, if yees can, give me a sign some time that something was saved from this mighty wrick. I will listen for the call in the dape night. I will listen by the timbers in the dape drifts; come back if yees can and give us a hope that there will be hand clasps and wilcomes for us whin the last shift shall be worked out."

So one after the other talked until the night stole away before the smile of the dawn. Harding pulled aside the curtains, and at that moment the sun, panoplied in glory, shed rosy tints all over the desert to the eastward.

"See." said Harding. "It was on such a morning as this that on the desert was painted the mirage which troubled poor Wright so much, until the clearer light drove it away. Let us hope that there are no refractions of the rays to bring fear to him where he is."

There was the usual inquest, and on the second day after his death, Wright was buried. After the funeral his effects were looked over; the bills were paid, a simple stone was ordered to be placed over his grave, and his money, some few hundred dollars, was divided among the hospitals of the city.

CHAPTER XVIII.

A few days more went by, but the old joy of the Club was no more.

Wright was gone, and all that had been heard from Miller was a brief note thanking the Club for their kindness, but giving no intimation that he contemplated returning.

One morning about the twenty-fifth of the month the five miners who were left went away to their work as usual, but all were unusually depressed, as though a sense of sorrow or of approaching sorrow was upon them.

As said before, Brewster was working in the Bullion. Toward noon of this day word was passed down into the other mines that an accident was reported in the Bullion; some said it was a cave and some that it was a fire, but it was not certainly known.

Each underground foreman and boss was instructed to see that the bulkheads, which, when closed, shut off the underground connections between the several mines, were made ready to be closed at a moment's notice, in case the accident proved to be a fire. The whisper of "fire in the mine" is a terrible one on the Comstock, for in the deeps there are dried timbers sufficient to build a great city, and once on fire they would make a roaring hell.

When the news of an accident in the Bullion was circulated in the other mines, but one thought took form in the minds of the other four members of the Club. Brewster was working in the Bullion, and it might be that he was in peril.

Within half an hour, and almost at the same moment, Carlin, Corrigan, Ashley and Harding appeared at the Bullion hoisting works.

The superintendent stood at the shaft, and though perfectly self-contained, he was very pale and it needed but a glance at his face to know that he was either suffering physically or was greatly troubled. By this time, too, the wives of the miners at work in the Bullion had commenced to gather around the works.

Mingled with the condensing vapors at the mouth of the shaft, there was the ominous odor of burning timbers.

Just as the Club miners entered the Bullion works, the bell struck and the cage came rapidly to the surface. There was nothing on the cage, but tied to one of the iron braces was a slip of paper. This the superintendent seized and eagerly scanned.

Turning to a miner who stood near, he said: "Sandy, go outside and tell those women to go home. Say to them that the accident involves only one man, and he has no family here. His name is Brewster, and we hope to save him yet."

At this the four members of the Club sprang to the shaft and demanded to be let down.

They were sternly ordered back by the superintendent.

"But," said Carlin, fiercely, "this man whom you have named is like a brother to us; if he is in danger we must go to his rescue."

The rest were quite as eager in their demands. Seeing how earnest they were, the superintendent said: "You are strangers to the mine. The whole working force from all the levels has been sent to the point of the accident. You would only be in the way."

But they still insisted, vehemently. Said Ashley: "Your men are working for money, and will take no risks; it is different with us."

"You do not know what you are doing in refusing us," said Harding; "that man's life is worth a thousand ordinary lives."

"Suppose your brother were in danger and some man stood in the way forbidding you to go to him, what would you think?" asked Carlin.

"Yees are superintindent and rule this mine," said Corrigan, "but you have no rule over min's lives, and this is a matter of the grandest life upon the lode, and yees have no right to refuse us."

"Very well," said the superintendent; "if you men can be of any possible use you shall be sent down."

On a bit of paper he wrote a brief note, tied it to the frame of the cage and sent it down. When the cage disappeared in the shaft, he turned to the men and explained that he had been upon the surface but a few minutes; that long before a drift had been run off from the main gallery at the twenty-one hundred-foot level some fifty feet through ground so hard that it had never required timbering. At the farther end soft ground had been encountered and a stringer of ore. Following this stringer a lateral drift had been run some fifty feet each way. This lateral drift was timbered when it was run. No ore of any value having been uncovered the work was abandoned, and since then the drift had been used as a storage place for powder and candles. That morning the foreman had gone into this drift with a surveyor to establish some point which the engineer required. To assist the surveyor the foreman had stuck his candlestick into a timber and had gone with the surveyor to one end of this lateral drift.

Looking back they saw that the candle had fallen against the timber, which was dry as tinder.

It had caught on fire and the flame had already run up and was in the logging.

They rushed back, and though not seriously injured, were pretty badly scorched. All the miners in the mine were called to that point, and the work of putting out the fire, or of keeping it from connecting with the main drift, was begun. The superintendent was at the time on the twenty-four hundred-foot level. He had hastened to the spot at the first alarm. A donkey pump was at the twenty-one hundred-foot station, with plenty of hose. This was running within fifteen minutes. The fire, after burning a little way in each direction along the lateral drift, exhausting the oxygen in the air, ceased to flame and just burrowed its way through the timbers. This produced a dense and sifting smoke.

A heavy stream of water was turned into this drift, the superintendent directing the work until, under the heat and smoke, he had fainted and been brought to the surface.

Holding up the note which had come up on the cage, he said the man Brewster who was holding the nozzle of the hose had gone too far into the drift, under where the logging had burned away and had been caught in a cave, but the rest were working to release him.

The bell sounded again and in three minutes the cage shot out of the shaft. The paper which it brought had only these few words: "If you can send two (2) first-class miners, all right, but not more. Any others would only be in the way. It is a very dangerous place, don't send any but thorough men." This was signed by the foreman.

When the superintendent read the note the four men rushed forward, and for a moment their clamors were indescribable.

"It is my place to go," said Ashley. "I have as little to live for as any of you. Do not hold me back."

"Stand back," said Harding. "I would rather never go home than not to go with Brewster."

Seizing Harding by the arm, Carlin hurled him back, exclaiming: "Art crazy, boy? Your bark is but just launched; this is work for old hulks that are used to rocks and storms."

Over all the voice of Corrigan rang out: "Hould, men! This is me place. Me life has been but a failure. I will make what amind I can," and he sprang upon the cage, and, seizing a brace with either hand, turned his glittering eyes upon his friends.

At length over the Babel the voice of the superintendent was heard commanding "Silence!"

"You all alike seem determined," he said, "but only two can go. You will have to draw lots to decide." This proposition was with many murmurs agreed to. The superintendent prepared four bits of paper, two long and two short ones. He placed the slips in his hat, and, holding it above the level of the men's eyes, said: "You will each draw a slip of paper; the two who draw the long slips will go, the others will remain. Go on with the drawing!"

The long slips were drawn by Corrigan and Carlin. With smiles of triumph these two shook hands with the others, who were weeping. Said Corrigan:

"Whativer may happen, do not grave, boys. I will see yees again before night, or—I will see me mither."

The two men stepped upon the cage. In his old careless way, Carlin said: "Don't worry about me, boys! I will come back by and by and bring Brewster, or I will know as much as Wright does before night."

With these words the two devoted men disappeared with the cage into the dreadful depths.

With bitter self-reproaches the two remaining men sat down and waited. A half hour went by, when the bell struck and the engine began to hoist. The cage again bore only a slip of paper. This the superintendent read as follows:

"We have had another cave; another man is hurt;

all the miners are much exhausted. Send a couple more men if possible."

The two men sprang upon the cage, the superintendent joined them, and they were rapidly lowered into the depths. Reaching the fatal level, they learned that Corrigan and Carlin, on going down, had insisted on taking the lead; that they had partly uncovered Brewster when another cave had come. It had caught and buried Corrigan, but Carlin, though stunned and bruised somewhat, had escaped. By this time the smoke had partially cleared, but the drift was intensely hot.

The superintendent again took charge. Timbers and heavy plank were brought. The drift was rapidly shored up, and within an hour Harding and Ashley recovered the body of Corrigan.

There was very little rock over him, but he was quite dead. He had been struck and crushed by a boulder from the roof of the drift. He was bending down at the time, the boulder struck him fairly in the back of the neck and he must have died instantly.

Very soon Brewster's body, too, was uncovered. He also was dead. He had been buried by decomposed rock, and had died from asphyxia.

The bodies were carried to the shaft; each was wrapped in a blanket, and that of Corrigan was placed upon the cage. The superintendent, with Carlin and two other miners, stepped on the cage and it was hoisted to the surface. It returned in a few minutes, and this time Brewster's body was placed upon it, and Harding and Ashley, with two other miners, accompanied it to the surface.

In the daylight the faces of the dead were both peaceful, as though in sleep. The bodies were sent away to an undertaker. and as Brewster had been heard to say. at Wright's funeral, that if he should die in the West, he would want his body sent East to be buried beside that of his wife, word was sent to the undertaker to try and get the coroner's permission and then to embalm the body of Brewster.

The three remaining members of the Club were carried to their dreary home. Besides their sorrow. they were terribly exhausted. Harding had fainted once in the drift; Carlin was, besides being worn out, badly bruised. and Ashley was so exhausted that upon reaching the surface he was seized with chills and vomiting. The Professor, the Colonel and Alex were at the hoisting works when they were hoisted to the surface. They accompanied them home and remained, ministering to them until late in the night, when at last all were sleeping peacefully.

With the morning the desolateness of their situation seemed more oppressive than ever. Yap Sing had prepared a dainty breakfast, but when they entered the dining room and saw only three plates where a few days before there had been seven, it was impossible for them to eat a mouthful. Each drank a cup of black coffee, but neither tasted food.

Returned to the sitting room, it was determined to examine the effects of their dead friends. There was little in Corrigan's bundles except clothing and a memorandum book. This book had $150 in greenbacks, and a great many memorandums of stocks purchased, extending over a period of three years. These, a few words at the bottom of the pages showed, had almost all been sold either on too short margins or for assessments. Corrigan's humor ran all through the book in penciled remarks. The following are samples:

"I had a sure thing; was the only mon in the sacret. I was but one and I caught it."

"I bate Mr. Broker mon. He bought for me on a fifty per cint margin, and it broke that fast he could not get out from below it."

"This was a certain sure point. Bedad, I found it that same."

"I took the Scorpion to my bosom and, the blackguard, he stung me."

"I stuck to Jacket until I had not a ghoust of a jacket to me back."

"I made love to Julia. She was more ungrateful than Maggie Murphy."

But between these same pages was found the letter Corrigan had received announcing his mother's death, and this was almost illegible because of the tear stains upon it.

In Brewster's trunk everything was found in the perfect order which had marked all his ways.

A book showed every dollar that he had received since coming to the Comstock; his monthly expenses, the sums he had sent his sister for his children, and his bank book showed exactly how much was to his credit.

Another paper was found giving directions that if anything fatal should happen to him, his body should be returned to Taunton, Massachusetts, and if anything should be left above the necessary expenses of forwarding his body, the amount should be sent to his sister, Mrs. Martha Wolcott, of Taunton, for his children. The paper also contained an order on his banker for whatever money might be to his credit, and a statement that he owed no debts. There were also sealed letters directed to each of his children.

Another large package was tied up carefully and endorsed, "My children's letters. Please return them to Taunton without breaking the package."

The bank book showed that there was eleven hundred and sixty-three dollars to his credit.

Brewster was a man that even death could not surprise. He was always ready.

When the examination was completed, Carlin suggested to Ashley that he take the book, call at the bank, see if the amount was correct and if the bank would pay it on the order found in the book.

Ashley hesitated. "There is something else, Carlin, that should be done, but I do not know how to go about it. That sister should be advised of her brother's death, that she may communicate the news to Brewster's children."

"I have been thinking of that ever since yesterday," said Carlin, "but I can not do it."

"I have been thinking of it, too," said Harding, "but by evening we can determine when the body will be sent and can include everything in one dispatch."

Ashley went away, leaving Carlin and Harding together.

"I am not sure," said Harding, "but I begin to believe that the man who invented dealing in stocks was an enemy to his race. Look at the result of Corrigan's life; think what poor Wright had to show for all his years of toil. They could not have fared much worse had they dealt in poker or faro straight."

"And they are only two," responded Carlin. "There are three thousand more miners like them here and a hundred times three thousand other people scattered up and down this coast, trying to get rich in the same way, while here and in San Francisco a dozen men sit behind their counters and draw in the earnings of the coast. It is worse than folly, Harding. It is a kind of lunacy, a sort of an every day financial hari-kari."

By this time it was past eleven o'clock in the forenoon. Suddenly, without a preliminary knock, the door opened and Miller stood before the two men. They sprang to their feet and welcomed him, the tears starting to all their eyes as they shook hands."

"Oh, Miller!" said Harding, "why did you go away? We have had only trouble and sorrow since."

"It was not fair of you, Miller," said Carlin, "You held our friendship at a miserably low price."

"You are awfully good," said Miller; "but you are looking from your standpoint. I looked from mine, and I could not do differently. But tell me about this dreadful business. I saw about Wright, and read the account of this fearful accident of yesterday as I was coming up in the train, but still, there must have been some blundering somewhere."

Everything was explained, and also what had been discovered of the effects of the dead miners.

"Poor grand souls," said Miller. "It was a tough ending. Never before did three such royal hearts stop beating in a single fortnight on the Comstock."

Ashley returned, and, with words full of affectionate reproach, greeted Miller.

Ashley had found everything at the bank as the book indicated, and the undertaker had promised that Brewster's remains should be ready for shipment on the evening of the next day.

Then the question of the dispatch to the family came up again.

"Before deciding upon that," said Miller, "let me tell you something:

" When I took the money to pay the bills, I had, with a little of my own, something over seven hundred dollars. I bought on a margin of only twenty-five per cent.—the broker was my friend—all the Silver Hill that the money would purchase. I thought I had a sure thing. My informant was a Silver Hill miner. I believed I could multiply the money by three within as many days. In five days it fell thirty per cent. What could I do? A note from the broker asking me to call, received the evening before I went away, decided me. I went away, but when I saw by dispatches that Wright had been killed, and I could get nothing to do, I determined to come back.

" Well, I met my broker this morning. He asked me to call at his place. There he informed me that the day he purchased Silver Hill he met the superintendent and learned from him that there was not yet a development; that the stock was more liable to fall than to rise for two or three weeks to come, the rage being just then for north end stocks. He could not find me, and accordingly, on his own responsibility, he sold the stock, losing nothing but commissions and cost of dispatches.

" There was a little lull in Sierra Nevada that day, and, believing it was good, he bought with my money and on my account. As it shot up he kept buying. At last, a week ago, he had two thousand shares and sold five hundred, and by the sale paid himself all up except $21,000.

" Hearing day before yesterday that I had left the city, he sold the other fifteen hundred shares at $157. This morning he handed me a certificate of deposit in my favor for $213,000, and here it is."

Most heartily did the others congratulate Miller on his good fortune. 17

But Miller said: "Congratulate yourselves! I used the money of the Club. The profit I always intended should be the Club's. Wright and Corrigan and Brewster are gone, but you are left and Brewster's children are left. If I am correct, $213,000 divided by five, makes exactly $42,600. That is. you each have $42,600 on deposit in the bank, and a like sum is there for two fatherless and motherless children in Massachusetts."

It was useless to try to reason the matter with Miller. He merely said: "It shall be my way. It was a square deal. I meant it so from the first: only," he added, sadly. "I wish Wright and Corrigan and Brewster could have lived to know it." Then turning quickly to Harding, he said: "Harding, how much is that indebtedness which has worried you so long?"

Harding replied that the mortgage was $8,000, while the personal debts amounted to $3,000 more.

"Then." said Miller, "you can pay the debts and have nearly $30,000 more with which to build your house and barns, to stock and fix your place for a home."

The tears came to Harding's eyes, but he could not answer.

"Never mind, old boy," said Miller; "did I not tell you I would make things all right for you?"

Then Carlin got up, went into the adjoining room, brought out the watch which had been Wright's and told Miller how Wright, under the shadow of death, had bequeathed the watch to him.

For the first time Miller broke down and burst into tears.

When he recovered somewhat the command of himself, he said:

"Now, I have a proposition to make. Let us all give up this mining. It is a hard life, and generally ends either in poverty or in a fatal accident. I am going to San Francisco. The place to make money is where there is money, and I am going to try my skill at the other end of the line."

"You are right," said Carlin. "I am never going down into the Comstock again. I made up my mind to that yesterday. I am going back to Illinois."

"And I am going to Pennsylvania," said Ashley.

"I gave up mining yesterday, also," said Harding; "at least on the Comstock I do not mind the labor or the danger, but it is not a life that fits a man for a contented old age."

Suddenly Miller said: "Harding, were you ever in the Eastern States?"

"No," said Harding; "the present boundary of my life is limited to California and Nevada?"

"Well," said Miller, "if we all give ourselves credit for all the good we ever dreamed of doing, still neither of us, indeed, all of us together, are not worthy to be named on the same day with James Brewster. His body must go East, and on its arrival there only an aged woman and two little orphan children await to receive it. I think it would be shabby to send the dust of the great-hearted and great-souled man there unattended. What say you, Ashley and Harding, will you not escort the body to its old home?"

Both at once assented. A dispatch was prepared announcing Brewster's death, and adding that his body would be shipped the next evening escorted by two brother miners, Herbert Ashley and Samuel Harding. This was signed by the superintendent of the Bullion company.

The superintendent also made a written statement that he had examined the effects of Brewster and found that, less the expenses of embalming, transportation, etc., together with $80 due Brewster from the Bullion company, there was left the sum of $840.25. With this statement a bill of exchange on Boston for the $840.25 was enclosed, and Ashley took charge of it.

The bills were all paid. The money due Brewster's orphans, according to Miller's calculation, was also converted into a bill of exchange payable to Mabel and Mildred Brewster. Ashley and Harding took charge of the first and left the second of exchange to be forwarded by Colonel Savage, and before night all preparations for leaving the next day were made.

The next morning Corrigan's funeral took place with all the ostentatious parade which Virginia City was famous for in the flush times when some one who had been a favorite had passed away. At the hall of the Miners' Union Colonel Savage delivered a eulogy which was infinitely more beautiful than some of the orations which have been treasured among the gems of the century.

He was followed by Strong in a eulogy that touched every heart. Here is a sample:

"Gentle and unpretentious was Barney Corrigan. There was no disguise in his nature. Could his heart have been worn outside his breast, and could it, every moment, have thrown off pictures of the emotions that warmed it, to those who knew him well, those pictures would have thrown no new light on his nature.

"Generous and true was he; true as a man, a friend

a citizen. His walk through life was an humble one, but it was, nevertheless, grand. So brave was he that he performed heroic acts as a matter of course, and all unconscious that he was a hero.

"So he toiled on, his path lighted by his own genial eyes, and strewn behind him with generous deeds.

"When death came to him the blessed anæsthetic which made him indifferent to his sufferings was the thought that in a little while he would rescue a friend in peril, or feel the grasp of the spirit hand of his mother.

"Noble was his life: consecrated will be the ground that receives his mortal part. The world was better that he lived: it is sadder that he has died.

"With tears we part with him: our souls send tender 'all hails and farewells' out to his soul that has fled, and we pray that his sleep may be sweet."

The Colonel, Professor and Alex, with Miller, Carlin, Ashley and Harding, rode in the mourning carriages. These were followed by a long line of carriages and quite one thousand miners on foot. At the grave the services were simply a prayer and a hymn sung by the Cornish quartette. They made his grave close beside that of Wright's; they ordered a duplicate stone to be placed above it. and left him to his long sleep.

Yap Sing was paid off and a handsome present made him, the furniture and food in the Club house was distributed among poor families in the neighborhood, and on the evening train the four living men, with the body of their dead friend, moved out of Virginia City.

A great crowd was at the depot to see them off, and the last hands wrung were those of the Professor, the Colonel and Alex.

On the way to Reno, Carlin said to Miller: "One thing I cannot understand, Miller; whatever possessed that broker to turn over that money to you when he was not compelled to?"

"I have no idea in the world," said Miller, "except that we are old friends."

"But did you never do him any great favor, Miller—any particularly great favor?" asked Carlin.

"No," said Miller, "I cannot think of any." But after a moment's silence he added: "By the way, come to think of it, I did do him a little favor once. I saved his life."

"How was it?" asked Carlin. "Why," answered Miller, "he and myself had a running fight with a band of renegade Indians. There were seven or eight of them at first, and we got them reduced to four, when one of them killed the broker's horse. It was a very close game then. It required the promptest kind of work. When the horse fell the broker was thrown violently on his shoulder and the side of his head and was too stunned to gather his wits together for a few minutes. I had a gentle horse, so sprang down from him and let him go. I got behind a low rock and succeeded in stopping two of the Indians, when the others concluded it was no even thing and took the back track. But the broker was "powerful" nervous when I got up to him. The worst of all was, I had to ride and tie with him for seventeen miles, and he was so badly demoralized that I had to do all the walking."

At Reno Miller bade the others good-bye and took the west-bound train. Carlin sent a dispatch to an Illinois town. Late in the night the east-bound Overland express came in; the body of Brewster was put on board, the three friends entered a sleeper and the long ride began.

CHAPTER XIX.

Following a long established habit our three travelers were up next morning shortly after dawn.

The train was then thundering over the desert northeast of Wadsworth. Carlin noticed the country and said:

"This must be almost on the spot where poor Wright saw his wonderful mirage."

As he spoke the bending rays of the rising sun swept along the sterile earth, and a shimmer in the air close to the ground revealed how swiftly the heat waves were advancing.

"It is as Wright said; the desert grows warm at once, so soon as the morning sun strikes it," said Harding. "Heavens, how awful a desolation. It is as though the face-cloth had been lifted from a dead world."

"Do you remember what Wright told us, about the appalling stillness of this region?" asked Ashley. "One can realize a little of it by looking out. Were the train not here what would there be for sound to act upon?"

"Is it not pitiful," said Harding, "to think of a grand life like Wright's being worn out as his was? He met the terrors here when but a boy. From that time on there was but blow after blow of this merciless world's buffetings until the struggle closed in a violent and untimely death."

"You forget," said Ashley, "that a self-contained soul and royal heart like his, are their own comforters. He had joys that the selfish men of this world never know."

All that day the conversation was only awakened at intervals and then was not long continued. Not only the sorrow in their hearts was claiming their thoughts and imposing the silence which real sorrow covets; but the swift changes wrought in the week just passed, had really resulted in an entire revolution in all their thoughts and plans.

It was to them an epoch. The breakfast station came, later the dinner, later the supper station. All the day the train swept on up the Humboldt valley. Along the river bottom were meadows, but about the only change in the monotonous scenery, was from desert plains to desert mountains and back again to the plains.

Night came down in Eastern Nevada. When they awoke next morning the train was skirting the northwest shore of Great Salt Lake and the rising sun was painting the splendors that, with lavish extravagance, the dawn always pictures there on clear days, and no spot has more clear days during the year.

Ogden was reached at nine o'clock in the morning, the transfer to the Union Pacific train was made; breakfast eaten, and toward noon, the beauties of Echo Canyon began to unfold. Green River was crossed in the gloaming; in the morning Laramie was passed, at noon Cheyenne, and the train was now on a down grade toward the East. With the next morning men were seen gathering their crops; the desert had been left behind and the travelers were now entering the granary of the Republic.

Late that night the train entered Omaha. The usual delay was made: the transfers effected and early next morning the journey across Iowa, so wonderful to one who has been long in the desert, began. Ashley darted from side to side of the coach that he might not lose one bit of the view; but Harding sat still, by the window, hardly moving, but straining his eyes over the low waves of green, which, in the stillness of the summer day, seemed like a sea transfixed.

Carlin was strangely restless. He did not seem to heed the scenery around him. He studied his guide-book and every quarter of an hour looked at his watch. When spoken to, he answered in an absent-minded way; it was plain that he was absorbed by some overmastering thought.

Noon came at length, then one o'clock, then two; the train gave a long whistle, slackened speed, and in a moment was brought to a standstill in front of a station.

With the first signal Carlin had sprang from his seat and walked rapidly toward the end of the car.

"What can the matter be with Carlin?" asked Harding. "He has been half wild all day and altogether different from his usual self."

"He will be home sometime to-night," replied Ashley. "He has been absent a long time, and I do not wonder at his unrest. I expect to have my attack next week when the southern hills of Pennsylvania lift up their crests, and the old familiar haunts begin to take form."

"Look! Look!" said Harding. "Carlin's unrest is taking a delicious form, truly."

Two ladies were standing on the platform. Carlin had leaped from the train while yet it was moving quite rapidly. He bent and kissed the first lady, but the second one he caught in his arms, held her in a long embrace and kissed her over and over again.

" He has struck a bonanza," said Ashley.

"And the formation is kindly," said Harding.

"The indications are splendid." said Ashley. " Mark the trend of the vein; it is exquisite."

"It does not seem to be rebellious or obstinate ore to manipulate either. Carlin's process seems to work like a fire assay," said Harding.

"Just by the surface showing the claim is worth a thousand dollars a share," said Ashley. " I wonder if Carlin has secured a patent yet?"

"And I wonder," said Harding, "if we are not a pair of blackguards to be talking this way. Let us go and meet them."

The friends arose and started for the platform, but were met half way by Carlin and the ladies. There were formal introductions to Mrs. and Miss Richards. Under the blushes of the young lady could be traced the lineaments of the "Susie Dick" that Carlin had shown to the Club in the photograph.

Crimson, but still smiling. the young lady said: "Gentlemen. did you see Mr. Carlin at the station. before a whole depot of giggling ninnies, too? Was ever anything half so ridiculous?" Then glancing up at Carlin with a forgiving look, but still in a delicious scolding tone. she added: " I really had hoped that the West had partly civilized him."

Harding and Ashley glanced at each other with a look which said plainly enough. "Carlin has proved up without any contest: even if the patent is not already issued, his title is secure."

The friends had the drawing room and a section outside. With a quick instinct Ashley seated the elder lady in the section, bade Harding entertain her, then swinging back the drawing room door, said: "Miss Richards, I know that you want to scold Carlin for the next hour, and he deserves it. Right in here is the best place on the car for the purpose. Please walk in." Saying which he stepped back and seated himself beside Harding.

The elder lady was a charming traveling companion. She wanted to know all about the West. She knew all about the region they were passing through, and the whole afternoon ride was a delight.

During the journey Harding and Ashley had been begging Carlin to accompany them to Massachusetts, and he had finally promised to give them a positive answer that day. After a while he emerged from the drawing room and said: "I am sorry, but I cannot go East with you. These ladies have been good enough to come out and meet me. We will all go on as far as Chicago and see you off, but we cannot very well extend the journey further. Indeed, Miss Susie intimates that I am too awkward a man to be safe east of Chicago."

The others saw how it was and did not further importune him. Next day they separated, Carlin's last words being, "If you ever come within five hundred miles of Peoria stop and stay a month."

The grand city was passed. The train swung around the end of Lake Michigan, leaving the magical city in its wake. Through the beautiful region of Southern Michigan it hurried on. Detroit was reached and passed; the arm of the Dominion was crossed, and finally, when in the early morning the train stopped, the boom of Niagara filled the air, and the enchantment of the picture which the river and the sunlight suspend there before mortals, was in full view. Next the valley of the Genesee was unfolded, and with each increasing mile more and more distinct grew the clamors of toiling millions, jubilant with life and measureless in energy. Swifter and more frequent was the rush of the chariots on which modern commerce is borne, and all the time to the eyes of the men of the desert the lovely homes which fill that region flitted by like the castles of dreamland. •

Later in the day the panorama of the Mohawk Valley began to unroll and was drawn out in picture after picture of rare loveliness.

Ashley and Harding were enchanted. It was as though they had emerged into a new world.

"Think of it, Ashley," said Harding. "It is but eight days—at this very hour—since we were having that wrestle with death in the depths of the Bullion mine. Think of that and then look around upon these serene homes and the lavish loveliness of this scenery."

"I know now how Moses felt, when from the crest of Pisgah he looked down to where the Promised Land was outstretched before him," was the reply. "I feel as I fancy a soul must feel, when at last it realizes there is a second birth."

Said Harding: "I dread more and more to meet these people where we are going. How uncouth we will seem to them and to ourselves."

"Our errand will plead our excuses," said Ashley; "besides they will be too much absorbed with something else to pay much attention to us. Moreover they will know that our lives of late have been passed mostly under ground, and they will not expect us to reflect much light."

"What are your plans, Ashley, for the near future, after this business which we have in hand shall be over?" asked Harding.

"A home in old Pennsylvania is to be purchased." said Ashley, "and then a trial with my fellow men for a fortune and for such honors as may be fairly won. And you Harding, what have you marked out?"

Said Harding: "My father's estate is to be redeemed; after that, whatever a strong right arm backing an honest purpose, can win. But one thing we must not forget. We must be the semi-guardians of those children of Brewster, until they shall pass beyond our care."

"You are very right, my boy," said Ashley. Brewster was altogether grand and his children must ever be our concernment."

In the early night the Hudson was crossed and the train plunged on through the hills beyond. At Walpole early next morning the train was boarded by three gentlemen who searched out Harding and Ashley and introduced themselves as old friends of Brewster and his family. They had come out to escort the body of Brewster to Taunton, now only a few miles off. The names of these men were respectively Hartwell, Hill and Burroughs.

Hartwell explained that the remains would be taken to an undertaker, and examined to see if it would be possible for the children and Mrs. Wolcott, the sister of Brewster, to look upon their father's and brother's face. He also said the funeral would be on the succeeding day. Then the particulars of the accident were asked.

A full and graphic account of the whole affair had been published in the Virginia City papers.

Copies of these were produced and handed over as giving a full idea of the calamity.

The statement made by the superintendent of the Bullion including the smaller certificate of deposit, also the other effects of Brewster, all but the money obtained from Miller, were transferred to Mr. Hartwell.

On reaching Taunton a great number of sympathizing friends were in waiting, for Brewster had lived there all his life until he went West three years before, and he was much esteemed. The manner of his death added to the general sympathy.

A hearse in waiting, at once took the body away. The young men were taken to his home by Mr. Hartwell. They begged to be permitted to go to a hotel, but the request would not be listened to.

On examination it was found that the work of the embalmer had been most thorough. The face of Brewster was quite natural and placid. as though in sleep.

Breakfast was in waiting for the young men, and when it was disposed of they were shown again to the parlors and introduced to a score of people who had gathered in to hear the story of Brewster's death from the lips of the men who had taken his body from the deep pit and brought it home for burial.

In the conversation which followed two or three hours were consumed.

When the callers had gone, Hartwell said:

"Gentlemen, I advise you to go to your rooms and try and get some rest. In two or three hours I shall want you to go and make a call with me, if the poor family of my friend can bear it."

Late that afternoon Hartwell knocked on the door of the sitting room, which, with sleeping apartments on either side, had been given Harding and Ashley. and when the door was opened, he said:

"Gentlemen, please come with me, the children of James Brewster desire to see you!"

The young men arose and followed their host. Brewster had always referred to his daughters as his "little girls;" the man who had the young men to go and meet them, spoke of them as "the children of James Brewster." Both Harding and Ashley. as they followed Hartwell, were mentally framing words of comfort to speak to school misses just entering their teens, who were in sorrow.

When then, they were ushered into the presence of two thoroughly accomplished young women, and when these ladies. with tears streaming down their faces, came forward. shook their hands, and. in broken words of warmest gratitude. thanked them for all they had done and were doing. and for all they had been to their father in life and in death, the men from the desert were lost in surprise and astonishment.

As Harding said later: "I felt as though I was in a drift on the 2,800-foot level, into which no air pipe had been carried."

This apparition was all the more startling to them, because during the two or three years that they had been at work on the Comstock, the very nature of their occupation forbade their mingling in the society of refined women to any but a most limited extent.

From the papers given the family by Hartwell that day, matters were fully understood by the sister of Brewster and the young ladies, so no explanations were asked. At first the conversation was little more than warm thanks on the part of the young ladies and modest and half incoherent replies.

The ladies were in the humble home of their father's widowed sister, Mrs. Wolcott. That they were all poor was apparent from all the surroundings. This fact at length forced its way through the bewildered brain of Harding and furnished him a happy expedient to say something without advertising himself the idiot that he, in that hour, would have been willing to make an affidavit that he was. Said he:

"Ladies, amid all the sorrows that we bring to you, we have, what but for your grief would be good news. Tell them, Ashley!"

"Oh, yes." said Ashley, "we have something which is yours. and which, while no balm for sorrow like yours, will, we sincerely hope, be the means of driving some cares from your lives."

Taking a memorandum from his pocket, he continued:

"Your father left more property than he himself knew of. How it was Harding and myself will explain at some other time, if you desire. At present it is only necessary to say that the amount is forty-two thousand and six hundred dollars, for which we have brought you a bill of exchange." With that he extended the paper to Miss Brewster. Then these brave girls began to tremble and quake indeed. "It can not be," said Mabel. "There must be some mistake," said Mildred.

"Indeed, there is no mistake," said Harding. "See, it is a banker's order on a Boston bank, and is payable to your joint order. No one can draw it until you have both endorsed it, for it is yours."

Then these girls fell into each others arms and sobbed afresh.

As soon as they could the miners retired.

Mabel Brewster was tall, of slender form and severely classic face. She had blue eyes, inherited from her mother, and that shade of hair which is dusky in a faint light, but which turns to gold in sunlight. Her complexion was very fair, her hands and arms were exquisite and her manners most winsome.

Mildred, her sister, was of quite another type. A year and a half younger than Mabel, she looked older than her sister. She had her father's black eyes, and like him, a prominent nose and resolute mouth. She was lower of statue and fuller of form than her sister. She had also a larger hand and stronger arm. Over all was poised a superb head, crowned with masses of tawny hair.

Standing in their simple mourning robes, with the afternoon sun shining around them, they looked as Helen and Cassandra might have looked, while yet the innocence and splendor of early womanhood were upon them.

Mabel was such a woman as men dream of and struggle to possess; Mildred was such an one as men die for when necessary, and do not count it a sacrifice.

From the house the young men walked rapidly away, and so busy were they with their own thoughts that neither spoke until they entered a wooded park or common, and finding a rustic bench sat down.

Harding was the first to speak. "After all his mighty toil; after his self-sacrificing life; after all his struggles, Brewster died and was not permitted to see his children. It is most pitiable."

"May be he sees them now," said Ashley, softly. "It can not be far from here to Heaven."

"I wish I had never seen her," said Harding, im-

18

petuously. And then all his reserve breaking down he arose, stretched out his arms and cried:

"I wish I had died in Brewster's stead."

"Is she not divine?" said Ashley. "A very Iris, goddess of the rainbow, bringing divine commands to man, his guide and his adviser."

"Say not so," said Harding. "Rather she is Ceres, in her original purity returned to earth: flowers bloom under the soft light of her divine eyes, and all bountifulness rests in the heaven of her white arms. I tell you, Ashley. the man who could have that woman's eyes to smile up approvingly upon him, would have to move on from conquest to conquest so long as life lasted."

An anxious look came over the face of Ashley. "Which lady do you mean?" he asked.

"Mean!" echoed Harding. "I mean she of the royal brow and starry eyes, Mildred Brewster."

"Thank God," said Ashley with a great sigh of relief.

"And why do you thank God?" asked Harding.

"Because," said Ashley, "to me Mabel is the dainty, the divine one. She comes upon the eye as a perfect soprano voice smites on a musical ear."

"You are growing musical. are you?" said Harding. "Well then, the other is a celestial contralto, deep-toned and full and sweet. materalized."

After this both were silent for a moment and then Ashley began to laugh low to himself.

"What is your hilarity occasioned by?" asked Harding.

"I was thinking what fools we have been making of ourselves," said Ashley.

"And how did you reach that estimate, pray?" asked Harding.

"Why, Harding," was the answer, "an hour ago we met two ladies. They were not what we expected to find, and they brought a sort of enchantment to us. We saw them first an hour ago; we will to-morrow see them once more, and that will be all; and still we have been raving like two lunatics for the past half hour about them."

MABEL AND MILDRED.

"You are right," was the sad reply. "See yonder on the street corner."

Just then a dainty carriage and a set of heavy trucks met on the corner and passed each other, the carriage turning to the east, the trucks to the west.

"Typical. is it not?" said Ashley. "The trucks go west—at least they will to-morrow night."

"Most true." said Harding. "and still I think I would like to kiss the carpet that has been sanctified by the footfalls of Mildred Brewster."

Ashley reached out. seized Harding's wrist and felt his pulse.

"You have got it bad, Harding," said he, "and I don't feel very well myself. If poor Corrigan were alive again and here we would get him to tell us about Maggie Murphy."

"We have had a mirage, Ashley. Let us pray that it will soon pass by." said Harding.

And then without another word being spoken, they returned to the hospitable house of Hartwell.

CHAPTER XX.

The following is the copy of a letter written by Mrs. Wolcott to the widow of her deceased husband's brother, Mrs. Abby Roberts, of Eastport, Maine:

TAUNTON, Sept. 20th, 1878.

MY DEAR SISTER:—I wrote you briefly of the dispatch announcing the death of my brother James, in a Nevada mine, and that his embalmed body was being brought home by two miners. Since then events have crowded upon me so swiftly that I have not had composure enough to think of writing.

The remains of my brother reached here on the 29th ultimo. Mr. Hartwell, Mr. Hill and Mr. Burroughs went out as far as Walpole on the railroad to meet the train on which the body was being brought.

The miners were taken home by Mr. Hartwell. On examination my poor brother's face was found to look quite natural, and it wore an expression so restful that I could not help but feel as though it was an in dication that after his hard physical toil and fierce mental troubles, he was at peace at last.

Mabel, you know, has been with me since she graduated in June. On receiving the dispatch we telegraphed to Mildred at Mt. Holyoke to come home at once, so both girls were with me when the remains arrived.

From the two miners who came with the body Mr. Hartwell received the Nevada papers giving an account of the accident in which James was killed; also a letter from the superintendent of the mine, stating that after all expenses were paid my poor brother left eight hundred and forty dollars to his children. This we all thought was most wonderful, considering the amount regularly sent the children. It shows that poor James lived a most economical life in the West and that the wages paid there are generous.

The letter of the superintendent stated that the two miners who were to accompany the remains home had risked their lives in trying to rescue James, and the published account showed that one of them had fainted in the dreadful chamber of the mine while the exhaustion of the other was so extreme that he was entirely prostrated and seized with chills and vomiting upon being brought out into the open air.

Of course myself and the girls were anxious to meet and thank these men, but I confess that at the same time we all dreaded the interview awfully. Good land! You know what we have been reading about Western miners for the last twenty-five years, and we could not help but feel that if they should prove to be quiet men it would only at best be a case of wild beast with a collar and chain on. And what to do with them at the funeral was something which had been troubling us ever since the receipt of the dispatch. It was to be in church and on Sunday and it was certain that there would be a church full of people. How to be polite, and at the same time how to get those men in and out of a church without their doing something dreadful was a question which I confess had worried me and I could see that it was worrying Mabel, too. Mildred did not seem to think much about it.

Mr. Hartwell called upon us and told us he was going to bring them over at once and we sat down in fear and trembling to wait their arrival.

You can never imagine our surprise when Mr. Hartwell showed them into our parlor and we saw them for the first time. Both were young men, one not more than thirty, and the other not more than twenty-four years of age; both were dressed with perfect taste, in dark business suits of fashionable clothes, and though slightly confused--I guess startled is a better word - both, with considerate gentleness, and with a grave courtesy, in low voices, addressed me first and then the children.

They expected to find school children, they met young ladies—I may say beautiful young ladies if I am their aunt—and I think the surprise for a moment threw them off their guard.

But they certainly were not more astonished than were we. Mabel well nigh broke down, but Mildred, with her more matter of-fact nature, bore the ordeal nobly.

While the girls were talking I stole the opportunity to look more closely at the men. My surprise increased every moment. Instead of a pair of bronzed bruisers, they stood there with faces that were as free from tan as the face of a closely-housed woman. They were each of about medium height, but with broad shoulders, tremendous chests and powerful arms. The younger one had a firm foot and large hand and the frankest open face you ever looked into. The other had smaller hands, feet and features, but their heads were both superb, and the first words they spoke revealed that both were fairly educated. The younger one was light with auburn hair. He wore a heavy mustache; the rest of his face was clean shaven. The other was darker with gray eyes, brown hair, with full beard, but neatly trimmed, and the hair of both was of fashionable cut. I tell you, sister, as they stood there they would have borne inspection even in Boston.

After the first greetings were over and we had all gained a little composure, the men explained to us that James was possessed of more property than he himself was aware of, and one of them handed to Mabel a paper which he called "a bill of exchange" on a Boston bank for forty two thousand six hundred dollars. Since then they have explained that the money was made by a friend of my brother, and that it was accomplished by buying stocks when they were low and selling them when they were high, which seems to me to be a most profitable business. You see it makes the girls rich when they thought they were so poor, and were counting only on lives of hard work.

The visit of the young men was only a very brief one, not five minutes in duration it seemed to me, but they were moments of great excitement to our little household as you may well believe. When they were gone Mabel said: "Are they not perfectly splendid?" and I said: "Indeed, they are," but Mildred merely said: "They seem to be real gentlemen." That Mildred is the strangest girl.

The funeral was to be the next day, and in anticipation of it we had bought cheap mourning hats and plain bombazine mourning habits, such as I thought would be becoming to people in our circumstances. But when I learned that the girls were no longer poor, I thought it would be only proper that they should have more expensive dresses. So, as soon as the young men had gone, I sent a message to Mrs. Buffets, the dressmaker, and Mrs. Tibbetts, the milliner, asking them to do me the favor to call upon me at once, if possible. They both called within a few minutes. Before they came, however, I explained to the girls what I had done, at which Mabel was very glad, but Mildred seemed perfectly indifferent. She hardly spoke after the young men went away for several minutes. I think their coming had turned her thoughts back more intently upon her father. Mrs. Tibbetts came first and from her Mabel ordered three expensive hats. I expostulated against her buying a hat for me but she would have it so. When we explained what was wanted to Mrs. Buffets, she declared at first that it was impossible without working after twelve o'clock on Saturday night which she did not like to do as she was a member in good standing in the First Baptist church, but she finally agreed that she would try, provided we would pay what would be extra for her sewing girls. This she estimated would amount on three dresses to at least seven dollars and a half. I have no idea that the girls got more than half a dollar apiece extra and there were but seven of them, and that the rest was clear gain to Mrs. Buffets, but that is the advantage which is always taken of people when there is a funeral.

We had a hard time with Mildred. She insisted that two dresses and hats were all that were required, one for Mabel and one for aunty; that as yet she was a school girl and the cheap raiment was good enough for her. I think she would have refused to yield had I not told her that unless she did I would not accept either hat or habit; then she consented.

Of course, it may seem like vanity to speak of such a thing in so sad a connection, but the dresses were most lovely. The girls' were of rich and soft cashmere, mine was of Henrietta cloth. I must say that in the new clothes the girls did look beautiful at the funeral, and I was as proud of them as I could be on so sad an occasion.

That Saturday evening after we talked the matter over, the girls sent an invitation over to Mr. Hartwell's house to the miners to attend the funeral with us. The invitation was answered by the younger miner, Harding. He accepted the invitation for himself and his friend, stating that Ashley (the other one) was temporarily absent in the city. The note was beautifully written and every word was spelled correctly.

Next morning, a few minutes before it was time to proceed to the church, the young men came in.

They were scrupulously dressed in black and their attire even to their hats and gloves was in perfect taste.

Mildred betrayed more agitation than on the first meeting. She is a strange girl and the loss of her father almost crushed her. Mabel, however, received them with a grace which was queenly and in her new robes she looked like a queen indeed.

When it came time to go to the church, I supposed, of course, the young men would offer to escort the girls. Besides Mildred, Mabel and myself, Aunt Abigail, James' wife's grandmother had come down to the funeral. You know she is old now—past 73; she never was very pretty and coming down from the country her dress and bonnet—good land, she was a sight.

Mabel could not conceal her mortification, and I must say I should have been glad if she had not come.

As we stood up to go, the younger miner said gently: "Ashley, will you not see to Mrs. Wolcott?" and then he went up to Aunt Abigail and with as much kindly politeness as I ever saw displayed, asked her to lean upon him in the walk to the church. The other one gave me his arm, at the same time saying: "The young ladies are the nearer relatives, they should walk in front." His face was fair, but the arm I took was as hard as iron.

I said: "No matter, Mildred take the other arm of Mr. Ashley and Mabel take that of Mr. Harding!" This was done except that somehow in the confusion Mildred took the arm of Harding and Mabel sought the disengaged arm of Ashley.

At the church we were seated in the front pew, of course. You never saw such a crowd at a funeral. I noticed as we worked our way up the aisle, men there that had not been in a church before for years.

There were, besides, the Brown, the Smith and the Jones families, who were never before known to attend an ordinary funeral.

I mention this merely to show how much James was respected.

The services were most impressive. The organ was played as we entered the church. When we were seated there was a short prayer, then a chant with organ accompaniment was rendered. Professor Van Dyke, the music teacher at the seminary, presided at the organ and Jane Emerson led the sopranos. She sang her best and people do tell me that they have paid money to hear women sing in concerts that could not sing as well as Jane Emerson. If Jane was only a little better looking and knew how to dress in better style and if her father only belonged to a better family, there would not be a young woman in Taunton with brighter prospects than her's.

Mr. Ashman's main prayer was a most touching one and it moved many in the congregation to tears. He preached from John, the fourteenth chapter and eighteenth verse.

"I will not leave you comfortless, I will come to you."

It was generally conceded that the sermon was one of the minister's best efforts since he preached in Taunton. Miss Hume who was present says she never heard a finer discourse in Boston.

The burden of the sermon was that the promise to send a comforter to the disciples was a promise made for all time, to those in sorrow, that if they would but ask, the comforter would come to them.

When the sermon was over and the choir had sung again; the minister said, as many persons present would like to know the particulars of James' death he would read the account from the *Territorial Enterprise*, a paper published in Virginia City only a few miles from the Nevada mines. He said further that the report was written by a Mr. De Quille, who he presumed was a descendant of the distinguished family of France of that name, that the account showed that he was a very learned man and graphic writer, and such a man could only be retained by the receipt of an enormous salary.

He further explained that where the word shaft was used it meant a hole like a well which men sunk in order to get the rock out from underground that had silver in it, that drifts were places in the mines where the rock that had the silver in it lay in ridges like snow drifts; that stations were where men kept lunch stands for the miners, that tunnels were holes made in the shape of a funnel to get air down in the mine, that a winze was a corruption for windlass, and cages were simply elevators, like those in use in hotels, but made like cages so that men could not fall out, that run up and down in the well.

You never at a revival saw a congregation so excited as that one was during the reading of that account. They tell me that men were as pale as death all over the house while the sobbing of women could be heard above the reading.

But our two miners never showed a bit of emotion and never seemed conscious that every eye in the church was on them. The only things I noticed were that during the singing the older one was softly beating time on his hymn book, and both moved a little uneasily in their seats when the minister was explaining the mining terms.

After the children had looked for the last time on their father's face, the young men who had been standing at the foot of the coffin, walked up to the head, one on each side. After a long gaze at James' face they turned facing each other and stretching out their hands, clasped hands a moment over the coffin. I suppose that is a custom among miners in the west.

Brother's body was buried beside that of his wife.

The young men remained in Taunton two weeks after the funeral. We all went on a little excursion to Buzzards Bay and to Cape Cod. I never saw better behaved men, even those that come down from Boston, than those two miners. They received a great many attentions, too, here in Taunton and every day were obliged to decline invitations to dinner.

There is a story going around, but I do not believe it is true, that one morning early they went to a livery stable and asked for two wild horses, regular furies, that had thrown their riders the previous day, that they mounted them and the horses reared and plunged awfully but they rode rapidly out of town; that they were gone an hour and a half and when they returned the horses were covered with foam and seemed perfectly gentle.

Just before going away they came over one day to my house and telling the girls that they had received so many kindnesses from so many people that they wanted to make a little picnic festival in Mr. Hartwell's grounds, asked them to help suggest names for the invitations. The festival was to be the next afternoon. What do you think? That morning carpenters came and fixed benches and tables on the grounds, the three o'clock train brought the ——— Cornet Band from Boston, and at five o'clock in the afternoon the waiters in the ——— Hotel appeared, set the tables and waited on the guests. They had sent up to Boston for the dinner and I never saw anything like it in my life.

Mr. Hartwell says the expense must have been at least two hundred and twenty-five dollars. Those Western men are awfully extravagent.

Next morning they went away. The older one to Pennsylvania, where he will live hereafter, and the other one to California, where he has property. We have been real lonesome ever since they went away.

Mildred left us yesterday to return to school, and will graduate next June, she says on the day she is eighteen. Mabel, you know, was eighteen and a half when she graduated last June, but Mildred always was a little the most forward scholar of her age. Since the funeral the girls have purchased some beautiful clothing, and it would do your heart good to see them. My letter is pretty long but I could tell you as much more if I had time.   Your loving sister,

MARTHA WOLCOTT.

P. S.—I want to tell you a secret. I think that Ashey, the older miner, and Mabel have a liking for each other, though I don't know, except that I saw Ashley kiss Mabel as he was going away. All I can say is that if they should make a match, there would not be a handsomer couple in Massachusetts. It is only a surmise on my part that they are fond of each other. After the young men had been gone for several hours I asked Mabel if there were any serious relations between her and Ashley, and she answered: "Not the least serious auntie, our relations are altogether pleasant."   M. W.

The next letter from Mrs. Wolcott to Mrs. Roberts read like this:

TAUNTON, Sept. 13th, 1879.

MY DEAR SISTER:—It is now almost a year since I wrote you the letter telling you of brother James' funeral and that I half suspected a fondness had sprung up between one of the men who came with the remains of James and Mabel.

Well, I was correct in my suspicion for last Thursday they were married and left by the evening train for their future home in Pennsylvania. He has an iron mine in the mountains and reduction works at Pittsburg and is making money very fast. Their home is in Pittsburg.

I thought at first that I was mistaken because no letters came to Mabel, but it seems Mabel made a confident of her cousin George who is a conductor on a train which runs between here and Providence, he hired a box in the postoffice there, Mabel's letters were sent to that postoffice and George brought them to her. This was done to thwart the curiosity of the wife of the postmaster here. The postmaster himself is a good meaning man, but his wife is a real gossip and had frequent letters come from one place to Mabel the whole town would have known it in no time. When it was known that the girls had received a large amount of money the Browns, the Smiths and the Proctors, who had never called before, all came and begged Mabel, now that she had graduated, (look at the hypocrisy) to come out more in the world. Young Henry Proctor called several times and in less than a fortnight asked Mabel if he might not sit up with her on Saturday nights. He is a very proud young man and it is said he will have twelve thousand dollars when he goes out for himself next year, but Mabel declined any particular attentions from him. She did the same thing with half a dozen more young men of the best families. I was perplexed. Of course I was in no hurry for Mabel to marry, but good opportunities for girls are none too plenty, so many young men go West, and when I saw her throw away chance after chance, and some of them so eligible, I was afraid she would be sorry sometime, for careless as girls are, they all expect sometime to be married. It went on so until six weeks ago when suddenly one evening Mabel said: "Auntie come go with me to Boston to-morrow." "What are you going to Boston for?" I asked. "There is a young man coming here to carry me away in a few weeks, Aunty, and I need a few things," said she. "And who is the young man, Mabel?" I asked. "Herbert Ashley," was the answer, and then she fell on her knees and burying her face in my lap sobbed for joy. I cried a little, too, it was so sudden. "But when were you engaged?" I asked after she grew a little composed. "We have had a perfect understanding since the week after father's funeral," said she, and then added: "My heart followed him out of the house on that first day when I had only looked once in his eyes. Is he not grand, Auntie?" "But why have you never told me?" I asked. Then she put her arms around me and said: "Because, dear Aunty, you know you could not have kept my secret." I was hurt at this, because every body knows how close mouthed I am. But I went to Boston and, what do you think? that girl spent over seven hundred dollars just for clothes. I remonstrated, but she cut me short, saying, "I am going with my king, and I must not disgrace his court." Did you ever hear such talk? When I was married I had just two merino dresses, one brown and one blue, four muslin dresses and some plain underclothing. But I had a beautiful feather bed that I had made myself, four comforters, two quilted bed spreads in small patterns, and a full set of dishes that cost six dollars and a half in Portland. Things are greatly changed since I was a girl. Well, Mr. Ashley came; he is a splendid man. Mabel slipped away with her cousin and went down to Providence to meet him. He brought Mabel jewelry that the best judges here think cost as much as a thousand dollars. It is shameful, the extravagance of those Western men. Why, he gave the minister that married them fifty dollars, which you know yourself was a clear waste of forty-five dollars. Five dollars is certainly enough for five minutes work of a minister, especially if he and his wife are also given a fine supper. Mr. Ashley also gave Mildred some beautiful jewelry. It must have cost two hundred and fifty dollars, and he was most generous to me, too. On his wedding day he got five dispatches from the West; one from Illinois, two from Virginia City, Nevada, and two from California, congratulating him, and they must have cost the senders as much as fifty dollars. Thank goodness, they all came marked "paid." The wedding was in the church in the evening. It had been whispered around and the church was full. Land sakes, but they were a lovely couple. Mabel's dress was white satin with princesse train of brocaded satin. The front of the skirt was trimmed with lace flounces, headed with garlands of lilies of the valley and orange blossoms. She wore also a long tulle veil, with orange blossoms in the hair. Her dress cost one hundred and fifty-three dollars and thirty-seven cents. I did not think the train was necessary and there was no need of a veil, leastwise not so long a one, but it was Mabel's wish to have them, so I did not object. Mrs. White said she never saw a handsomer bride in Boston nor a more manly looking groom. I confess I was proud of them both. We had a quiet little party at my house and a supper, and at ten o'clock they went away by special train to Providence. Think of the foolishness of hiring a special train, when the regular train would have come by next morning. Mr. Ashley wanted to have what he called a "boss wedding;" wanted to ask half the town and, as he said, "shake up Taunton for once," but Mabel coaxed him out of the idea. He wanted me to sell or rent my place and with Mildred go and make his home mine, but I don't think that is the best way. Young married folks want to be let alone mostly, while they are getting acquainted with each other. Mildred has been home since she graduated in June. I think she has discouraged more men since she came home than ever Mabel did. She has improved greatly in her personal appearance and is a girl of most decided character. When she first came home we used to tease her about her

beaux, but we do not any more. When the young men were here last year, after we got pretty well acquainted, one day when they had called Mildred took a sheet of paper and pen and going to Mr. Harding, said: "Mr. Harding, please write an inscription to put upon Father's monument." He took the pen and wrote: "The truest, best of men." Well, one day about a month ago Mildred had gone down town for something when Mabel wanting scissors, or thimble or something which she had mislaid, went to Mildred's work basket to get hers. There under some soft wools that Mildred had been working upon Mabel saw the end of a ribbon and picking it up drew out a locket which was attached to it. She could not control her curiosity but brought it to me. I gave Mabel liberty to open it though my sense of perfect justice was a good deal shocked. To tell the truth I was dying to see what was in it. Mabel opened it and inside there was nothing but that bit of paper with the words in Harding's handwriting: "The truest, best of men." There were some stains on the paper but whether they were made by kisses or tears we could not make out though I put on my gold-rimmed spectacles, which are powerful magnifiers, and looked my best. Mabel put the locket back, but to this day there has not been a word said to give me any idea whether there is anything like an engagement or not. Mildred is so quiet and self-contained that if her heart was breaking I do not believe she would say a word. I should be glad to think they were engaged, for privately, I liked Mr. Harding a little the best, but if they had been it seems to me he would have been here to the wedding. I don't know when I have been so worked up about anything. If I was fifteen years younger, and I thought the majority of men in the West were like the two that I have seen, I would sell my place and go West, too.   Your affectionate sister,
                                                    MARTHA WOLCOTT.

P. S.—When Mr. Ashley was here he took the girls out to James' grave. We had put up a plain stone but Mr. Ashley did not like it. When he came in he ordered the finest monument in the marble works. Those that have seen it say it is real Italian marble, and that it is handsomer than the one that the banker Sherman erected over his wife and that cost over five hundred and fifty dollars.   M. W.

This letter explains itself:

Los ANGELES, Cal., March 20, 1880.

MY DARLING SISTER:—We reached our home here last night. While I write the perfume of almonds and orange blossoms, of climbing vines, and roses shedding their incense in lavish fragrance steals in through the open window. A mocking bird is mimicking an oriole's warblings, and I fancy I feel at this moment as do ransomed souls when amid the mansions of the redeemed they open their eyes and know that for them joy is to be eternal. You have always called me "Old Matter-of-Fact." Well, then, just imagine me sitting here half blinded by the tears of happiness that I can not restrain.

But let me tell you of my journey. You remember that though the sky was bright overhead—as bright as it can be in Pittsburg—on the morning that we were married, when we took the train in the evening it was snowing hard. Before morning the train was delayed by the snow. We worried along, however, and the next evening arrived at Peoria, Illinois. Here an old friend of my husband (is not that word husband lovely?) your husband and father's, with his wife met us at the depot and we had to go home with them and stay two days. The man's name is Carlin and he is "a splendid fellow," as they say out this way. He was one of the Club to which our husbands belonged. He has a mill, store and farm a few miles from Peoria and seems to be the first man in that region. He has, too, a charming wife whom he calls "Susie Dick," and a six months' old baby which he calls "Brewster Miller Carlin." They are as hearty people in their friendship as I ever met. They asked all about your husband, and yourself, and I had to get out your photograph to convince them that you were far more beautiful than myself. When we arrived Mr. Carlin sent out and got in some twenty couples, and to use his own expression, "we made a night of it," and "painted the town red," that is until midnight. They made me sing and play, and one old gentleman present made me proud, by telling me "you beat ord'nary primer donners." After the company retired Mr. Carlin asked me how I liked the old gentleman's pronunciation, and then husband said the old gentleman knew as much about music as our minister in Taunton did about mining. Then he told Mr. Carlin what Mr. Ashman said about tunnels, drifts, stations, etc., and the man laughed until the tears ran down his cheeks. Well, at length, with blessings, presents, and packed lunch baskets, we got away. All through Illinois and Iowa the world was hid by the snow, we passed Omaha, crossed Nebraska, climbed the Rocky Mountains and came down on this side, and swept across the desert of Nevada to Reno. Here we stopped and next day went to Virginia City. I wanted to visit the place where our father died. In Virginia City — which is a city on a desert mountain side—you cannot conceive of such a place —the wind was blowing a hurricane; blowing as at the old home, it comes in sometimes from the ocean in a southeaster. Husband took me to the fatal Bullion shaft. The men were just then changing shift as they call it; the men who had worked eight hours were coming out of the mine, those who were to work the next eight hours were going down. The shaft is half a mile deep and the cage loaded with nine men shoots up out of the dreadful gloom or drops back into it as though it were nothing. Many of the miners greeted husband warmly, and were hearty in their welcomes to me, though they were not encumbered by any great amount of clothing. I turned away from the shaft almost in a panic, I could not bear to look at it. But Virginia City is a wonderful place, I would tell you more of it, if you had not some one near you who can tell it much better than I can. We met a great many pleasant people there, especially a lawyer named Col. Savage, a journalist, a Mr. Strong and a Professor Stoneman. They met us like brothers and spoke of your Herbert as another brother. We left that same evening and returning to Reno started up the Sierras. I confess that a feeling of something like desolation took possession of me. The region was so dreary, it seemed to me that only my husband was between me and chaos. After leaving Reno a couple of hours. we entered the snow sheds and I went to sleep with a thought that I was under a mountain of snow. I wakened next morning in Sacramento and when I looked out the birds were singing and flowers were blooming around me. Before noon we reached San Francisco and drove to the Palace. There we were met by a gentleman named Miller, the one that made for father our money. He is very rich. He told husband that he had been "coppering" the market ever since he came to the city and had "taken every trick." Later I asked husband what "coppering" meant and he smiled and said: 'betting that it will not win." I do not quite understand it yet, but I know it is right for husband says so. This Mr. Miller told husband that he was going to make me a present and that he must not say a word at which Sammy said "go ahead." Then he handed me a little package but said I must not open it until I reached home. What do you think? It is a diamond cluster which the cost of must have been fifteen hundred dollars. In San Francisco I found the most delicious flowers I ever saw. Tell aunty, too, that there are no such hotels, as one or two in San Francisco, "not even in Boston." There are splendid churches and theatres. The Bay is beautiful, the park is going to be grand, the ladies dress most richly. We sailed over to Saucelito and San Rafael, looked out through the Golden Gate in short, ran around for a week. Then we came directly home, reaching this place last night.

A charming supper was in waiting, and, all smiles, the Chinaman who prepared it was in attendance. His name is Yap Sing, and he has been with husband ever since his first return from the East. He was the cook for the Club which you have heard our husbands talk about, and of course knew father. He fairly ran over with joy at our coming, and such a cook as he is. I would like to hear what Aunt Martha would say to one of his dinners. But husband pays him forty dollars a month. Is not that a dreadful price for a cook?

We have received good news since coming home. Husband's mine in Arizona is yielding him for his one-half interest twelve hundred and fifty dollars per month.

My house is a beautiful cottage, with broad halls and verandas, and is furnished elegantly all through.

My heart runs over with gratitude. My soul is on its knees in thankfulness all the time. I believe I am the happiest woman in the world. "The truest and best of men" sits across the room writing letter after letter, clearing up a delayed correspondence. He is handsomer than on that day when I first looked in his eyes, and knew in an instant that he was my fate, that I should worship him forever, whether he knew it or not : that if he did not ask me to be his wife, I should never be a wife, but by myself should walk through life bearing my burdens as humbly and bravely as I could, and keeping my heart warm by the flame in the vestal lamp which his smile had kindled within it.

Now heaven has opened to me, and so jubilant is my heart that I can feel it throbbing as I write, and with a thankfulness unspeakable I worship at my hero's feet.

With warmest love to you, dear sister, and to your husband and Auntie, in which my other self joins heartily, I am

Your loving sister,

MILDRED BREWSTER HARDING.

P. S.—Sister: This morning as we sat here I asked my lord why he and your husband clasped hands over our father's coffin. Waiting a moment, he answered that on the journey East with father's body, your husband and himself made a covenant together that henceforth, whatever might happen, they would watch over us as a sacred trust received from our father, and that the hand-clasp was but an involuntary pledge of the sincerity of that compact.

Can we ever be good enough wives to these men who do not half realize how grand they are?

Love and kisses,

MILDRED.

www.ingramcontent.com/pod-product-compliance
Lightning Source LLC
Chambersburg PA
CBHW020847020726
47497CB00005B/1290